DR. MARVELLUS DJINN'S ODD SCHOLARS

···

B. SHARISE MOORE

MVMEDIA, LLC
FAYETTEVILLE, GA

MVmedia, LLC
PO Box 143052
Fayetteville, GA 30214

Publisher's Note: This is a work of fiction. Names, characters, places, and incidents are a product of the author's imagination. Locales and public names are sometimes used for atmospheric purposes. Any resemblance to actual people, living or dead, or to businesses, companies, events, institutions, or locales is completely coincidental.

Book Layout ©2017 BookDesignTemplates.com
Cover Art by Marcellus Shane Jackson
Map by Sarah Macklin
Cover Design by Kecia Stovall

Ordering Information:
Quantity sales. Special discounts are available on quantity purchases by corporations, associations, and others. For details, contact the "Special Sales Department" at the address above.

Dr. Marvellus Djinn's Odd Scholars/ B. Sharise Moore. -- 1st ed.
ISBN: 978-1-7346279-9-2

CONTENTS

For Ellen E. Armstrong, Professor J. Hartford Armstrong,
Edna Moore, Brenda Moore, and all the "Colored Conjurers"
I've ever admired.

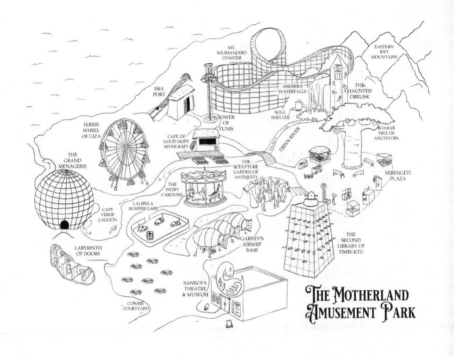

EASTERN RIFT MOUNTAINS

MT. KILIMANJARO COASTER

ERA PORT

ANDRIRA WATERFALLS

THE HAUNTED OBELISK

FERRIS WHEEL OF GIZA

TOWER OF TUNIS

SOUL SHELVES

BOABAB TREE OF ANCESTORS

CAPE OF GOOD HOPE RIVER RAFT

DJENN RIVER

THE GRAND MENAGERIE

THE SCULPTURE GARDEN OF ANTIQUITY

SERENGETI PLAZA

THE IVORY CAROUSEL

CAPE VERDE LAGOON

LALIBELA BUMPER CARS

THE SECOND LIBRARY OF TIMBUKTU

LABYRINTH OF DOORS

GARVEY'S AIRSHIP BASE

SANKOFA THEATRE & MUSEUM

COWRIE COURTYARD

THE MOTHERLAND AMUSEMENT PARK

PART ONE:
THE ODD SCHOLARSHIPS

The Negro World

Four Lucky Winners to Tour Dr. Marvellus Djinn's Colored Theme Park

April 1, 1920

Dr. Marvellus Djinn, internationally known Scholar of Sorcery, will award exclusive passes to *The Motherland*, her theme park of magic and mythological creatures in Hampton, VA in June. In addition to the tour, the winners will receive full financial support to attend Hampton Institute.

The odd scholarships will be awarded to four teens (ages 13-19) who prove victorious in competitions in the following categories: Strength, Ingenuity, Chemistry, and Magical Prowess. All who are interested should meet Dr. Djinn in the following cities: Altamonte Springs, FL (Mighty Biceps-Strength Competition May 2, 1920); Charleston, SC (Juvenile Ingenuity Competition May 5, 1920); Washington, DC (Boys Chemistry Competition May 10, 1920); and Charleston, SC (Dueling Crystal Balls-Magical Prowess Competition May 5, 1920). *For more information on how to register, see page E5.*

ONE

STRENGTH IS
THE FAMILY BUSINESS

Altamonte Springs, FL 1920

In a mere thirty minutes, the gathering of a few strapping workers assembling the stage swelled to over one hundred onlookers. Everyone within a twenty-mile radius of Altamonte Springs was in attendance to see if Omen could redeem himself after last year's defeat. His eyes roved over the audience of familiar faces. Sisters, brothers, wives, aunts, uncles, grandparents, cousins, neighbors—they'd all made the trip to see this year's *Mighty Bicep Competition*, the premier event to begin the summer.

"You beat Cairo once; you can beat him again. Still don't look to me like the boy's got it all up here." Omen's father, Ivan Crow, tapped his forehead. "Remember boy, strength is ninety percent mental."

"I know Pop, I know." Beads of sweat gathered at Omen's temples. He snatched a red checkered kerchief from his back pocket and dabbed at his hairline.

This was the ritual every year: the same crowd ripe with excitement, the same split of loyalty down the middle, and the same bad blood. Omen's father paced back and forth with his hands stuffed in the pockets of his overalls. Though there had always been twenty contestants, everyone knew the Crows and Armwoods were the only ones who mattered. The rivalry dated back to 1820 when Omen and Cairo's great-great grandfathers found themselves at odds over a red-bone gal with green eyes on the plantation on Fort George Island. According to the old folks, the dispute was settled over an arm-wrestling match. And ever since Omen's great-great grandfather's win, the scales had been slightly tipped in the Crow family's favor.

One by one, the competitors lined up for the announcement of the draw. Omen leaned against a curtain. A rumble of gator-mating calls traveled along the breeze from a patch of swamp across the clearing. His line of vision drifted to the crates and barrels enveloping the stage. Painted black, the red and green letters screamed the contents inside: *Biceps Galore, Love at First Kiss, Far East Trinkets and Charms, Salves for Spirit Sicknesses, Back to Africa Talismans.* An upright piano decorated with black and green symbols stood in the corner. The back wall had been covered with pictures of Marcus Garvey and clippings from *The Negro World* newspaper. Three iguanas moseyed around their cages on a table nearest the audience. Each lizard changed its color from red to black to green in unexpected synchronicity. For the first time ever, the *Mighty Biceps Competition* had partnered with a celebrity. He whistled to himself and turned to his competition. *Cairo.* From his calves as big around as tree trunks to his barrel chest, the boy looked burlier and more clueless than Omen remembered. Altamonte's old folks said the Armwood boys had never been babies. They were born big and stayed that way 'til they died.

"Yup, he's big alright, but don't let that fool ya," Uncle Dwight chimed in as if he'd been reading Omen's mind. "It's the skill that matters." He mopped his protruding brow with a bandana.

For 365 days straight Omen had heard the boos and whispers. They'd stuck to him like a wart no one knew how to remove. *Sometimes, the will skips a generation. Might be the mighty Crows are finally stepping aside for another family to take the crown. Ever seen that boy's arms? They right scrawny. He ain't got the genes. I'm tellin' ya he's a wee bit too small to challenge anybody. Ivan done trained the boy soft. I know Ole Fitzgerald is turnin' over in his grave.*

A shrill whistle pulled him back to the present and a shirtless man in a red vest stood before the crowd. Silver armbands choked his forearms as his silk pants flapped in the breeze.

"Welcome one and all to the *Annual Juvenile Mighty Biceps Arm Wrestling Competition!* I am Professor Bartholomew Blue and before I introduce our illustrious judge for today's contest, I'd like to announce the competitors!"

His accent was difficult to place. West Indian perhaps? Last year he'd met a man from the Bahaman islands off Florida's coast. Omen never forgot the ease of his words. Once they left the stranger's lips, they floated on the wind like a magic carpet in the stories his younger sister liked to read.

As one of the previous year's finalists, he and Cairo's names were the first to be called. After Cairo posed for the audience, Omen flashed a grin and waved to the cheering crowd.

Professor Blue rattled off the names quickly; all were familiar: King Tyrone, Donnie Dumbbell, John the

Menace, Duke the Rude, Big Glen. If a family had a boy who could beat a Crow or an Armwood, they had something good going.

"Allen the Outcast, Good Eatin' Gilbert, Smashmouth Steve," the man shouted among the cheers. "Chuck the Wailer, Hilliard the Wrench, and last, but certainly not least, Helena Hightower!"

Omen froze as his gaze swung to a girl with deep dimples and a long, onyx braid. Thickset and half his size, it didn't take long to determine she was strong—and beautiful.

A hush fell over the crowd. Omen glanced at his father. "Since when they allow girls to compete?" he asked out of the side of his mouth and stuffed his thumbs under the bib of his overalls.

"They been hollerin' 'bout girls bein' good as boys for a while now. Since Dr. Djinn is here, I reckon this gal," Ivan motioned toward Helena, "is tryna get her hands on a scholarship." He shrugged. "And who can blame her?"

It made perfect sense. He wasn't the only one who wanted the chance to see the world beyond Altamonte. There was so much more to life than gators and swamps. He'd promised himself when the opportunity came, he'd snatch it up.

"We took a vote the other day," his father continued.

Omen folded his arms across his chest, eyes glued to Helena. "How'd you vote, Pop?"

Ivan Crow tossed a towel over his shoulder. "I voted 'gainst it. Imagine if your mama had been demandin' she wrestle gators and lift dumbbells? You might not have been born." He cracked his knuckles above his head. "Never mind that though. Keep your eyes on the prize. That Dr. Djinn is a legend in her own right. You wait and see." He pulled a newspaper clipping from one of his pockets. "Your Uncle Dwight got a hold of this a few months back while handlin' business down in the bayou. Take a gander."

Omen unfolded the clipping and peered at the article.

𝕯𝖍𝖊 𝕯𝖎𝖒𝖊𝖘 𝕻𝖎𝖈𝖆𝖞𝖚𝖓𝖊

Race Riot near Lake Pontchartrain Leads to Lynching
New Orleans, LA

August 9, 1919

A disturbance at an outdoor market led to a lynching on the banks of Lake Pontchartrain on Saturday afternoon. Eyewitnesses say a group of vendors had been selling their wares peacefully when a scuffle broke out. According to Laura Lafayette of 21 Rue Charles, "an irate Colored woman refused to return the money of a White man who had bought one of her items and politely requested an exchange. The crowd dissolved into chaos as the Colored woman was carried off and hanged."

Diane LaFleur of Rue Dauphine, who witnessed the quarrel, furthered that it was for good reason as the Colored woman, since identified as Marvellus Djinn, "began chanting spells and hexes and foaming at the mouth with the intention of ridding New Orleans of its good White folks."

When authorities arrived to assess the damage, a single braid that looked to have come from the head of a Colored had been left behind, but no remains or body had been found. Nothing more is known at this time as the NOPD continues its investigation.

Omen folded the article, handed it to his father, and turned his attention to the stage.

"On behalf of *The Motherland*, the country's first Colored Amusement Park, I present to you the Mentor of Magic, the Scholar of Sorcery herself, Dr. Marvellus Djinn!" He raised his arms with a flourish.

In an instant, the crowd split down the middle and Dr. Djinn entered like the prophet Moses parting the Red Sea. Omen watched as she twirled a cane with a gem encrusted handle like a majorette.

"Those are real ruby and emerald stones in that topper." His father leaned in close. "She's one of the richest Colored Women in the country. No man in his right mind would be okay with a woman having all that power. And them pants—I reckon it's why she ain't married." He tugged at his beard.

Despite the Florida heat, Dr. Marvellus Djinn wore a green tuxedo with a matching top hat and tails. A black boa constrictor wound around her arms and its tongue slipped in and out of its mouth like flashes of pink lightning. She climbed the risers with outstretched arms.

"Thank you, Professor Blue." She spun back to her audience. "Greetings one and all and welcome to this year's *Mighty Biceps Juvenile Arm-Wrestling Competition!*"

Omen joined the crowd's whistles and chants.

"The Honorable Marcus Garvey says if you have no confidence in self, you are twice defeated in the race of life!" She spoke in a syncopated voice that matched her odd get-up. "I am Dr. Marvellus Djinn and today I offer one of you an Odd Scholarship which includes a fully-funded education at Hampton Normal and Agricultural Institute and a once in a lifetime opportunity to tour my magical amusement park! Without further ado, let's get this show on the road!"

Quickly, the contestants descended the risers and huddled with their teams.

"This is it, Omen. You get that scholarship; you write your ticket. With a little education, I reckon we may be able to incorporate the family business. Push us into the big leagues." Ivan Crow's eyes shifted. "Now, this is where you make your mark. Give 'em some leeway the first few seconds, feel 'em out. Then, move in for the kill."

Omen returned to the stage as his uncle thumped him between the shoulder blades. His heartbeat quickened. This was it. He figured he was about ninety minutes away from redemption. Somehow, he summoned calm as the audience rushed forward, choking the edges of the stage. A group of men dressed similarly to Professor Blue stepped in to secure the area.

The rules were simple: two preliminary rounds, a semifinal, and a final. Best two out of three in each. The winner would move on to the next round. For the preliminary bouts, two matches would take place at once. Omen took a look at his first opponent. *Allen the Outcast. As good a warm-up as any. Six-feet- two-inch frame. Solid build.* Despite it all, Allen had never been all that sure of himself and it showed. To him, losing wasn't a lesson; it was the end of the world. Losses came with the territory. It's the response to the loss that makes a champion. Allen wouldn't last in the Strength Business. Everyone knew it.

The two boys took their seats on a pair of stools. Omen craned his neck to make out the other two competitors. Cairo sat across from Good Eatin' Gilbert, the 300-pound hammer. Rolls of flesh strained against the gaps in Gilbert's overalls. *Don't you go puttin' the cart before the horse!* Omen's father's voice echoed inside his head. *You beat him once. You'll beat him again. It's your time.*

Omen looked toward the heavens and mouthed a silent prayer.

"Let's get ready now," Professor Blue shouted over the excited crowd.

Omen and Allen set their elbows on the barrel, each flexing their fingers and rotating their wrists in preparation. They locked hands as Blue cupped his palm over theirs.

"On the count of three. One. Two. Three!"

Omen gazed into Allen's eyes. Already, tiny lines of exertion had formed across the boy's forehead. He counted to three silently, then tightened his grip, crushing the boy's hand in his. Allen's eyes grew from slits to saucers. *Slam!* Omen forced Allen's arm to the barrel in record time.

The crowd went wild. A smile stretched across his face. The second game ended quicker than the first. Allen stared at the floor as Professor Blue held Omen's arm high in the air.

The preliminary bouts sped by in a blur. Cairo won easily. Then, King Tyrone took out John the Menace, two to nothing. Big Glen forced Chuck the Wailer to forfeit in a puddle of tears. Omen stood aside as Chuck's father, Big Lung Bruce, led him down the dirt road in shame. After the commotion of Chuck's exit, Donnie Dumbbell bested Hilliard Hard Hitter in a nail biter, two to one. But the biggest surprise of the day was Helena Hightower's decisive win over Smashmouth Steve.

"Whatever you do, you best not lose to no girl," Cairo's father shouted for all to hear. "You'll never live that down. Never."

Steve's dad, Bugsy Knuckles, wore a tight scowl as he steered Steve away from the crowd. By the end of the early rounds, four were left standing: Omen, Cairo, Donnie Dumbbell, and Helena Hightower. Dr. Djinn announced a fifteen-minute intermission and Omen and his corner headed to the family tent. Finally, he could breathe.

Uncle Ichabod was the first to greet him inside. "You got a clear path to that scholarship," he said thickly, a long pipe bobbing between his lips. "Two more matches and it's yours!" Omen held his breath to avoid the fumes of tobacco and liquor.

"Don't get that boy all pumped up for a letdown." Omen's mother sauntered toward them. Her Southern drawl sat on the ears like molasses on a flapjack, sweet and slow.

"This ain't no time for no woman to be interjecting philosophy," Ichabod scoffed. "I know you as headstrong as they come Elle, but he don't need to be hearin' no negativity right now."

"Ain't nobody bein' negative." Omen's mother folded her arms across her chest. "I'm only sayin' y'all are giving him a reason to let his guard down. And I'll interject philosophy wherever my son is concerned any time I'd like, Ichabod."

A shrill whistle brought the conversation to a halt.

"Lineage roll call!" Omen's father marched inside.

On cue, the Crow children formed a line. Omen's six-year-old brother, Night, rattled off the history of an ancestor born in 1857, followed by his younger sister Sage. Finally, Omen brought up the rear. He closed his eyes before speaking in the loudest voice he could muster. "Fitzgerald Crow. Born 1850. Strong Man and Gator Wrestler. Fitzgerald Crow holds the record for besting the largest gator on record in Florida at 450 pounds and 10 feet. The prize was a three-inch tooth, the Crow family heirloom, passed down to the most deserving, skilled, and talented member of the Crow family line." Omen pulled his shoulders back. The mention of his grandfather's feat filled him with pride.

The Crow family erupted in applause.

"Well done." Ivan gave each of his children a brisk nod as they hurried off. Then, Uncle Ichabod, Bub, and Cousin Owl formed a line alongside Ivan. They stood shoulder to shoulder, four men ranging in age from twenty to sixty. Ichabod retrieved a suede pouch from a knapsack and handed it to Ivan. Omen held his breath.

"No matter what happens today, Omen deserves this. Truth is, it was his long ago. Not when he won, but when he lost." He motioned for Omen to step forward.

Big Bub slapped him on the shoulder. "We're proud of how you conducted yourself last year. It was a tough loss. But Cairo's an Armwood; beating that clan ain't never gonna be easy," he said in a voice drier than an ashtray.

Uncle Nubs sucked on his gums. "Them Armwoods is somethin' else," he said with a heavy lisp. "We don't like to give 'em they due. But they right good at wrestlin'."

Omen's eyes swung to the pouch. With care, his father reached inside and pulled out the alligator tooth captured by his grandfather, Fitzgerald Crow, over fifty years ago. Now, the tooth dangled from a chain offset with two smooth chunks of turquoise. He could barely contain his excitement as his father slipped the prize over his head and stood back to admire his son with a smile.

"What is strength?" Ivan grunted.

Omen took a deep breath. "Strength is the family business."

Ivan turned to the Crow family. "What is strength?" he called again.

"Strength is the family business!" They shouted in unison.

"What is strength?"

"Strength is the family business!"

Ivan pumped his fist in the air. "Now, let's win this thing!"

* * *

Dr. Djinn returned in all black with a bright green parrot perched on her shoulder. She tipped her hat to signal quiet. "We started with twenty, now we're down to four. Give our boys—" she turned to wink in Helena's direction, "—and girl a round of applause!" The crowd obliged with whistles and shouts. "And now, let's meet our semi-finalists."

Omen held his breath. He'd much rather face Cairo in the final. That would make the victory sweeter.

"In bout one we have Cairo Armwood versus Helena Hightower and in bout two we have Omen Crow versus Donnie Dumbbell!"

Omen breathed a sigh of relief seconds before chaos broke out.

"We protest!" Cairo and his corner yelled in unison. "We protest!"

The crowd settled into a hush.

Dr. Djinn's eyes narrowed into slits. "You protest?'

"We do. Wrestlin' a girl is 'gainst everything we stand for," Cairo's father huffed.

The crowd stirred in the late afternoon heat. Whispers of agreement rocked the gathering as they stood, on edge.

"Well then, does this mean your son is forfeiting his semi-final match?" Dr. Djinn studied her nails.

The Armwoods slapped their knees in mock laughter. "Never," Cairo's father growled. "It wouldn't be wise for my son to wrestle a... girl," he spat.

Omen glanced at Helena's corner, a knot of copper-skinned, black-haired women. If they'd been at all bothered by this display of disrespect, none of them showed it.

"It wouldn't be wise?" Dr. Djinn snickered.

Cairo's scowl crumbled. His father poked out his massive chest. "Arm wrestling is a man's sport!" Mr. Armwood prattled on, tiny bits of spittle flying from his mouth.

"A man's sport! A man's sport!" mocked the parrot.

Dr. Djinn leaned forward, placing her weight on her cane, and lacing her fingers around its topper. "Correct me if I'm wrong, but your union recently voted on the inclusion of women and girls in arm wrestling and other strength competitions. How did your union vote, Mr. Armwood?"

Cairo's father's eyes flashed in anger. "They…they voted yes."

"They voted yes! They voted yes!" The parrot strut from one of Dr. Djinn's shoulders to the other.

She cupped a hand over her ear. "I didn't quite catch that."

Again, Dr. Djinn's parrot let out a piercing squawk. "Yes! They voted yes! They voted yes!" The parrot screeched as it puffed up its feathers before settling down.

Laughter spread through the gathering as Cairo lumbered across the stage. "I'm not arm wrestling a girl. I won't do it!"

Dr. Djinn rolled her eyes. "Very well. I will grant you your wish. You will not have to wrestle a girl."

"Not have to wrestle a girl! Not have to wrestle a girl!" the parrot squawked in turn.

Dr. Djinn turned on her heels. "Before we move on, are there any others who feel this way? Please, speak now."

One by one, the men in Donnie Dumbbell's corner raised their hands.

Dr. Djinn looked out into the crowd. "Anyone else?"

"Anyone else?" the parrot shrieked. "Anyone else?"

Omen turned to his corner. Beating a girl in the final bout wasn't ideal. In fact, his victory might be questioned due to the "quality" of the match. Still, there was nothing he wanted more than to win, regardless of his opponent. He'd trained 364 days for this very moment. Before his father could raise a hand, he gripped his chain inside his fist and pleaded with his eyes. "No!" he hissed.

Ivan and Big Bub exchanged a frown, but honored his request.

Dr. Djinn faced the crowd. "It seems Omen Crow is the only competitor willing to take his chances against Helena Hightower."

"Take his chances! Squawk! Take his chances!" the parrot declared.

"As the final judge of this tournament, I reserve the right to make an executive decision." She formed a tent with her fingers. "Mr. Dumbbell and Mr. Armwood, by refusing to engage in competition with Miss Hightower, you hereby forfeit your rights to continue in the tournament."

The Armwood and Dumbbell corners erupted in angry curses. Omen held his breath, waiting for an all-out brawl. But before any such thing could happen, the men were ushered away by Professor Blue and his silk pant wearing associates.

Dr. Djinn winked. "Good. And now we have our final match! Seats please!"

For the third time that day, Omen placed his elbows on the wooden barrel as shouts rippled through the crowd. He looked in Helena's coal black eyes. He expected a fight.

They locked hands as Blue cupped his palm over theirs.

"On the count of three. One. Two. Three!"

Omen won in seconds. It was too easy.

"Omen! Omen! Omen!" Out of the corner of his eye, he saw his younger brother, Night, beginning a chant.

During the second match, the girl's grip tightened. Beads of sweat lined his temples. He'd never felt such pressure from a peer, not even Cairo. Still, he fought back, tightening his hold on her sweaty hand. A moan escaped from her lips. In a flash, his arm slammed on the barrel.

Gasps echoed throughout the clearing. Omen sucked in air as the memory of last year flooded back in a giant wave. *Sometimes, the will skips a generation. Might be the mighty Crows are finally stepping aside for another family to take the crown. He ain't got the genes. Ivan done trained the boy soft. I know Old man Fitzgerald Crow is turning over in his grave.*

Omen leaned over in his chair to catch his breath. When he opened his eyes, he saw the tooth dangling in front of him. His grandfather had wrestled a ten-foot gator and won. *His grandfather.* Those were the people he came from. *Strength is the family business.*

Omen bit his lip and set his elbow on the barrel. Professor Blue placed a palm over the two competitors' hands for one last time.

"On three. One, two..."

Again, came the crushing force and Omen nearly pinned Helena's arm in the opening seconds. Moments later, she regained the advantage. Seconds passed with neither competitor gaining ground. Omen held his breath. In his mind's eye, he saw his grandfather pouncing on a gator and its thick tail thrashing back and forth. Sharp teeth poised to tear into his flesh. Omen swallowed hard, but the girl's arm wouldn't budge. Quickly, the tables turned, Omen watched his arm bending backward. *Strength is the family business.* The voices of doubt echoed in his head. *Sometimes, the will skips a generation. He ain't got the genes.* With a roar from deep in his gut, he regained the edge and pinned the girl's sturdy arm to the barrel. He jumped up as his chair went clattering to the floor.

The crowd roared. After a few moments of hysteria, Dr. Djinn waved her hands high and Professor Blue whistled for calm.

"It is my vision that the Odd Scholars will be the best of the best. The scholarships will be awarded to those who show sportsmanship and character at all times."

"Squawk! Character at all times. Character at all times. Squawk!" the parrot chirped.

With that being said, this year's *Mighty Bicep Competition* winner is—" She held his hand up high. "Omen Crow! Congratulations young man. You are the winner of the *Mighty Biceps Juvenile Arm-Wrestling Competition* and my very first Odd Scholar!" She spun on her heels. "One down, three to go!"

TWO

THE KLEPTOMANIAC INVENTOR

Charleston, SC 1920

After three grueling hours of demonstrations, the contestants finally reached the end of Charleston's *Juvenile Ingenuity Competition*. A cluster of wooden tables covered with cogs, gears, and other mechanical instruments formed a circle under a pavilion in the middle of the marketplace. Brenda watched in silence as Dr. Djinn inspected her latest invention in the palm of her hand. No more than two inches in length, the contraption had a steel outer shell with a slender glass barrel inside. Minuscule wires looped around the bottom and an inch-long syringe poked from its end. Tiny copper buttons covered the barrel's side. Brenda cracked her knuckles behind her back.

"Never seen anything like it," Dr. Djinn said under her breath. "What's it made of?"

"Ninety-two percent inox. Copper, wire, and glass make up the remaining eight percent." Brenda cleared her throat. "Inox is steel. It's lightweight and resistant to staining."

Dr. Djinn looked in the direction of a tall man at her side with ink-black skin. He responded with a stiff nod. She turned back to Brenda. "Demonstrate."

Brenda took the contraption out of the magician's palm. "It's a siphoning mechanism." Her eyes settled on a jar dangling from the man's belt. Now and again, its contents would bubble and flash as if possessed by some unseen force. She motioned toward it. "May I use the jar?"

Gasps and chatter tore through the gathering. The man's eyes grew wide. "Only a Taint—someone with magic blood, can properly handle the contents of a Soul Jar—"

"This is an ingenuity competition, Professor Blue." Dr. Djinn rubbed her palms together. "If anything goes wrong, we can deal with it. Let's see what she can do."

The Professor stared at Dr. Djinn through narrowed eyes. "Very well." He threw her a side-long glance. "But we must protect our potential Scholars at all costs. We both know what's inside that Jar." His West Indian lilt floated through the heavy Charleston air as he lifted the clasp on his belt.

Brenda watched as he sat it on the table in front of her. The audience crept forward, tightening around them.

With the utmost care, she balanced her invention between her thumb and index finger and pressed one of the buttons on its side. A tiny blue flame emanated from the syringe, gradually penetrating the glass. The Jar rattled and screeched. Out of the corner of her eye, Brenda could see Professor Blue reaching for it as Dr. Djinn blocked his efforts.

After the syringe cleanly broke through the glass, Brenda pushed another button. Instantly, the mucous like substance from the Soul Jar filled the glass barrel. With a subtle click, the syringe retracted and the tiny opening in the Jar closed like a healed wound. Brenda reached for the glass barrel, now filled with demonic fluid.

"The barrel is heat and cold resistant. You can use it to inject or draw out poison or any substance you'd like." She held the barrel up high. "I call it a Fire Needle."

Dr. Djinn tipped her top hat, bright green like her tuxedo. "Well done, young lady."

Resounding applause and whistles rippled through the crowd as Brenda replaced the barrel inside the Fire Needle with a click, injected the goo back into the Soul Jar, and pushed it toward the Professor.

Blue reattached it to his belt loop and gave her a small smile. "Impressive."

Dr. Djinn raised an arm up high, silencing the chatter.

"Thank you all for your inventions. Each of you has mesmerized, inspired, and surprised me this afternoon. After a one-hour intermission, I will announce the winner of the *Juvenile Ingenuity Competition* and our second Odd Scholarship."

Back at her station, Brenda glanced at her stopwatch, reached for her briefcase, and dismantled her invention, piece by piece. A tiny woman squeezed through the crowd and hurried toward her.

"A whole hour, Aunt Squeak!" Brenda huffed as the woman reached her side.

"Patience Beebee, patience." Squeak rubbed her shoulder.

Brenda frowned at the invention, now a pile of tiny cogs and screws. "It shouldn't take an hour to make a decision."

"They want to make sure they choose well," Squeak said. "The competition is top notch."

Brenda turned back to her briefcase and pushed a button on its side. The case popped open to reveal a slew of flaps, snaps, buttons, and drawers. Tiny lights blinked on and off in a strange rhythm. After she unzipped a felt-lined pocket, she scraped the parts of the Fire Needle inside.

"Your uncle loved that briefcase." Aunt Squeak stared at the contraption with a longing in her eyes.

Brenda kept her eyes fastened to the pile of mechanical parts. She opened another drawer soaked in ul-tra-violet rays.

"Seeing you here and doing such a fantastic job—" Squeak dabbed at her eyes with a lacy kerchief.

"I know. I know. Uncle Rufus would be proud," Brenda sighed.

Squeak stuffed the kerchief in her purse. "Sure would," she sniffled. "You were fantastic Beebee! Imagine, a fully funded education at the Hampton Normal and Agricultural Institute!" Her aunt pulled a newspaper clipping from her purse and gently unfolded the tiny squares. "Take a look...for extra motivation."

Brenda turned from the briefcase and peered at the clipping.

The Negro World

Dr. Marvellus Djinn, The Motherland, and Resistance

May 1, 1920

Though the grand opening of *The Motherland* is less than 60 days away, the national buzz surrounding it is a potent reminder of the intrigue of its creator, Dr. Marvellus Djinn.

The nation was introduced to Dr. Djinn when she worked as an assistant to the incomparable magician, Black Herman, in the early 1910s. After setting off on her own in 1915, she amassed a fortune selling tonics and talismans during her impressive traveling one-woman magic show. In 1916, she and fellow UNIA member, Professor Bartholomew Blue, discussed their ideas for *The Motherland* with H.D. Woodson, the brilliant Negro Architect of several buildings in Washington, DC, including portions (and portals) of Union Station. The project broke ground with Woodson at the helm later that year. Djinn describes the park as a "simmering stew of myth, history, science, magic, and suspense." Though she remains tight-lipped about the park's Grand Menagerie and the creatures inside, she was more forthcoming about its dedication to invention and architecture.

"I wanted to create a place that showcases the brilliance of innovation and the pride of our history," Djinn told *The Negro World*. In partnership with the Hampton Institute, Djinn is constructing "an inventor's playground with state-of-the-art equipment" inside the park's replica of the Eastern Rift Mountains. The innovation lab will serve as an incubator for the ideas of young Negro inventors and scientists. Patents will be plentiful as well as the money needed to fund them. The innovation lab is set to open this fall.

"*The Motherland* is my way of giving Colored folks a much-needed escape from Jim Crow," she said by phone on Monday. "This park is my resistance."

The Motherland's grand opening is set for June 15, 1920.
For more information on discounted tickets for Bona fide UNIA members, see page C12.

A smile slid across Brenda's face. She could already see herself inside the lab, rummaging through cogs, screws, and scrap metal inventing anything she wanted, with more tools at her disposal than she'd ever had.

"That scholarship is yours, Beebee." Aunt Squeak chucked her under the chin. "Now, let's look around." Squeak pointed at a storefront and lowered her voice. "That's a Two-headed woman's shop." She jabbed her playfully in the arm. "Want a reading?"

Her aunt was from the Low Country. Initially, she'd downplayed those roots for Brenda's uncle, the big city man from Philadelphia she'd fallen in love with. Funny thing is her strangeness is what reeled him in. He would have married her regardless. Uncle Rufus had told Brenda as much many times before.

A shiver ran through Brenda's thin frame despite the summer heat. "No thanks."

"Well, suit yourself." Squeak shrugged. She doubled back to meet her niece's eyes. "Dr. Djinn is the best Colored magician the world has ever seen. It's about time everyone knew your name, too. And fix that skirt!" Squeak fumbled with Brenda's hemline and gave her a once over. She licked one of her thumbs, smoothed her dark eyebrows, and stifled a groan as her aunt tugged at the thick cornrows dusting her shoulders. Squeak squinted through the sunshine, admiring her handiwork. "Go on and have a look around." She raised an eyebrow. "One hour. No funny business. We ain't in Philly."

Brenda forced a smile. "Yes, ma'am." The moment Squeak turned her back and moseyed toward the two-headed woman's shop, Brenda hiked up her skirt. She chuckled to herself as her aunt disappeared in the crowd.

"I hate when they do all that fussin.' Ain't no need," a voice called over her shoulder.

Brenda turned to face a girl with two bushy plaits on either side of her head. She recognized the girl right away as one of her competitors.

She stuck out a skinny arm. "I'm Constance." She narrowed her eyes. "Seems to me you're in the way of me getting one of those scholarships."

What Constance didn't know was her name didn't matter one bit. From the moment Brenda saw that bushy hair, she knew she'd be calling her Plaits. Brenda cocked her head to the side. "Brenda from Philadelphia. And the only person I ever compete with is myself; you should try it."

Plaits looked her up and down like she wanted a fight. And that's when Brenda caught sight of the girl's shoulder bag, beige, brand new, and almost as big as she was. One of the clasps to secure it shut had been left open and several crumpled bills peeked from inside. *Bad move Plaits, bad move.*

"Well, you sure did come a long way to go back empty handed." Plaits ran her tongue across her bucked teeth.

"You think way too much of yourself," Brenda snapped.

"How old are you?" Plaits sneered.

"Old enough," Brenda countered.

"Yeah? When I saw you, I thought you were 'bout twelve or thirteen. Couldn't be no more than that." Plaits placed a hand on one of her non-existent hips.

"Why do you care?"

Plaits chuckled. "You and your big city confidence. The bigger they are—"

"Leave me alone," she said, annoyed.

"And if I don't?" Plaits rolled her neck in a circle.

Brenda walked off, nudging Plaits just enough to brush her open satchel. With one deft movement, Brenda stuffed the bills in her fist. The flawless exchange made her three dollars richer. Some people deserved what was coming to them and some were in the wrong place at the wrong time. Plaits was a little bit of both. Briefcase slung across her middle, she headed in the opposite direction, pushing her way through the thick crowd.

Cabbage row had always been Aunt Squeak's favorite place. The maze of tents, carts, and storefronts created playful shadows in the late afternoon. She'd visited Charleston every year for as long as she could remember. Brenda walked briskly past a pyramid of ripe peaches. A heavy-set vendor smiled in her direction.

"Peaches! Only a nickel! Fresh peaches!"

The moment the vendor turned her head, Brenda slipped between two tables and swiped a ripe peach from the pile, tender and fuzzy in her palm. She took a bite as she hurried on. A river of sticky liquid dripped into the crevices of her fingers. *So good.* Though she'd never admit it to Aunt Squeak, Cabbage Row had become one of her favorite places as well. Haggling customers, a cacophony of odors: flowers mixed with ripe fruit and raw meat fresh from the slaughter. She gazed at the long, flowy skirts spread out over wooden tables and carts covered with perfume bottles. Fish with their heads still attached stared at her from trays overflowing with ice. A tent caught Brenda's attention. Emerald ferns sprouted from clay jars. Colorful glass bottles and bowls sat on wooden shelves. A squat container of gold mud sat beside a triangular tin filled to the brim with cobalt blue. The aroma of spiced sandalwood incense drifted beneath her nostrils. She wandered toward one of the shelves. A bottle with raised indentations caught her eye. Without so much as a thought, she reached for it, mesmerized. It was like fire and ice in her palm. Her eyes narrowed. *Why not?* She felt lucky enough.

"Tonic's been in my family for years," a voice drifted over the tinkle of wind chimes.

Brenda froze. *Damn.* She'd never been this close to being caught. "What's in it?" she asked, turning the bottle over in her trembling hands.

"Ginger, milkweed, and mint. Brings peace to an anxious mind," the voice answered.

Brenda turned to face the stranger. Where she expected a face, she saw nothing but long, twisting braids adorned with silver beads. Layers of black skirts covered her from waist to ankle. She wore a white blouse, thin enough to rustle in the stingy breeze. The braids covered the left side of the girl's face like a veil. Her single visible eye was large and dark brown. Brenda blinked. The girl couldn't have been more than a year or two older than her, if that.

In response, the girl returned Brenda's stare with a bone deep gaze. It was as if she could see her birth, the thoughts in her skull, and all her fears stenciled inside a single breath. Uneasy, she shifted her weight, stepped backward, and nearly knocked over a shelf. Nearly a dozen tins and bottles rattled on their shelves, tilting at dangerous angles, all threatening to tumble to the ground. The girl dove forward in time to save a rainbow-colored substance in an expensive-looking crystal vial. Brenda jostled a tin filled with glitter and two other bottles in her arms before placing each back on the shelf. Cheeks hot with embarrassment, she turned to leave.

"Want a reading? Might aid what's troublin' you," the girl said as she straightened the shelf.

"You don't know anything about me," Brenda spat over her shoulder.

"I don't. But what if I could show you who you'll be in ten years, ten days? Who you mighta been in the past?" She smiled. "Hi Brenda, I'm Clair. Follow me."

Brenda stood as still as a statue. She hadn't given her name. Half terrified, half curious, she followed the girl toward a table and chair in the back of the tent. Clair motioned for Brenda to sit, then pulled a wooden bowl toward her. Brenda adjusted her briefcase still dangling across her middle and sat. Inside the bowl, she saw a tooth, two shiny pennies, a flamingo feather, and a chunk of bark from a palmetto tree. Clair filled the bowl with water. As the water rippled, an image formed. Brenda recognized it immediately: trees with pink blossoms, a tall bell tower, horse-drawn carriages. *Philadelphia. Center City.*

Brenda pulled her eyes away from the image as Clair fell into a trance. Brenda's eyes darted around the room. She wanted to run but couldn't move. An unknown force kept her glued to the chair.

"Look," Clair said in a gargled whisper.

Brenda swallowed hard, heart slamming against her chest. She saw herself standing beside her Uncle Rufus in his antique shop on Lombard Street. She could see it all: the crow's feet clawing at the edges of his gray eyes, the deep dimples in his cheeks, and a white halo of hair stretching from ear to ear. Her favorite uncle had a smile as easy as a breeze. He pushed his tortoiseshell frames up the bridge of his nose. Brenda inhaled deeply. Sure enough, the familiar scent met her nose: mothballs, pine cleaner, and furniture polish.

"Be careful with that spring, Beebee. You're too heavy handed," Uncle Rufus warned.

Rufus' Rare Antiques wasn't your run of the mill antique shop. They were surrounded by oak armoires, Victorian lamps, and books. Each artifact had a story her uncle sought to preserve. Brenda focused on the tiny rods, springs, and wheels spread before her.

"Come on now. It's your birthday. You know what happens," Uncle Rufus coaxed.

Brenda watched herself inside the memory. "I know," she heard herself say.

The packages began arriving on her tenth birthday. They came wrapped in old newspaper, with no return address, and written in a curious cursive script. It wasn't long before Uncle Rufus became obsessed. Brenda had no idea why Benjamin Banneker had chosen her, the great, great, great niece he'd never known, to construct inventions he hadn't lived to complete.

"Well, open it!" Uncle Rufus leaned over her shoulder.

Brenda turned the cylindrical box over in her hands. It looked different from the first she'd received five years ago. This one was made of segmented cherry wood while the others had been metal, locked, and with the same cylindrical shape. She surveyed the tiny squares, each labeled with a letter or symbol.

"Uncle Rufus, when was Uncle Benjamin born?" Brenda chewed on her lip.

"November 9, 1731," Rufus paused. "But that clue unlocked the last one. I don't think it will be that easy."

Brenda cleaned the lens on her magnifying glass with a cloth. "Where's the almanac?"

Uncle Rufus turned to a nearby shelf and pulled the book from its resting place. "Be careful with it. Those pages are older than us both."

With utmost care, she searched the delicate pages, checking for clues and combing through the index. After thirty fruitless minutes, she put down the almanac with a grunt.

"Maybe we're overthinking. Look, there's seven panels." Rufus pointed at the box. "Try, 'almanac.'"

Brenda did as she was told. A subtle click sounded. Two pieces of parchment slid from the wooden cylinder. The larger revealed a blueprint for a pair of intricate eyeglasses made of tiny wires, copper scraps, glass panels, and cogs.

"He trusts you from the grave, BeeBee!" Uncle Rufus grasped her by the shoulders.

The smaller parchment featured words written in the same cursive script.

An eye for an eye.

Brenda blinked back tears as the memory melted into the pennies, feather, bark, and tooth. Her lip quivered. "That was the last time I saw him alive. He was so happy." She wiped the tears from her cheeks.

Clair pushed the braids covering her left eye aside. To Brenda's surprise, she wore a jet-black eye patch with silver sequins sewn on its surface.

Brenda covered her mouth. "How?"

"An accident when I was two." Clair pointed to her eye patch. "A woman wanted revenge against my mama. I was the target."

"I'm sorry," Brenda said in a small voice.

Clair's lips curled into a smile as she threw her head back in laughter. "Kidding!" She winked and lifted the patch to reveal another brown eye framed by long lashes.

"But—"

"Caught pink-eye a few years ago. Wore a patch so my eye could heal. It also kept Big Mama's healing herbs and ointment in place." Clair shrugged. "Got used to it. Besides, the patch goes well with the ambiance." She gestured around the tent. "Mystery sells."

"Isn't that dishonest?" Brenda raised her eyebrow.

"Dishonest? You mean like stealing a peach from a vendor? Or a tonic from my shop?" Clair replied with a wink.

Brenda shifted uncomfortably in her chair. "What about what I just saw? Was that—?"

"I'm a Bona fide Sage, that's for sure," Clair chuckled. "Sometimes you gotta add a little extra to draw folks in—did you ever make the glasses in that memory?"

Brenda's mouth upturned into a smile. "Sure did."

"There you are!"

Brenda whirled around to see her Aunt Squeak, lips spread in a disappointed frown.

"I've been looking all over for you!"

"Aunt Squeak--" Brenda stammered.

"Never mind that now!" She thrust a finger at her wristwatch. "We have three minutes to get back to the pavilion. You had better come on here, gal!"

Brenda turned back to Clair. "Thank you. Take this, please." She reached inside her pocket and pulled out three crumpled bills.

Clair grinned and accepted the payment. "Somethin' tells me I'll be seein' you again."

The two girls exchanged a smile before Brenda darted out of the tent.

Brenda rushed between bustling shoppers, carts, and tables. She followed close as her aunt squeezed her tiny frame between tents and around poles. Stomach growling, she resisted the urge to swipe another peach from the big-bellied vendor and continued on. Nearly out of breath, she dashed toward the gathering.

"Go on BeeBee, I'll catch up! You get up there!" Squeak sputtered through heavy gasps.

Brenda pushed through the crowd beyond the pavilion's edge. By the time she reached the center, the contestants were standing behind their tables with their inventions displayed in front of them. From the looks of it, Dr. Djinn hadn't revealed the winner yet. Instead, the Professor stood in the center, his West Indian accent coating the air like honey on a wooden dipper.

"Equipped with state-of-the-art amusement rides, a safari of creatures you've never seen before, and an ancient library, *The Motherland* is like nothing the world has ever seen!" Professor Blue exclaimed with the flair of a showman. The crowd applauded.

Brenda tip-toed back to her table, flung open her briefcase, and quickly re-assembled her invention. Out of the corner of her eye, she saw Plaits smirk in her direction. Brenda thought of the three dollars she'd lifted from her open satchel and shook her head.

"Welcome back to the *Annual Junior Ingenuity Competition!*" The crowd parted as Dr. Djinn strolled to Professor Blue's side. A brown ferret wearing a tiny top hat peaked over her shoulder. "The competition was stiff." She held her breath as Dr. Djinn approached each table. "Each of these young people showed tremendous creativity and intelligence beyond their years."

"Well beyond," Professor Blue chimed in.

Dr. Djinn spun around to face her audience. "But there was one particular invention that was fashioned with such intricacy that we could not stop raving about it."

"Impressive indeed." Professor Blue's bald head bobbed up and down in agreement.

She held her breath as Dr. Djinn removed her hat. "Please put your hands together to congratulate Brenda Banneker, our second Odd Scholar!"

Brenda beamed with pride from behind her table as Aunt Squeak made her way through the crowd.

"I had a feeling, Beebee! I had a feeling!" Squeak said while squeezing her tight.

"I know, Auntie," she said as she wrapped her arms around her tiny waist. "I think I had a feeling, too."

THREE

A CURE FOR BIGOTRY

Washington, DC 1920

Thelonious lowered his voice. "They say she killed a man…maybe two."

"Well, I can think of a lot of reasons why someone might kill someone in the South. Namely, self-defense." Elliot removed his protective goggles and turned his attention back to a beaker filled with smoke.

Arthur squeezed his nostrils closed with his fingers and hurried past Thelonious's station. "True. Stuff happens down there."

"*Down there?*" Moses frowned. "Did you forget what happened last summer?"

Art's eyes shifted to the ground. "Never," he said in a whisper.

Thelonious pulled a crumpled newspaper article from his shirt pocket. "Take a look at this."

𝕿𝖍𝖊 𝕹𝖊𝖌𝖗𝖔 𝖂𝖔𝖗𝖑𝖉

Who is Dr. Marvellus Djinn?

September 1, 1919

Storming the world in the early 1910s, Dr. Marvellus Djinn is most famously known for her inclusion in the 1915 San Francisco World's Fair. There, she shocked the world as the first magician to successfully extract souls from cadavers and store them outside of the body. Her pavilion at the fair was one of the most widely attended and talked about for years to come.

While traveling to Harlem in 1916, she attended one of the Honorable Marcus Mosiah Garvey's lectures. In May 1917, Dr. Djinn became one of the original members of the Universal Negro Improvement Association. As a Bona fide member of the UNIA, she used her talents to spread the Honorable Marcus Mosiah Garvey's teachings throughout the United States and Canada. In 1917, she and fellow UNIA member Professor Bartholomew Blue, a Jamaican native and one of the Honorable Marcus Mosiah Garvey's closest confidantes, dreamed up *The Motherland*, a magical theme park for Negroes and a replica of Mother Africa herself in Hampton, VA.

Dr. Djinn has thwarted all efforts by those in power to destroy her. From launching a successful campaign for the funding of the multi-million-dollar park to surviving a lynching, she is worthy of our support. *The Motherland* will open to the public on June 15, 1920 in Hampton, VA. As a proud sponsor of the park, U.N.I.A members will receive half price admission during the month of June for its grand opening. *(See page F12 for more information.)*

Arthur shrugged. "So what?"

Thelonious slapped his forehead and thrust his index finger in the direction of the article. "She survived a lynching! Did you read that?"

Elliot stroked his chin. "Wish I could bottle up whatever courage she had and make it into a cure."

Thelonious shook his head. "She's a Taint," he said as his eyes darted around the room before settling on Elliot and Moses. "Might even be a Time Thief."

Art shrugged. "If she's a Taint, she'll have a Mark. They're easy enough to find to be sure."

"Mark?" Elliot frowned.

Art flashed a slick smile and nudged Elliot in the arm with his elbow. "Word of advice little brother, never get so caught up in books that you don't know what's hip. All Taints have Art Marks. The Marks let you know the order they're in."

"Yup," Thelonious began counting on his fingers. "There's Time Thieves, Artists, Shifters, and Sages. Each has their own special mark in a different place on their body."

"What are you some kind of Taint expert?" Moses smirked.

"Well, there was this Shifter girl I was trying to court." Thelonious's eyes narrowed to slits as he rubbed his palms together.

Arthur and Moses doubled over in laughter. "The one who stood you up at Hilliard's Ice Cream Shop back in September?" Arthur gasped through a belly laugh.

"Aww man, whatever." Thelonious crossed his arms. "She ain't stand me up. She was a Shifter. She looked different and I didn't know who she was."

Elliot patted his best friend on the back before heading back to his station. "It's okay, man. It happens to the best of us."

It was Elliot's third consecutive year participating in *The Boys Chemistry Competition* and clearly, his nerves were getting the best of him. He needed to walk. As he weaved between picnic tables, he sized up his competition. A Venus flytrap surrounded by sealed containers filled to the brim with flies sat on one tabletop. He glanced at the flies as they shot around inside, unaware of their fate. On the table beside the plant sat several perfume bottles with colorful spray bulbs. He watched as his best friend, Thelonious, grinned from ear to ear. The pungent odor of citrus and sulfur wafted in his direction. Elliot held his breath. He didn't have the heart to tell Thelonious the perfumes smelled like death in a skillet. No one did. And that's when he saw it, everything he needed stuffed behind a curtain.

The back of the tent had been converted into a makeshift supply center. Shelves were stacked with extra vials, Bunsen burners, beakers, clamps, and anything else a budding chemist might need. Satisfied with his stash, he grabbed an extra set of tongs and set his sights on the rickety fence in the distance. Nothing. Still no sign of her, just a clown, children with sticky, candied apple hands, and the tinkling sound of laughter. A sign with the words, *Welcome Dr. Marvellus Djinn,* rippled between two poles above the fence. The boys had known one another for most of their lives. Elliot's best friend, Thelonious, lived next door and Moses was Elliot's cousin on his mama's side. Elliot smiled as he recalled them starting a small fire in his father's lab when they were eight. Turned out to be one of the best days of his life. His smile dissolved into a frown. *Until Art ruined it.* Arthur was his older brother by 11 months. Elliot scowled. There was nothing written that said you had to like your kin. Life was like that sometimes. He had avoided Arthur's eyes the entire morning. He knew how badly his brother wanted the scholarship, but he wanted it too. A fully funded education would change their lives.

"They say she's a Time Thief." Thelonious glanced over his shoulder as if he was sharing top secret information.

Elliot looked up, intrigued. Time Thieves were more than your regular, run of the mill magicians. They were the PhDs of their order. Time Thieves bought wisdom from antiquity that average people didn't have, magical or not. Elliot didn't come from magic. His kin were scientists, professors, and surgeons, not Sages or Thieves. They weren't born with Tainted blood to help them avoid the hardships of being Colored. He groaned under his breath. None of the boys at the fair were Taints, but they could all use the opportunity to tour a magical park and attend one of the best Colored schools in the country free of charge.

"Anybody seen her mark?" Moses asked. "That would settle it for good."

"Nope. That's why she's always wearing sleeves. Never seen a photograph of the woman without a full tuxedo." Thelonious leaned over his cauldron. "And the killings ain't all. I heard all that money ain't really hers."

"Now you're talking crazy, Moses," Elliot scoffed. "Next you'll be saying wearing pants makes her dangerous."

A pulsing vein appeared above Moses's temple. "Y'all act like none of this stuff is possible!" He paused. "And she does wear pants every day! It's all my mama and dad could talk about when I entered the competition! What kind of woman does that?"

"A rich one," Thelonious chimed in as the others chuckled.

"I mean, yeah she wears pants," Arthur interjected. "Who cares I guess, but there's gotta be a limit to what she can do. Killing folks, stealing money without getting caught, time traveling... nobody's God, but God, right?"

"And yet we're all here. All trying to figure out how we can win this scholarship. All trying to be the next scholar who can say he's studied with the great Dr. Marvellus Djinn...who wears pants!" Elliot narrowed his eyes in Moses' direction. "Either we believe what Moses says or we don't. Either we compete or we don't. Science is our magic. As far as I'm concerned, science is magic, too."

The boys went quiet aside from the soft clink of glass on glass. Elliot's gaze swung back to the gate; nothing.

"Look, you guys can sit around gossiping all you want. I've got work to do." Elliot returned to his station and retrieved one of his most prized possessions, the brown leather bag he'd received for his thirteenth birthday. He ran his fingers along an inside pocket lined with notes and haphazard doodles. The texture of suede and butter-soft leather made him smile. The bag was an extension of himself. Every idea he had in the last three years had been stuffed inside. He peered at one of the notes, crumpled and covered with scribbles. *This one was special.* He plucked it with his thumb and index finger.

A shrill whistle snatched him back to the present. The liquid in his beakers were at a boil. He fumbled with the note and stuffed it back in the bag. Large, loosely connected ribbons of smoke danced across the lip of the glass. *Perfect.* He steadied his hand and removed the stopper from a tiny test tube. In one fluid motion, he poured a sky-blue substance into a bowl filled with thick, canary yellow liquid releasing a puff of green smoke. He sniffed the scent of spearmint and bottled a bit of the mixture into a crystal vial.

"Good luck. I know this is hard."

Elliot turned to meet his brother's eyes. They were at eye level on account of Elliot's growth spurt a few months ago.

"Don't take it personal when I beat you." Art had a smile like an oil slick. There was always something underneath it, something slimy and insincere. He smoothed his lab coat and gestured toward the materials strewn across his station. "How do you like your chances?"

"I like them just fine, thanks."

"May the best man win." Art clasped him on the shoulder and they exchanged an awkward glance before he walked off.

Before he could give his brother another thought, a disturbance erupted at the fair's entrance. He craned his neck as a crowd gathered outside. A man in red and white checkered pants on stilts lumbered under the tent. The megaphone attached to his belt bobbed above their heads.

"Make way, make way, make way one and all." A tornado of noise and color gathered nearby. A flurry of reporters holding flashing cameras formed a knot around the man on stilts. Elliot spotted a black top hat somewhere in the center of the commotion and a woman with dark brown skin and round, shining eyes smiled wide. Though curiously dressed in a bright yellow tuxedo, she was beautiful. *No one had mentioned she was beautiful.* The newspaper clippings hadn't done her justice. He adjusted his glasses for a better view.

She cleared her throat. "The Honorable Marcus Garvey tells us to try to associate with people from whom we can learn something. All the knowledge that you want is in the world, and all you must do is go and seek it. Good morning, gentleman!" She flashed a thousand-watt grin. "I'm so happy to be with you today at the Latimer School for Gifted Boys! I am the noble, the honorable, the magical—" She weaved through the labyrinth of tables while emphasizing each word. "--Mistress of Mysticism, Dr. Marvellus Djinn!" Red, black, and green confetti rained down on them. "I look forward to meeting all of you as well as your concoctions. Good luck!" In an instant, she was swallowed inside the growing mob.

In an instant, the boys hurried to practice their presentations and set up their elixirs. According to scholarship guidelines, they would be judged on creativity, choice of ingredients, and overall quality of product. Easy enough. The hard part was pitching to a famous magician and keeping cool. Elliot's stomach did a somersault before landing somewhere near his knees.

Art was first. Elliot watched from afar as the crowd migrated toward his demonstration. To Elliot's surprise, he appeared nervous and continued to fiddle with his lab coat, pushing the sleeves to his elbows. As much as he hated to admit it, his brother was a complete charmer. Girls loved him and almost every teenage boy under that tent wanted *to be* him. It was an odd sight to behold.

When Elliot spotted his father peering over the shoulder of a woman with a cane, he grinned. Ernest Just was one of the best Colored scientists in the country. He was the reason he and his brother pushed themselves to be the best they could be. He hadn't thought his father would make it to the event due to prior commitments. Now he had two people to impress.

All eyes were glued to Art as he spoke. Elliot caught Thelonious's eye. Together, they moved closer. When the faint smell of mint wafted toward him, his heart sank. He craned his neck to see over the crowd. Sure enough, his burner had been lit and a bowl of a canary yellow liquid sat next to a tiny vial of sky-blue. Elliot's cheeks grew hot. Everyone in the tent held a collective breath as Art gently pulled the stopper from his test tube and poured with the precision of a master chemist.

"And this, ladies and gentlemen, is my—"

"Kiss of Love." Elliot pounded a fist in his palm and shoved his hands in his lab coat before walking briskly back to his station.

Thelonious looked at him with wide eyes of concern. "What're you gonna do? You only have twenty minutes tops."

In his mind's eye, Elliot envisioned himself socking his brother in the jaw, but of course that wouldn't be received well. Not here, anyway. He shook his head, reached for his leather bag, and rifled through his notes. *Quick and impressive. I need something quick and impressive.*

"Everything okay, son?"

His father's deep baritone caught him off guard. He held Elliot's eyes with a questioning gaze.

"Fine, dad. Doing some last-minute prep work."

"Good. You know I believe in you." Ernest Just smiled and after a hearty clasp on the back, he moved on.

Elliot tuned out the demonstrations, applause, and occasional pockets of laughter. Lucky for him, Thelonious had spread the word to stall. Moses and the others were laying it on thick. Thelonious had invited several onlookers to feed his Venus Fly Trap before Dr. Djinn and her sidekick could move on to the next table. His best friend winked in his direction. Great. He needed as much time as he could get.

He poured over his notes. *Too long. Incomplete. Unimpressive.* This couldn't be any old elixir. It had to be dynamic enough to win. Again, he stumbled upon the note with the faded writing. He felt a pang of anticipation. It was certainly good enough, great even. *Maybe. Why not?* He rubbed his palms together and combed the contents until he came to a small phial of purplish-pink powder. Crushed passion flower petals. After glancing at his watch, he looked up to gauge his progress. Time was ticking. Two more presentations and he was up. He made a dash for more supplies in the back. Once he retrieved a vial of turmeric, now reduced to a golden liquid, he pulled out its stopper and poured the contents into a larger beaker. He held it up to a ray of sunlight and gave it a quick swish. Then, he turned up the fire on his burner and added the liquid to a vial suspended above the flame. Something was missing. *Yes!*

One of the benefits of being the son of a scientist was access to rare concoctions. Ernest didn't believe in living in his lab. His father had always said the cures for everyday diseases were in the forests, rivers, and trees humans ignored each day. He pulled out a vial of brown chunks. Ginseng. Boosts brain health. Next, he snatched a plastic bag of bright green leaves. "Gotu Kola and Ginkgo Biloba for mental clarity and cognitive function," he muttered before tearing the leaves into shreds. With a flick of his wrist, he dropped the leaves inside his simmering mixture. He shut his eyes before grabbing another vial of clear liquid. Carefully, he opened the top and added a few drops. The smell of lemon wafted toward him as the mixture came to a rolling boil. *Perfect.* He smoothed his mustache and lifted the vial from above the flame with a pair of tongs. The contents were now a striking black with flecks of silver. He bottled the mixture in an empty beaker and gave it a final swish. *Showtime.* The crowd shuffled toward him.

Dr. Djinn stuck out her hand and pumped his arm. She peered at his nametag before looking over her shoulder in Art's direction. "Brothers?"

Elliot responded with a curt nod. By now, everyone had gathered around. As a final touch, he'd shifted the beaker full of gleaming black liquid directly in a stream of sunlight. He took a deep breath. "My name is Elliot Just, and this—" he pointed at the glass "—is a cure for bigotry."

A hush fell over the tent. His line of vision swung to Art. His brother looked on in shock. Win or lose, his introduction had the desired effect.

Dr. Djinn narrowed her eyes. "I'm sorry, but did you say that this—" she pointed at the beaker, "contains the cure for bigotry?"

"I did. I call it Formula: 0619, The Black Gaze."

"What's the significance of the name?" asked the man in stilts.

Elliot chewed on his bottom lip. "Juneteenth— and it honors a time when my uncle was lynched by a mob."

Chatter tore through the tent. Dr. Djinn patted his shoulder. "My deepest sympathies to you, your uncle, and your family."

Overwhelmed by a wave of sudden grief, he bit his lip. "Thank you, Dr. Djinn. My family appreciates your condolences."

The magician looked at her stilted companion as he bent low enough to whisper in her ear. After they exchanged a look, she continued. "How do I know this works? Where are your control and experimental groups? There isn't anyone here to test it on."

All eyes focused on Elliot. He inhaled sharply before answering. "The Black Gaze is like no other," he said. "It contains lemon extract and passion flower petals, Gotu Kola, Ginseng, and Ginkgo Biloba. All improve cognitive function and mental clarity." He caught a glimpse of his father's pensive glare out of the corner of his eye and continued. "What is bigotry? I, for one, think it's a disease of the mind. Bigotry is spread through ignorance and then, it seeps into the fabric of a country. It becomes culture. Bigotry is Colored water fountains

and Colored entrances. Colored hospitals and Colored
restaurants. Bigotry is my uncle Baron shot in the head
for being a Colored man in the wrong place at the wrong
time."

Elliot could sense the discomfort in the room.
The air was thick like a hearty sweat after a marathon
run. He could feel it all, from rising anger to profound
sadness. "But what if we could eliminate it?" He
snapped his fingers. "Just as scientists have discovered
treatments and cures for disease—" he looked at his father, "imagine if this beaker," Elliot held up the glass,
"holds a cure? We'd be legendary. Iconic. We'd change
the world." He paused and focused on the magician.
"Your odd scholarships are for the best and brightest, Dr.
Djinn. They will be among the most innovative Colored
teens in the country. All of the herbs I've chosen target
the brain. This elixir is potential in a bottle. My scientific
skill merged with your sorcery would be a heck of a
pair."

The murmurs grew louder as Dr. Djinn turned to
Elliot and tipped her hat. "Thank you, Mr. Just." She
spun around to face the surrounding audience. "Ladies
and Gentlemen, I'd like to thank you all for supporting
these fine young men. Please, join me in giving them all
a round of applause!" There were claps and whistles and
raucous shouts as the boys bowed and the cameras
flashed. "But unfortunately, there can only be one winner." A path formed as she walked to the center of the
tent. "Arthur Just has truly impressed me today with his
Kiss of Love tonic that he so brilliantly demonstrated for
the crowd. Extremely entertaining! And it looks like he's
stolen some hearts!"

A few people laughed as Art poked his chest out
and smiled from ear to ear. Those within his vicinity patted him on the back.

"Thelonious Jones' Venus Fly Trap musk was also a favorite of ours." Elliot clapped as Thelonious flashed a surprised grin. "As was Moses McCormick's smelling salts. I will need to deliberate before deciding. I'll be back with the name of the winning entry in ten minutes!" she shouted before rushing away.

Elliot wiped the sweat from his brow and leaned over his table, heart racing as his father pulled him into a hug.

"What made you decide on that experiment? That was a gamble, a big one. With no control or experimental groups, your hypothesis appears flimsy." His father stood back and adjusted his tie. "But, coupled with a bit of her magic," he shrugged, "you never know."

"I had to go for it. Art didn't give me a choice."

His father let out a breath. "I'm sorry about that. I'm going to have a talk with him when we—"

"No need, Pop. He's doing what he's always done. This isn't the first time and probably won't be the last."

"And now the day is yours. Something tells me you're going to take this one home," his voice cracked. "Your uncle would be so..."

Elliot's smile faded.

"Proud." The two embraced as tears welled in the corners of their eyes.

A camera's flash interrupted the sentimental scene as Dr. Djinn and her companion returned. Again, a knot of eager reporters shadowed their every move.

"The Honorable Marcus Garvey says that with confidence, you have won before you have started. All of you demonstrated a great deal of confidence. I was truly blown away by your creativity, ability, and scientific knowledge." She paused as her eyes roved over the contestants, one by one. "But there is one competitor who has exceeded my expectations with his creativity, scientific know-how, and performance under pressure. This young man has impressed me more than any other to-day."

His father thumped him on the back.

"Elliot Just, I invite you to join the other Odd Scholars as we develop the biggest and best Colored owned and operated amusement park the world has ever seen. Well done scholar, well done."

FOUR

DUELING CRYSTAL BALLS

Charleston, SC 1920

Clair hurried down a dimly lit street clutching three crumpled bills in her fist. Her knapsack whacked against her shoulder blades as she ran. The clock on St. Michael's Cathedral struck nine. *Almost there.* She gathered her skirts and hurried through the shadows. *I got a right to compete for one of those scholarships.* She glanced down at the bills. She wouldn't be turned away.

"Well, well, well..."

Clair tumbled into a pair of strong arms and blinked. *Lonnie.* She looked back at the clock. Time ticked without regard. *Ain't no time for this! Not now!*

"Hey, what's the rush?"

Lonnie had always been the sugar to her sweet tooth. A seventeen-year-old bad boy with skin smooth as a caramel treat, a smile like a thousand South Carolina suns, and a good head on his shoulders to boot, the boy was triple jeopardy. As usual, he was dressed to the nines in a tweed newsboy cap, matching vest, and trousers. He lit a cigarette, the embers lighting up the darkness. His eyes settled on her knapsack as he grabbed her gently by the wrist.

"Got somewhere to be, Lonnie."

Lonnie raised an eyebrow. "Where you off to this time of night?"

Clair's gaze shifted to a streetlight. "Nowhere." She bit her lip.

"C'mon now Clair. You know I ain't buyin' that."

She rolled her eyes and opened her palm to reveal the three crumpled bills. "Did a reading earlier and thought I might try my hand at that competition in the paper."

"Dr. Djinn's competition?" He cocked his head to the side. "Sounds good. Want some company?"

"Not really." She folded her arms across her chest.

He leaned in for a kiss. "After all we've been through?"

She dodged his advances like a boxer in the ring. "I ain't studying you. The competition starts in ten minutes—"

His eyes sparkled. "Ok. Hear me out." He grabbed hold of her hands and pulled her close. "How about I come with you to the competition. Then, later on, we do what we do best?" he lowered his voice. "Got a shipment of rum coming in tomorrow, early. Accordin' to my people it's a big batch." He pushed his sleeves up to his elbows and licked his lips. "If you'll help me with the bootlegging, I reckon we can split it down the middle like old times."

"I don't think so."

He looked at her in disbelief. "Between your Sage magic and my Shifting—" With a snap of a finger, he morphed before her eyes. His light brown skin and captivating smile became a ruddy faced man with crooked teeth, then a chubby-cheeked woman with a toothless grin. For his final trick, she watched as his face thinned, now displaying high cheekbones, deep brown skin, long braids, and a black sequin eye patch. She shook off a shiver as she stared at her own image. Then, as quickly as he'd shifted, he returned to his old handsome self. "I wouldn't keep askin' if you wasn't any good at it." He softened his gaze.

"Bootlegging ain't my thing no more." She bit her lip and took a breath. "Matter of fact, I don't think you're my thing no more."

He rubbed his hands together. "But I'm talking a bigger—wait, you're breakin' up with me?" He frowned. "Now?"

Clair sidestepped his large frame and stilled herself, blocking out all the sounds in the immediate vicinity: Lonnie's breathing, chirping crickets, singing cicadas, the hum of streetlights. Then, she pictured the club in her mind and muttered an incantation. The last thing she saw were Lonnie's outstretched arms reaching for her. She was a blur, shooting down a few blocks and around a corner until she stood in front of her destination. She cracked her knuckles and shook it off. *The Legendary Black Magic Flapper.* Only Taints could locate it and enter. Ordinary folks simply saw an abandoned basement club boarded up after a fire. Yet here it was, vibrant and alive. Heart pounding, she descended the steps.

At the bottom of the landing, she saw a mural of a woman in flapper attire holding a three-dimensional crystal ball. In the distance, she heard the chime of the clock tower. *Dammit, Lonnie!* She ran a hand over the mural in search of a clue to enter.

In seconds, she spotted a box set inside the crystal ball. When she leaned in to inspect it further, it opened wide, exposing a miniature keyboard. A sheet of music had been glued to the inside of the box. Each note shimmered in red, black, and green dust. *A musical password. Simple chords.* She exhaled and arched her fingers over the black and white keys. *Here goes nothing.* She played the chords as written and closed her eyes. *Not bad for someone who hadn't taken a lesson in years.* She held her breath as the keyboard retracted and the brick wall dissolved like a desert mirage. A dimly lit lounge appeared. Ragtime music blared through speakers and tiny golden orbs floated about, illuminating the room. Nearby, teenagers chatted and played games on triangular pool tables with hovering billiards and chess boards. Several bowling lanes caught her eye from the other side of the room. White pins dodged red, black, and green bowling balls covered in blinking quotes. A cheer ricocheted through the crowd at the sound of a strike. The walls were covered with pictures of Marcus Garvey, the man trying to take Black people back to Africa. Lonnie had mentioned him in passing not long ago. A woman carrying a platter of food zoomed by on a hover board. The aroma of golden fried chicken and waffles wafted toward her nose. Her stomach grumbled. *Focus.* She turned to the host podium covered in flyers for the night's event. Her eyes zeroed in on a short poem below a picture of Dr. Marvellus Djinn. After several seconds, it shifted into a new poem. Each poem told a story.

The Onyx Conjuring Stick
her conjuring stick
was a gathering of chants
congealed into
ebony, ice, and juju.

Time
time is an onion

and a spell
a culture
and a lie
a council
a shifter
and a thief.

She blinked as the poems disappeared, drawing her back to the present. She tapped a tiny bell.

In no time, a plump man of no more than four feet waddled toward her. He wore a bright red zoot suit decorated with tiny symbols of the African continent, and a fresh conk. His hair was an oil slick of deep waves entrenched in his scalp.

"How can I help you?"

"I-I'm here…here to compete," she stammered.

His lips stretched into a warm smile as he examined her from head to toe, stopping abruptly at her eye patch. "Ah yes. Welcome to *The Black Magic Flapper*, home of the *Annual Crystal Ball Duel*." He peered at her again. "Thief, Artist, Shifter, or Sage?" He laced his stubby fingers together. "Wait, don't answer that; I'm gonna guess." He narrowed his beady eyes. "Sage."

"You're good!" She wagged an index finger in his direction. "Sixth generation."

"It's a gift," he said with a smug grin. "Hang around here as much as I have and you can spot the types a mile away." He turned his attention to a sheet of paper on the podium. "Oh. Where are my manners? The name's Russell Rouge, second generation Thief. And you?" He extended one of his hands.

"Clair Drayton. I signed up using the cerebral option right there." She pointed to a blinking box on the page.

Russell glanced at his watch. "Oh my, we'll be beginning shortly, follow me!"

Clair followed the diminutive host between tables and chairs. By now, the lights had dimmed to darkness and the boisterous crowd had settled into their seats. Russell shooed her toward a line of wicker chairs and tables below darkened spotlights.

"There, at the end."

Heart thumping, she hurried and slid into a seat. A hush washed over the room as the music faded.

"Ladies and gentlemen, welcome to the *Dueling Crystal Balls Competition* sponsored by *The Motherland Amusement Park*. Four of our best and brightest teens will create their own conjuring crystal balls in front of our eyes!" boomed a phantom voice from the speakers. "My name is Dr. Marvellus Djinn, and not only will I be your host for tonight, but I will also be the judge in tonight's competition for an Odd Scholarship!" A spotlight appeared. "And now, the contestants!"

The spotlight spliced into four, illuminating each chair.

"She's a Charleston native and fifth generation Artist who enjoys shrimp and grits! Please welcome, Constance Pepperdine!"

A girl with reddish-brown plaits rose from her chair and waved.

"Next, he's a third generation Time Thief who enjoys Hip-hop, a kind of music that hasn't been invented yet, and blackberry cobbler. Please welcome, Cedric Lamar!"

A young man with neat cornrows waved to the clapping audience.

"He's the shapeshifting son of a Geechee Shaman who appreciates his tailor. Please welcome, Lonnie Thompson!"

Her jaw dropped as Lonnie rose from his seat. Her nostrils flared. This had been his plan all along. Enter the competition himself, tour The Motherland, and take advantage of the scholarship to Hampton Institute. She shook her head.

"And finally, she's a sixth generation Sage who says her eye is a secret weapon. Please, give it up for Clair Drayton!"

Clair forced a smile and stood as the spotlight swallowed her whole.

Moments later, Dr. Djinn materialized in a red top hat, matching tuxedo, and silver cane. Deafening applause consumed the club. "And these," she gestured toward the teens seated in the chairs behind her, "are our contestants!" Cheers and whistles rang out as the competitors waved. Lonnie shot her a wink as she resisted the urge to run over and strangle him with her bare hands.

"Now the rules!" She turned to the four contestants. "You have thirty minutes to build your crystal ball. It can be as creative as you'd like, but it must be in working order. The best divination tools are artfully designed for any Taint of any class to use." She smiled in the direction of the crowd. "Periodically, I will ask questions and stop to interview the contestants at random. Once time is up, I will examine each of your work. You will be graded on a five-point system, with a score of 5 being the highest and 1 the lowest. The person with the highest point total at the end will be named winner of the Dueling Crystal Balls and given an Odd Scholarship!" The crowd applauded as Dr. Djinn raised the parchment high. "Constance, Cedric, Lonnie, and Clair, please take out your materials."

Clair hoisted her bag from the floor and poured its contents onto the table.

Noting the potent stares from the audience, Lonnie muttered an incantation and snapped his fingers. Instantly, his bag appeared in front of him. A ghost-like hand gathered the materials and spread them on his table for all to see. The crowd went wild.

"Gotta play to the crowd, Sweet Thang. Gotta play to the crowd," he said and blew Clair a kiss.

Clair returned the kiss with a scowl before visualizing her spell. In an instant, her materials levitated and spun in an axis around her head. The crowd responded with a cheer. She turned back to Lonnie and winked. "Thanks for the advice, Sweet Thang."

"And your time starts now!" Dr. Djinn shouted.

Clair took a deep breath and guided her materials back to within eye level. As they hovered above the table's surface, she took inventory. Five gris-gris bags, each a different color, bobbed in front of her. She'd been simplifying the steps for months. First, create the base. Next, comes the heart of the crystal ball. Skilled diviners knew the guts of divination tools should never be taken for granted. Last, came the ball itself. The shell had to be sturdy enough to hold the sorcery inside. A shaky shell meant for a disastrous reading.

She set all the materials on the table's surface with a blink. Though she'd been leaning toward a bronze base, she decided the silver would be more appealing. According to the rules, all materials had to be in their rawest states of matter. She pulled a silver block toward her and went to work.

Telekinetics were the most coveted of the Sage Order. The ability to manipulate objects ranked high in the magical world. Her heart pounded as she carved symbols in the silver block using her telekinetic gifts. Arguably the most delicate and difficult of all conjuring skills, Sage magic could only be achieved through the right combination of caloric heat, visualization, and vibration. It required a layering of spells with additional incantations and an in-depth understanding of science.

She stood back to admire her handiwork. Still smoldering from the heat, she set it aside to cool.

"Tell me more about what you're using." Clair looked up to find Dr. Djinn standing near Lonnie's table. She took a breath and tuned it out. Now, color. When building a divination tool, the diviner had to be mindful of colors and texture. Better to use lighter colors than heavier hues to "see" properly. Otherwise, the prediction could quickly turn murky and unreliable. She grabbed a glass bowl and her gris-gris bags. Indigo, lavender, sky blue, pink, and orange. Next, she pulled out two larger pouches, each filled with black and white powder. Each color had a larger meaning: wisdom (indigo), tranquility (lavender), peace (sky blue), intuition (pink), and knowledge (orange). One by one, she emptied the bags into the bowl. The order had to be perfect for optimum use. Dark to light. The heavy energy needed to find its way to the bottom first. Onyx and indigo, then lavender, light blue followed by orange, and finally, pink and ivory. As she prepared to mix, Dr. Djinn approached her station.

"Clair Drayton, ladies and gentlemen, the only Sage in this competition." Dr. Djinn addressed the audience. "Please explain what you're doing at the moment."

"It's called a psychic mix." She focused on the tiny bits of powder in the bowl.

"What's it made from? Herbs? Stones? Sand?" Her eyes roved over Clair's station.

"Some of everything. Crystals, powders, dust—. The indigo is from my Big Mama's favorite dress. She was a slave on an Indigo plantation. Sewed and dyed it with her bare hands. The lavender is crushed amethyst. Came from a ring my daddy bought my momma. When he died, momma thought it would be best as a charm." Her voice quivered. "The light blue came from a pebble I found. It—speaks to me. The onyx came from an iron

collar my Granddaddy had to wear after he was caught
trying to escape his master. Carried it with him even after he got free. Said he wanted it passed down, so
wouldn't no one forget." A tear slipped from her eye.
"The ivory, well that came from my momma's gris-gris.
Been passed down among the women in my family for
generations."

"Heavy." Dr. Djinn looked on, deep in thought.

"Yes, but my Big Mama used to say there's a
time for everything. A time for tears and a time for
laughter. Peaks and valleys. That's life. These ain't just
herbs and crystals—they're bits and pieces of history
ground to shards and dust. The history is the spell. The
history is the magic, not the other way around." Clair
shrugged. "Finally, the orange and pink are dried roses.
Got 'em from my first love." She caught a glimpse of the
tug of war in Lonnie's eyes as he tried to pull himself
away from her interview. "Put love in everything you
make, and you won't fail."

"Excellent young lady, very impressive. Give it
up for Clair!" The crowd clapped as Dr. Djinn hurried to
speak with another contestant.

Focus. She homed in on the mixture in the bowl
and raised her hand. In response, the ingredients rose
from the dish. She blinked, causing them to fall again
like sugar through a sieve and muttered another incantation. The powders, now finer in consistency, gathered
into a thick braid. She snapped her fingers and the substance morphed into a funnel rotating on an axis. To the
naked eye, it looked like a tornado made of rainbow-
colored threads. Dr. Djinn stood transfixed as Clair
traced a butterfly in the air with the powdery residue. In
a flash, the bewitched insect flew across the room, its
wings opening and closing with grace. It circled the contestants' wicker chairs and doubled around Dr. Djinn's
top hat before swallowing the funnel and settling inside

the empty bowl. Then, the butterfly dissolved into an opal-colored puddle, and finally, a cloud of shimmering smoke.

Now for the shell. The glass bowl extended, rising in waves of transparent liquid. Her visible eyelid fluttered as she exerted all her energy toward completing the shell. *Plop.* She muttered yet another incantation, sealing the shell tight before blowing it cool.

Nearly finished, she glanced at the others. Competition was fierce. Constance, the Artist, had abandoned the traditional spherical shape of a crystal ball in favor of a pyramid. Golden smoke spiraled inside. Meanwhile, Cedric, the Thief, conjured a cube. A soul-stirring rhythm emanated from his creation. Clair swallowed hard. Lonnie looked to be in good shape as well. He'd chosen an octagon. His hair color changed like a stoplight while he worked.

"Five minutes remaining! Five minutes remaining!" Dr. Djinn shouted.

Attaching the bowl to the base was the final step. Clair reached for the silver block and blinked. The bowl clicked in place perfectly. The liquid inside the ball morphed from butterfly to funnel to puddle to cloud. *Thirty seconds to spare.* Again, she stole a glance at her competition. Constance stood with her arms behind her back. Cedric appeared to be using a peculiar looking ear plug to listen to his crystal ball and Lonnie stood in his favorite pose, arms crossed in front of his chest.

"Five, four, three, two, one! Hands at your sides!"

The crowd whistled and clapped. Now, Dr. Djinn granted them permission to walk through the room. They moseyed along inspecting the crystal balls up close and from a distance. The four contestants stood back and answered questions when asked.

Clair watched as Russell waddled to the middle of the stage carrying a box slightly larger than his body.

"Thirty seconds remain. Thirty seconds!" Dr. Djinn shouted over the din.

As time wound down, Clair allowed her thoughts to wander. She could see herself enjoying a playground of carnival rides beyond her wildest dreams. She could imagine sitting in a classroom surrounded by books. Everything she'd hoped for was within her reach.

"Hands at your sides!"

Clair froze before taking one last look at each table. All of the presentations were fantastic: a pyramid, an octagon, and a cube. Suddenly, her crystal ball appeared ordinary. Her stomach dropped. The day's events came flooding back. All of the fuss with Lonnie. A random reading for a stranger. The unexpected three-dollar entrance fee. All of that to leave empty handed. She shook her head. *No way.* She exhaled and took solace in doing her absolute best. That would have to do at this stage in the competition.

Clair summoned a modicum of calm as Russell hurriedly placed a chair in front of each station. It was time.

"All contestants will be graded on a five-point system, with a score of 5 being the highest and 1 the lowest. The person with the highest point total will be named winner of the Dueling Crystal Balls. "Now, let's see what these young sorcerers have created."

She began with Constance, then Cedric and Lonnie, spending no more than a few minutes at each station.

Now, it was her turn. Clair gulped as the magician took a seat and handed Russell her cane. She placed an expensive-looking monocle with golden gears and at least a dozen lenses over one of her eyes before reaching for Clair's crystal ball. She exhaled as she fiddled with the monocle's lenses.

"Gotta get the right lens," she called over her shoulder. "One moment."

The crowd remained silent. Dr. Djinn leaned forward and placed a palm on the ball. All at once its contents became a blinding blur. She grinded her teeth together, eyes shut.

As planned, the butterfly appeared from ether. Floating with grace, it flitted about inside, diving in delicate spirals while trailing pinpricks of silver in its path. Then, a dark, indigo cloud formed near the top of the crystal ball. After hovering angrily for a few moments, it grew to twice its size. Clair watched helplessly as a bolt of lightning lit up the sphere and the butterfly's wings crumbled to ash mid-flight.

Dr. Djinn recoiled as the residue became a swirling funnel then a blood red puddle, before dissolving before her eyes. Breathing heavily, she stumbled from her chair and beckoned for her cane. Russell and another assistant rushed to her side as she hobbled out of sight.

"Ten minutes!" Russell yelled into the shocked crowd as he steered Dr. Djinn offstage. "Ten-minute intermission!"

The crowd dissolved into chatter.

"Well, I think we all know who didn't win," Constance sneered in Clair's direction.

"The winner hasn't been announced. Who knows who won and who didn't?" Lonnie shot back.

Constance folded her arms. "All I know is this, if you want to win a competition, you should try not to kill the judge!"

Cedric rolled his eyes. "Quit being dramatic. Dr. Djinn ain't dead. She just looked a little…unsteady."

"Unsteady my behind! That woman almost passed out." Constance rounded on Clair. "How are you a Sage and don't realize the dust from slave chains and bones is too much for one divination tool? Come on!"

Lonnie stepped between the two girls before he met Constance's eyes. "Hey, this is a competition. You play to win. Just because Dr. Djinn looked a little woozy doesn't mean she almost died. And like you said, what do you know? You're an Artist!"

Clair took a breath and thanked him with a small smile.

Once the lights dimmed, they hurried to their stations. Dr. Djinn appeared, bathed in a green spotlight.

"On behalf of the *Black Magic Flapper*, *The Motherland*, and *Dr. Djinn's Black Magic Medicine Show*, I'd like to thank you all for coming out."

Clair crossed and uncrossed her legs in anticipation.

"In fourth place, please give it up for Constance!"

Unable to disguise her disappointment, the girl with the plaits strode toward Dr. Djinn and retrieved an envelope from Russell Rouge.

"In third place, please give it up for Cedric!"

Unlike Constance, Cedric grinned and turned to acknowledge Lonnie and Clair before joining Constance onstage.

Lonnie winked and leaned in. "I think we both know you got this," he whispered.

"And in second place, please give it up for Lonnie! Our grand prize and Odd Scholarship winner is Clair!"

She shot up from her seat and rushed to Dr. Djinn's side to the tune of deafening cheers. Russell pumped her arm while handing her a piece of rolled parchment and a full envelope. Finally, she was on her way. In her mind's eye she could see her Big Mama smiling. Everything had changed and she was ready to embrace it all.

PART TWO:
THE MOTHERLAND

B. SHARISE MOORE

FIVE

THE SANKOFA THEATER
AND MUSEUM

June 1, 1920
Hampton, VA

Omen peered at the slivers of golden sunlight as the Model T sped up the road. *You're about to have the opportunity of a lifetime, son. Be smart. Don't take no wooden nickels. Strength is the Family Business.* His father's words echoed in his head as he shifted in the leather seat. Never had he experienced such luxury. The shack he was raised in and his uncle's rusty pick-up truck were all he knew. He smoothed his trousers with his palms.

Life after winning the *Mighty Biceps Competition* had been almost manic. He'd entertained a different reporter each day. Most had been concerned with the rumors about Dr. Marvellus Djinn. *How had she become so rich? Did she really survive a lynching? Was she a Time Thief?* Often, he'd stare at them blankly after answering the questions as best he could. He didn't know the woman. He'd won a prize. That was it. The end. About a week later, he received a letter with strict instructions to pack a suitcase with enough clothing and toiletries for a week. The letter went on to say that on the morning of June 1st, all scholars would be picked up from their homes and transported to Hampton, Virginia. Today was the day. At 6 a.m., a shiny black Model T inched its way down the gravelly road in front of his home. In spite of the hour, his entire family had gathered to see him off. After a few strong handshakes and hugs, he was on his way. He'd been on the road with no one to talk to for several hours. Every now and then the driver, an old Colored man with a salt and pepper mustache, would glance in his rearview and ask Omen if he needed anything, but all in all the ride had been quiet. His mind drifted to his family's legacy. Making them proud had always been at the forefront of his mind. He rubbed the alligator tooth dangling from the chain around his neck.

"We're coming up on the park now," the driver quipped from the front, interrupting his thoughts. "It's around this here corner."

Omen plastered his face to the window as the car slowed to a stop.

"I'll get your bag from the trunk," the driver called.

Omen reached for a quarter in his pocket and slid it into the driver's outstretched palm. Then, he opened the door and stepped from the car. It felt good to stretch his long legs after only a few rest stops during the eleven-hour trip. He took a deep breath and gazed at the sky filled with puffy clouds giving way to cracks of brilliant light. Then, he froze. "A picture show theater?"

"Yup." A boy in his teens with a slender build and glasses turned toward him. An expensive looking briefcase hung from one of his shoulders.

"Enjoy yourselves gentlemen." The driver tipped his hat. "Y'all be careful in there, ya hear?"

Omen and the boy waved as the driver stepped back inside the car, turned on the engine, and disappeared down the road. Omen scanned the area. They'd been let off in some sort of cul-de-sac with the picture show theater at the top of the semi-circle. He and the boy were the only two people for as far as he could see. Definitely odd for 7 p.m. in June.

"This place looks...strange." Omen gestured toward the theater. Whitewashed brick and decorated with posters, an oversized billboard surrounded by lights and lettering jutted out from two stories above. It cast a shadow in the approaching sunset. "What picture shows are these? Never heard of any of them."

The boy walked toward one of the posters plastered on the building's side.

"*The Black Star Line: Starring Ernest Whitman as Marcus Garvey,*" Omen read. The poster featured a boat at sea. The craft appeared to sail toward him. Omen backed away.

"*The Pharaohs of Egypt: Starring Paul Robeson and Lillian Randolph,*" said the boy with the briefcase. "These aren't real, but it'd be great if they were!"

On cue, the lights surrounding the billboard blinked once before illuminating. The letters inside scrambled and unscrambled before their eyes until finally settling into a legible advertisement.

Now Showing to both Taints and Aints:
The Life and Times of Dr. Marvellus Djinn
at
The Motherland

Omen glanced at the billboard. "Which are you?"

The boy pushed his glasses up the bridge of his nose. "Not a magical bone in my body." He extended his hand. "Elliot Just."

Omen pumped the boy's hand and smiled. "Me neither. Omen Crow. Where from?"

Elliot wandered up a short flight of stairs to a set of green double doors. "Born and raised in Washington, DC. You?" he said while continuing to roam. The doors had heavy silver handles in the shape of elephant heads. He gave them all a tug.

"Country boy. Whole family's from Altamonte Springs, Florida. Ever been?" Omen followed Elliot and fixed his attention on a ticket booth. He ran one of his large hands over a silver grate above an open slot for the exchange of money and tickets.

"Yep. My Pop is a scientist and recently took a liking to botany. Me and my brother traveled with him to the Okefenokee, Everglades, and Kissimmee swamps to study plants."

"Whoa. Guess those swamps are kind of interesting when you think about it. I've only ever seen them as nests for mosquitos, dragonflies, and gators," Omen said with a raised eyebrow. "Perspective."

"What about you? Ever been to Washington?" Elliot stared at another poster.

"Only heard of Washington, DC. Never been." Omen shrugged. "Maybe one day." He bent down so he was at eye level with the grate. A speaker roared to life.

Welcome to The South Entrance of The Mother- land. Dr. Djinn requires a password.

Elliot rushed to Omen's side. "What did it say?"

The speaker responded with a loud crackle. *Password. You'll need a password.*

Out of nowhere, two Model Ts, both red, approached. Omen watched as the cars sped to a halt at the bottom of the stairs. The back doors opened slowly to reveal two girls about their age or slightly older. One was dressed plainly in a paper sack brown skirt and white shirt. She carried a leather briefcase. Her hair was pulled into two bushy ponytails on either side of her head. The other girl couldn't have been more different. She wore a flowing white skirt and a bright yellow top. Her hair was full of dark braids that flowed over her shoulders. A black eye patch covered one of her eyes and a bulky bag was strapped across her middle.

Omen's gaze swung between the two girls. Eye patch gathered her skirt and climbed the stairs as the other girl followed. She extended one of her hands toward Elliot. "Clair Drayton. And you are?"

"Elliot Just," he sputtered before erupting into a coughing spell. He turned away, removed his glasses, and wiped at his tearing eyes. "From Washington, DC."

Sensing it was his moment to make a move, Omen stepped in front of Elliot, bowed, took the girl's hand in his own, and kissed it. "Omen Crow. The pleasure is mine."

Clair smiled sweetly. "Nice to meet you Omen." She turned to Elliot. "Are you alright?"

"Yup. I'm fine." Elliot cleared his throat and shoved his glasses back on his face.

The other girl turned on her heels. "Brenda from Philadelphia. Might as well get all the introductions out of the way so we can get to where we're going," she said with a wave while shifting her briefcase and knapsack.

"Omen, from Florida. Nice to meet you." He kept his eyes fastened to Clair.

Dr. Djinn requires a password. Dr. Djinn requires a password. The speaker crackled.

Brenda craned her neck in the direction of the booth. "Password? What kind of password?"

Elliot shook his head. "We were trying to figure that out."

"Yeah, your guess is as good as mine," Omen added.

Clair poked her lip out. "I think I remember seeing something that might help." She slung her bag over her shoulder. It hit the ground with a clunk. After rummaging around inside for a few seconds, she retrieved a piece of parchment, yellowing at the edges. She picked at the bright green wax seal and unfurled it with a flick of her wrist.

The invitation. Of course. The others gathered around and rifled through their items for their letters.

"I know I read this right after I received it. But, it's...changed," Brenda said, squinting at her letter.

Elliot rubbed his chin. "Right. I've never seen these words in my life. They're different. I'll bet money on it."

Brenda held out a hand. "How much?"

Elliot frowned and turned back to the invitation.

"We're talkin' 'bout Dr. Djinn here. Things are gonna be strange." Clair shrugged.

"I think I got it," Elliot coughed.

Dearest Odd Scholars,

By now, you've reached my famous Motherland Theater. The Honorable Marcus Mosiah Garvey says, "Look for me in the whirlwind and in the storm." It is my hope that the four of you will be whirlwinds of strength, wit, innovation, and magic during your stay here. But remember, what you see in the park, must not leave it. There will be secrets and enigmas that push you to think and act in ways you never have in your short lives. You will be challenged, but this is the reason you were chosen. From here on out, you are stepping inside a storm of creativity. You will see things that you didn't know existed. I have prepared for you a film for your viewing pleasure. It will give you more insight into my life and what I need from you. *Look for me in the whirlwind and in the storm.*

   Sincerely,

   Dr. Marvellus Djinn

Omen rolled back on his heels as Clair reapplied the parchment's wax seal and put it away. "She kept quoting Marcus Garvey during my competition. She does the same thing here."

   Clair looked up. "Mine too."

   "Yup, she did the same thing at mine." Elliot wrinkled his nose and walked toward the speaker. "Look for me in the whirlwind and the storm," he spoke clearly into the speaker.

   Welcome and enjoy The Motherland. You may enter. The speaker roared to life and went dead again along with the lights surrounding the billboard. Elliot stepped backward in surprise as the green double doors opened wide to reveal a set of circular stairs.

   "She said she's prepared a film for us." Clair lifted her skirt and climbed the stairs.

   "Picture shows are okay, but all I really need is food." Omen rubbed his stomach and followed. The stairs coiled round and round until they reached a landing. His eyes settled on the back of Clair's head. He had to get to know her. There was no doubt about it.

   "Well, you got your wish!" Clair grinned.

   A concession stand with four large bags of popcorn and fountain drinks opened before them. Omen snatched a bag sheepishly as the others grabbed their snacks.

   The Life and Times of Dr. Marvellus Djinn will begin in two minutes. Please take your seats. The loudspeaker droned. An arrow on the wall showed them the way.

"Well," Omen said between chews, "let's go see 'bout this picture show." He fell in lock step with Clair and followed the blinking arrow.

The theater was larger than any Omen had seen. He looked up to find a balcony decorated with gilded steel. "Wow."

"If the park is anything like this, we're in for a treat." Brenda rubber her palms together.

The scholars settled into their seats as the theater went black and a film reel roared to life. A black and white picture appeared on the big screen. Immediately, Omen recognized two familiar figures on the screen: Dr. Marvellus Djinn and her companion, Professor Bartholomew Blue.

SIX

PICTURE SHOW

1920
Hampton, VA

Dr. Marvellus Djinn stumbled backward as a boat careened into the shoreline. Frothy waves crashed ashore as golden sparks crackled through the air. Professor Bartholomew Blue, the vessel's captain, dove from the deck headfirst in a forward roll onto the sand.

"One of the demons escaped, be on guard!" The Professor clambered to his feet, wild eyed as the winds came alive, whipping his cape against his broad shoulders. "I have a Soul Jar. I can seal the demon inside," he yelled, breathless. "The wax is on deck!"

She braced herself as a swirling mass knocked the wind out of her. On impact, it exploded into static shards. She struggled to stand. Not far from where she lay, the demon gathered itself, reformed into a cyclone, and charged again. This time she flung an immobilizing spell in its direction. It hung in mid-air like a bleeding cloud.

"I can grab the wax or hold off the demon. It's your call!" she shouted.

Professor Blue glanced at the demon as it writhed in pain. "Get the wax," he yelled.

The demon reared back on its tail and unfurled with an ear-splitting screech. The Professor dashed in front of it before it could strike a second time. Electric sparks rained down on them like white hot needles. Dr. Djinn gagged and climbed aboard the vessel. After making her way through the tangled rope and nets, she spotted an iridescent glob the size of her palm lodged between two wooden planks. She glanced over her shoulder as the Professor hurled spells at the demon. She grabbed hold of the wax and quickly flattened it into a disc. Red welts covered her fingers and palms. Light headed and swaying, she secured it in her breast pocket before returning to the fray.

"Got it!" She jostled the disc as it burned a hole in her tuxedo jacket. Shuddering in pain, she tossed it into the Professor's open palm.

He shouted an incantation over the din as the demon slowed to a crawl, then hung suspended in air like a puddle of pulsing slime. Armed with more incantations, Professor Blue raised his arms, pulling the demon toward him like a marionette on a string. At last, the entity shrunk into a mass the size of a golf ball. A deafening pop marked the end of the fight. In a flash, he stuffed it inside the Soul Jar and clipped it on one of his belt loops.

"Professor Bartholomew Blue: Master Teacher. Elite Conjurer. Ghoul Gatherer. Time Thief, Extraordinaire," she gasped in her best attempt at a West Indian accent.

The Professor pulled her into a bone crushing embrace. "Wah gwaan?"[1]

"Fair to middling I suppose." She grimaced and gestured toward the Jar. "Where'd you find that one, 18th century?"

"1776." Professor Blue cracked his knuckles.

"You went home to Kingston, didn't you?" She knelt to the water's edge and submerged her hands in saltwater.

"Had to, been too long." The Professor trudged through the sand and sat.

"The more irredeemable the soul, the better the fuel." Her eyes fluttered as the saltwater worked its magic.

"Makes sense, all things considered. Wicked energy is potent." Professor Blue wiped his brow with the edge of his cape. "Who knew the souls of dead slave owners could propel us through the Time Stitch?"

"Right. Who knew?" Dr. Djinn's eyes settled on the net stuffed with glowing Jars on deck. "Lemme guess, a graveyard dig?"

"Best one in recent memory. A cluster of slave masters and their descendants. Found 'em beside Dunn's River at the base of a waterfall." Professor Blue smoothed his mustache.

She raised an eyebrow. "How many graves?"

"A hundred, give or take."

Dr. Djinn motioned toward the demon in the Jar. "Who was that?"

The Professor narrowed his eyes. "Thomas Thistlewood—a rapist and a mad man."

---

[1] In Jamaican Patois, "Wah gwaan?" is a greeting that means "What's going on or How are things?"

"I know of a staff that's been sculpted by an Impundulu and stitched with shards of lightning—perfect for extracting souls," she said.

"I prefer the old way, builds character."

The water lapped against the sand as the Professor tossed the bulky net over his shoulder. Dr. Djinn stared at the Jar where the demon glowed inside. Now and again, a tiny bolt of electricity flashed as gooey translucent droplets bubbled to the surface. Then, out of nowhere, a tiny handprint appeared, ghostlike. She recoiled as it thumped against his coal black thigh.

"I don't understand why you keep the Soul Jars so close. Drop them all in the net. It's safer—"

"There's this saying about enemies," he said as he spun around to face her. "I think you've heard it." He tapped the Jar and trekked ahead. "Doing my duty as a Ghoul Gatherer. We go. We gather. We recoup what's been taken from us. Things. Resources. Knowledge. We gather wicked souls. We bottle them up. We return."

Dr. Djinn turned away. "I saw something."

He slowed to a stop. "We're Time Thieves; we all see things."

Clair nudged Omen ever so slightly and leaned into a whisper. "Time Thieves! I knew it!"

Omen took a sip of his drink and trained his eyes on the screen.

"They murder a man in Memphis. His name is King. He means a lot to the people," Dr. Djinn blurted out in a tiny voice.

"What year?" the Professor croaked.

Dr. Djinn bit her lip. "1968. He's shot. It's made to look like a lone gunman, but you know how that goes—"

"How do the people react?"

"Cities burn for days. Lots of us die, Blue. Too many of us die," her voice cracked.

"Consider yourself lucky."

"How can you say that?" She turned to face him. "How is it lucky to see a man assassinated? To see him waving to a crowd one moment and covered in blood the next?"

"Yuh mash up gal."[2] His West Indian accent returned thick as sweet potato soup. "Be glad ya ain't see a boy floatin' in tha wata!"

She stopped in her tracks. "What boy? What water? Floating where?"

He spat in the sand. "August 28, 1955. Emmett Till. Accused of whistling at a White gal. I saw how they hunted him down. Beat him. Dragged him. Tied barbed wire around his neck. Anchored him to a fan and dropped him in the river. Haunted me for months."

"And you did nothing?"

"Don't you dare judge me for it." His eyes flashed in anger. "I been at this longer than you, Marvellus. This ain't for the faint of heart. You'll see things. You'll hear things. You'll want to do things, but you can't. Only fools try and step in—"

"Well, if it's foolish to try and save Colored folks, then I guess I'll have to be a fool."

He turned to face her. "You're a Time Thief, not a savior!" The pained look on her face softened his tone. He took one of her hands in his. "Dabbling in time means death, Marvellus, or worse."

"What's worse than watching our people be killed and standing by, helpless? Like cowards?"

"We don't have the means, Marvellus. There is no undo." Professor Blue dropped his head as if in prayer before moving along.

For the next half a mile they walked in silence. A thicket of pines towered above them like sentinels guard-

---

[2] The phrase "mash-up" means slow-down in Jamaican Patois.

ing a secret. Dr. Djinn struggled to keep pace with the Professor's long strides.

"How's the park coming along? Still on pace to open on June fifteenth?" Professor Blue called over his shoulder.

"That's the plan."

"Good."

Dr. Djinn quickened her pace. "I've been thinking. What if we allowed early access?"

"You have my attention." Professor Blue tilted his head to one side.

"Odd Scholars. Dr. Djinn's Odd Scholars." A broad smile stretched across her face. "They'd compete for a scholarship and we'd choose only the best and brightest teens."

"What do you have in mind?"

She smiled. "Strength, ingenuity, science, conjuring?"

"Taints and Aints?"

"Yes, all Colored folks should experience The Motherland."

"This is a lot, Marvellus." Professor Blue narrowed his eyes.

"I wouldn't have it any other way." She winked.

"I'm on board as long as those kids are safe. Promise me!" He waved an index finger.

"You have my word." She clasped him on the shoulders.

Brenda leaned over the back of Omen's chair. "Is she sending us some kind of message?"

"Looks like it," Elliot whispered.

Omen shoved a hand inside his bag of popcorn as the scene faded to black.

The next scene opened with a maze of multicolored signs, tents, rides, and exhibits in the background. A steel track snaked around and between two steep hills looming above a river. Dr. Djinn and Professor Blue strolled through the park as if they were conducting an inspection. The click-clack of her shoes on the cobblestone path fell into a rhythm with the clang of hammers against nails. Men scrambled between bolts, beams, and two by fours, all in a hurry.

"You've outdone yourself." Professor Blue pulled at his beard. "I've only been gone a week and it looks twice as good as when I left."

Dr. Djinn rolled up the sleeves of her suit jacket. "This place is gonna be the greatest park the world has ever seen. Mark my words."

He placed two fingers to his lips and let out a shrill whistle. Quickly, the men migrated toward them.

Dr. Djinn smoothed the lapels on her jacket. "I want everyone to know how much we appreciate the work you do. Your dedication to this park isn't lost on us."

Professor Blue cleared his throat. "In the coming weeks, there will be guests. We've decided the park will be home to four teenagers—"

"Odd Scholars. Dr. Djinn's Odd Scholars," she cut in. "They'll be discovering the park on their own."

Omen frowned. "Did she say we'd be discovering the park on our own? I thought this was a tour?"

Clair shifted in her seat. "That's what I thought."

The gathering inside the picture show looked up as the sound of wheels on gravel interrupted the gathering. Dr. Djinn peered down the path as a lone police car made its way toward them. Once the car stopped, the doors creaked open and four men climbed from the vehicle. A lanky White man in a tan uniform strolled toward her with the others in tow.

Dr. Djinn tipped her hat. "Officer Goode, a pleasure to see you. How's Delilah?"

The man extended one of his long arms. "Well, if it isn't my favorite magician." He smiled warmly. "Delilah's gettin' stronger every day. Thanks for inquirin'."

Her eyes roved over the men in his entourage. "How can we help you, officer?"

Officer Goode pulled a kerchief from his pocket and wiped his brow. "I'm here to make a few introductions and clear up what I believe to be a small misunderstandin'." His smile vanished. "As you know, I've been the acting sheriff in the county for the last few years until we found someone qualified to take over." He motioned toward a large man behind him. "Well, seems we've found our man. This here's Sheriff Dodge. He comes highly recommended all the way from Charleston, South Carolina. He'll be takin' over, effective immediately."

Dodge adjusted his hat and grinned. He had stained, crooked teeth. The pebbles crunched beneath his feet as he lumbered forward, out of breath and wheezing. "Would you happen to have something cold to drink? I'm a bit...parched."

Dr. Djinn turned to one of the workers. "Get Hampton's new Sheriff a glass of Mama Cool's lemonade, please." The young man laid down his hammer and dashed toward a cluster of food stands in the distance.

"Well now, I hate to begin our relationship on a sour note, but I've come to investigate a complaint. Seems you might not be the rightful owner of this here land." Dodge gnashed on his tobacco chew and surveyed the area.

"This land's been in my family's possession for more than fifty years." She glanced at Officer Goode who avoided her eyes.

The sheriff rolled back on his heels. "It's my understandin' that this is the story you've provided for some time. But, you're gonna have to show me some papers because these fellas say otherwise."

Dr. Djinn looked in the direction of two men in dingy overalls. Their long, brown hair clung to their necks in the sticky Virginia heat.

"Professor, go get the papers."

Professor Blue disappeared up the path as the young man returned with a glass of lemonade in a mason jar. Dodge grabbed the jar and spat a mouthful of snuff on the ground before gulping down the lemonade. The space grew silent aside from the hum of insects. The sheriff wiped his mouth with the back of his hand. "Pretty day, isn't it? Ah, where's my manners? This here's Franklin." He pointed to the taller of the two men. "And this is Fred. They're the Jefferson brothers."

Officer Goode stepped forward. "I'm…I'm sorry for the inconvenience Dr. Djinn—" he stammered.

Sheriff Dodge waved him off. "Now, now, I'm sure she understands us lawmen gotta do our jobs. Your apologies ain't necessary." He spat again before looking around. "So, this is the little Hoodoo Juju Park you were telling me about, Officer?"

"Yes, sir," Goode said in a shaky voice.

"How…quaint. I understand opening day is coming soon. Think you'll be ready?"

"Once I produce the deed to the land, you can be on your way, sheriff," Dr. Djinn said through clenched teeth. "I'm sure there's some more important police work you could be doing instead of wasting your time here."

He wheezed. "Now, now, Mrs. Drew, I'm here to try and keep the peace. But when someone reports they might have a claim to some stolen land, well, I gotta check it out." He tipped his hat. "I know you understand."

A pang of anger crept into her chest. No one dared refer to her as Mrs. Drew. She dug her fists into her sides. "Dr. Djinn. My name is Dr. Djinn." In the nick of time, Professor Blue arrived, papers in hand.

She held out the document.

Sheriff Dodge snatched the deed and held it up to the light.

"Dr. Djinn, eh? So, who's this Charity Drew and why do you have her land?"

"My birth name is Charity Armstrong. When I married, I became Charity Drew. Are you unfamiliar with the custom of a woman changing her last name?"

His tiny eyes narrowed. "Where's Mr. Drew?" He gave her tuxedo a once over. "Or could it be you're Mr. Drew? You do know that men are the ones s'posed to be wearin' the pants, right?" The brothers and Sheriff Dodge slapped their knees in mocking laughter.

"There is no Mr. Drew, Sheriff. I haven't gone by that name in some time. Now if you don't mind, we'd like to get on with what we're doing in our little Hoodoo Juju park." She extended an open hand. "My deed?"

"Now Mister," he smirked as he placed the document in her hand. "I'm sorry, *Mrs.* Drew, you might wanna look into changing that name of yours legally. Wouldn't want nobody gettin' any ideas about all these acres of land that were turned over to you and your family. It's a suggestion." He took one last gulp of the lemonade and spat again. This time, a glob of brown saliva and snuff found its way to the toe of her shoe. "Thank you for your time, Mrs. Drew. I tend to like magic myself, so you can expect to see me 'round here often." He handed her the mason jar and headed toward the police car. Officer Goode followed; head bowed.

Once the hum of the police car's engine traveled a distance down the road, Dr. Djinn locked eyes with Professor Blue.

"Be on alert everyone, there's a new sheriff in town."

* * *

"Well one thing's for sure, she's a Time Thief."
Elliot removed his glasses and wiped them clean as they
filed out of the theater. "She said as much. Professor
Blue, too."

Brenda bit her lip. "Aunt Bird said the same thing
and I didn't believe her." She slowed to a stop.

"Bet you there's an Era Port somewhere 'round
here," Clair said as she examined the theater like a seasoned detective.

Elliot frowned. "What's that?"

Omen and Brenda looked at Clair with questioning eyes.

Clair raised an eyebrow. "You've never heard of
an Era Port?"

They shook their heads.

"It's like a train station, but for Time Travel.
Time Thieves never gather too far from Era Ports. It's
how they get around."

"Would you know it if you saw it?" Elliot asked.

"*You'd* know it if you saw it," Clair retorted.

Beyond the theater and concession stand, the
room opened into a courtyard. Everywhere Elliot looked,
he saw shells. They reminded him of smooth, white lips
with jagged smiles. The shells had been soldered to
wooden chairs and attached to an assortment of trees in
delicate designs surrounding the courtyard's perimeter.

"I still can't believe we'll be exploring this place
on our own." Omen shook his head.

"Right. The *Odd Scholarships* were sold to us as
a tour of the park and the chance to attend Hampton."
Elliot wiped his glasses clean and squinted at a banner
hanging across the courtyard. *Welcome, Odd Scholars.*
He blinked. "Are those…"

"Food!" Omen rushed toward a thicket of trees. At least a dozen platters piled with food hung in mid-air. Mounds of rice and peas smothered in steam. Extra-large shrimp soaked in savory sauces. Large fish with their heads still attached floated on a bed of greens, tomatoes, and bubbling soup. Slabs of meat curried to perfection. Bread and more bread, some of it toasted, some spongey, some buttered and filled with nuts.

Not one to ignore his rumbling stomach, Elliot moved closer to read the labels next to each dish: Egos soup, Jollof rice, Pounded yam, Beer meat, Suya, Okra soup, Potato leaf and rice, Fufu, Moi, Pepper Soup. Carefully, he grasped a piece of the sponge-like bread and read the label beside it. *Injera bread, Ethiopia. Use to sop up stew.* Cater corner to the bread was a reddish-brown mixture. He read the accompanying label. *Mesir Wat, Ethiopia. Red lentils, onion, ginger, garlic, and spices.* He breathed in the aroma and sopped up some of the stew with the bread. *Delicious.* For a time, no one spoke as Clair, Omen, and Elliot scarfed down dinner and dessert. Brenda wandered through the courtyard.

"What's Dr. Djinn gonna do about the sheriff? He's trying to prove this land isn't hers." Elliot asked between bites. "What if we've been chosen to help her keep this land?"

"Why would we be chosen to help with her land? That's her business," Brenda said with an eye roll and her arms folded across her chest. "You ask too many questions."

"Eat something." Clair nudged Brenda in the arm. "Ain't no telling when we'll be able to eat again."

Reluctantly, Brenda grabbed a small dish, stuck a fork inside a fileted fish, and transferred it to her plate. "I didn't expect to be solving mysteries."

"Expect the unexpected," Clair added through a mouthful of Jollof rice. "She's a Time Thief. We know that now for sure."

Elliot dipped his bread into the lentil stew. "Speaking of expectations, I did expect Professor Blue to greet us at least." He dabbed at the sides of his mouth with a cloth napkin. "It would be nice to have a guide."

Clair shook her head in agreement. "True. Guides are always good, but knowing Taints the way I do, we'll have clues to help us along."

"What kind of clues?" Brenda pushed her fork around her plate.

Clair tore into some of the bread and stew and groaned with pleasure. "Who knows? But they'll be there. Trust me."

"Yeah, I like adventure, but this one sounds a little, I dunno…strange," Omen chimed in after licking his fingers.

"Right. I also want to know where we'll be sleeping. I can already tell I'm gonna need my rest." Elliot scanned the courtyard as if a bed would magically appear.

"Rest? All this magic and mystery and you're thinking about rest?" Brenda rolled her eyes after swallowing a forkful of steaming rice.

Elliot exhaled. "I need to recharge. It's a long ride from DC to Hampton. And I know there'll be a lot to see."

Brenda shrugged and reached for another helping.

"What do you know about Dr. Djinn?" Omen turned to Clair. "You're the only one here with magic blood, right?"

"To be honest, I don't know much more than you. Mostly rumors." She lifted a glass of water to her lips. "That picture show revealed as much to y'all as it did to me."

"My dad showed me an article in *The Times Picayune* about a lynching." Omen rubbed his chin.

Brenda frowned. "A lynching?"

Omen shrugged. "There was some type of disturbance down in New Orleans. Dr. Djinn was selling her tonics and got into it with some White man. Then, a mob carried her off to hang her. Thing is, she survived."

"My best friend from home told me the same story," Elliot said between gulps.

"Time Thieves are already the most powerful conjurors in the world. If she survived a lynching, that's major." Clair took another swig from her cup.

"What do Time Thieves do anyway?" Brenda raised an eyebrow.

"Now who's asking a lot of questions?" Elliot shot at Brenda.

"What it sounds like." Clair ignored their bickering and turned to Brenda. "They steal time and resources."

Brenda took a deep breath. "Remember those packages from the vision? This makes me wonder if—"

Please proceed through the doors. Please proceed through the doors to your cabins. Enjoy your night.

On the opposite side of the courtyard, a pair of doors opened to reveal a grassy field.

"Well, let the journey begin." Elliot gathered his empty dishes and turned to the nearest trash bin. His heart pumped faster as he grabbed his briefcase and followed the others to a set of cabins bathed in moonlight. Brenda was right, he couldn't sleep with all of this adventure and mystery ahead of him. No way.

SEVEN

MAMA COOL'S COTTON CANDY

Elliot hardly slept that night. Between the picture show and Thelonious's words of warning on the day of the Boys Chemistry competition, he'd barely closed his eyes. Luckily, morning came quickly and after meeting outside their cabins, Elliot and the others found themselves once again sorting out their thoughts over a delectable spread of fruit and bread. This was how it went for the first few days at the park. After a bite to eat, they were whisked away to Hampton Institute a few miles down the road in the same Model T that brought him to the park. Once they arrived, they toured the campus and met with staff, all under the watchful eye of Professor Blue who'd encouraged them to ask questions and think long and hard about their courses of study. Elliot was a scientist through and through. There wasn't a question in his mind, especially after seeing Hampton's science department up close.

While Omen and Clair mulled over their courses, Brenda, the girl with the razor-sharp tongue and wit to match, settled on an engineering program. Elliot listened intently as she shared her views on microscope design with one of the school's seasoned professors. Though he agreed with some of Brenda's points, he disagreed with her argument about alloy being superior to steel in every instance. A month ago, he'd been complaining to his father about how easy it was for alloy to bend and break when one of their new microscopes crashed to the floor. He kept his mouth shut; however, it was clear that Brenda loved a challenge and he didn't feel like arguing.

As he lay in bed that night, his thoughts drifted back to the Picture Show. *What was Dr. Djinn's endgame? Why show them those scenes? Was she asking for help? Where was she?* Hopefully, he'd have more answers in the coming days. The suspense was becoming too much to bear.

*   *   *

"Something tells me she needs our help. That picture show ended with a lot of questions, and zero answers," Elliot said over toast and cantaloupe on the fourth day of their stay.

Brenda rolled her eyes and helped herself to a short stack of pancakes. "According to Clair, Time Thieves are the most powerful conjurers in the world. Why would they need help from a bunch of teenagers?"

"I know what I said, but now, my gut is telling me different. If she didn't need help, why show that picture show? It means something." Clair took a swig of grapefruit juice.

"She put us together for a reason. We were chosen." Omen made a tent with his fingers. "A strongman, a sage, an inventor, a chemist." He looked at each of them as he spoke. "Like it or not, we're all part of this puzzle. We fit."

Elliot shook his head in agreement. For weeks, he'd thought he'd won a full scholarship and a once in a lifetime tour of a magical amusement park. Now, he felt more like a guinea pig plopped in a maze. He wiped his hands and stood. "What's on today's agenda?"

"Looks like we head to Garvey's Airship Base in five minutes," Brenda said as she read the itinerary. "Finally, we get to see the park."

Omen stood and stretched. "About time. Hampton Institute is interesting and all, but I wanna have some fun."

"Well, I guess today's the day." Elliot rubbed his hands together in anticipation.

* * *

A gymnasium-sized room filled with vendors selling sweets, game booths, and dunk tanks stretched beyond the courtyard. The smell of pretzels and roasting peanuts wafted toward Elliot's nose. Had he not eaten minutes before, he would have made a beeline for the soft pretzels. He peered inside a booth with glass bottles stacked in the shape of a pyramid. A row of black baseballs with red and green stitching sat in front. It wasn't the game, but the prizes that caught his attention. Most, if not all of them were some kind of UNIA paraphernalia. Marcus Garvey buttons flashed his famous sayings. Stickers and decals of the African continent glowed and shifted to display different countries and their flags. Stuffed animals dressed in miniature red, black, and green hats and tee shirts looked out from their shelves.

Elliot wandered inside a gift shop. Along the walls, he saw posters of creatures he'd never seen before. *Ninki Nanka.* The words were written in a cursive script under a painting of a dragon-like creature with mirrors for scales. A large diamond protruded from the top of its head. He pulled off his glasses and wiped them clean again. His gaze swung to the next photo. *Jengu.* In the poster, a black woman with a halo of blue hair and a golden fin rested on a rock surrounded by ocean waves.

Fascinating. The entire store was filled with everything a visitor to the park would have wanted: shirts with the slogans, *Africa for the Africans* or *I Survived the Kilimanjaro Coaster,* coffee mugs, red, black, and green flags, postcards, bookmarks, and of course stuffed-animal likenesses of the strange creatures. Finally, his line of vision settled on a wall lined with books. He leaned in closer for a better look. *Inside the Optic Congress. The History of the House of the Evolving. Fangs, Feathers, and Folklore: Africa's Amazing Beasts.* Each book was unique. He ran his thumb over the gold and silver foiled letters on their spines.

"Look!"

Clair tugged on his arm and guided him from the store and back into the larger room. She pointed at the ceiling. A giant tank filled with brilliantly colored fish and other animals he couldn't identify zipped around the dome. An animal the size of a whale swam into view. Elliot stared at its gray belly from below.

Elliot scratched his temple. "But if that's the ceiling. How are we—where are we?"

She shrugged. "Expect the unexpected."

"Now this is more like what I expected at a park." Omen stopped and stared at a High Striker Strongman's game complete with a giant mallet and flashing lights.

Elliot took it all in. It was obvious that Dr. Djinn had taken great care to weave geography and history into the ball throwing games, darts, and ring tosses. Even the popcorn, peanut, pretzel, and candy apple stands had some interpretation of the red, black, and green motif. His gaze shifted from one corner of the room to the next and stopped. *Mama Cool's Sweets and Cotton Candy.* A heavyset woman with a poof of white hair pulled in a giant bun shuffled around inside. A pair of odd-looking spectacles with too many lenses dangled from a chain around her neck.

He took a few steps closer, his eyes settling on a mechanical arm inside a glass box near the woman's elbow. She used the arm to stretch and pull strands of sugar into miniscule ropes as fine as the hairs on the back of his hands. Each strand shimmered as if it had been scraped from a cave of crystals. The woman manipulated the mechanical arm like a weaver. It reminded him of the hats and scarves his grandmother crocheted while humming church songs in her old rocking chair. Though he didn't have an ounce of magic blood, there was something familiar about the process. He crept closer. Sticks of sparkling red, black, and green cotton candy rotated of their own volition. Some spun round and round. Others floated end over end. The sound of white noise and static assaulted his ears. Then, as quickly as they had come, the sounds were gone. He crept closer and pushed his tortoise shell frames up the bridge of his nose. After a few timid steps, he spoke. "Mama Cool?"

The woman looked up. "That's me."

"Is that sugar?" Elliot pointed at the sparkling threads between her hands.

The woman narrowed her eyes, reached for the eyeglasses strung haphazardly around her neck, and put them on. "Sugar, but not sugar. Sugar and spells. Sugar and spells. Sweets and Taints. Taints and sweets."

She had a heavy voice like the gospel singers in his mother's church choir. Elliot half expected her to break out in song. She turned her back to him. On one of the booth's walls, he spotted aging photographs of people he didn't recognize along with newspaper clippings, maps, brochures, and advertisements. Sprinkled in with the nondescript images was a black and white photo of an ever-confident Marcus Garvey wearing an assured smile. The shelves were stacked to the ceiling with silver bowls. Forks engraved with strange symbols, both foreign and familiar, hung from wooden pegs. Elliot rubbed the hairs on his chin.

"Cotton Candy? You choose. Red, black, green, or a combination." Mama Cool pointed at the rotating candy clouds.

Elliot rolled back on his heels. "What's the difference?"

"An Ain't, huh?" A smile spread across her face.

He bit his lip. "Yes, ma'am, but—"

"Ever wanted to know what it feels like to be a Taint?" She winked.

He looked at the woman with questioning eyes. "But—"

"Hush!" Mama Cool put a pudgy index finger to her lips. "Choose a color. Red, black, green, or a combination. The more color, the richer the journey."

"Journey?" He stepped back and looked at the sign above his head. Beneath it was a quote written in a neat, cursive script. He hadn't noticed it before.

It is crooked wood that shows the best sculptor.
~African Proverb

"Sculptor?" He raised an eyebrow.

She rested her chin in her palms. "Yes, you are the sculptor. Become a Taint with a single bite." Her husky drawl reminded him of red dirt and collard greens. "Step into the shoes of a Thief, a Shifter, or a Sage." She reached to the back of her booth, grabbed one of the strange forks and twirled threads of the sugary black cloud around its tines. Even as she held it, the threads pulsed to a rhythm. With her fingertips, she tore a piece from the larger cloud and popped it into her mouth. "With the Black, you become a Shifter. There is no other feeling quite like it. Black is best."

Elliot blinked as the woman's smooth brown skin and oval eyes stretched and darkened. She smirked as her features contorted. Her button nose widened and flattened. Her cheekbones sharpened and became more distinct. He gulped. Staring back at him was his father's easy smile. She spoke with his voice, low and rumbling. He could see the widow's peak at the top of his forehead. Stunned, Elliot stood rooted to the ground. In an instant, she shifted back and moved through the booth freely. He watched as she juggled black threads between her ringed fingers. Once she released her grip, the threads spun in mid-air.

Next, she removed one of the red clouds from its box. "Red. With red you feel, see, and know. With red you experience what it is to be a Sage." Her voice grew louder and more dramatic with each word. She popped a morsel of red cotton candy into her mouth and held his eyes in a penetrating glare. "You will have the revenge you seek. The cure is within reach." Before Elliot could reply, she'd shifted her focus to another rotating cloud. "And the green. Yes, the green." She rubbed her hands together. "The green is what it feels like to be a Thief! Ride a camel through the pyramids of Giza!" She pointed to the brochure of Egypt attached to a wall. "Climb Kilimanjaro!" She thrust a finger in the direction of a map of Zambia. "Smell the Zanzibar Marketplace! Travel through the Then and the Now!" Her eyes grew wide as she pushed a map toward him.

He turned the map over in his hands. It was warm to the touch. "All this in a bite?"

"Yes, young man." She laced her fingers together.

Elliot stared at the candy treat. "And if I get more than one, I get—"

"The entire experience."

"How much?"

Mama Cool rubbed one of her earlobes. "Nothing and everything. Free and not."

"How can something be everything and nothing? Free and not?" He grunted. "It's impossible."

"What did it cost you to become an Odd Scholar?" She peered over her spectacles.

"Nothing. I entered the competition and—"

"There is always a cost young man. Time, energy, family, trust . . ."

For a moment they stood in silence. Elliot stared at his shoes.

"That competition pushed you farther away from your brother." Mama Cool folded her arms across her chest. "There are things you should know. There is history here." She patted his hand. "You have a journey ahead of you that will require you to know as much as possible."

He shook his head. "It feels like I'm in a maze."

"You're right. This place holds secrets and you must find them." She snatched another fork from the back and muttered an incantation under her breath. Then, she pulled a page of newspaper from one of the booth's wall pegs. Its headline read:

Who is Dr. Marvellus Djinn?

It was the same clipping Thelonious had shown him on the day of the chemistry competition.

"What's your choice?"

Elliot took a look at the map and smoothed his mustache. He loved to travel and he certainly wanted to feel everything he saw. The shifting hadn't been appealing at all. "Red and green."

In a flash, Mama Cool folded the paper into a cylindrical shape, stuffed the candy clouds inside, and handed it over. "Remember to breathe, young man. Breathe. It's a lot to take in at once."

"Here goes nothing," he mumbled. He closed his eyes tight and sunk his teeth into the sweet, fluffy threads. The white noise returned. After a rush of warmth, the air turned blazing hot as an August afternoon. He zipped forward, weightless as bits of sand pricked his skin. Frames of ancient history zipped before him. Aset collecting the fragmented pieces of her husband's body. Imhotep gathering herbs and roots from the banks of the Nile. Hatshepsut in a golden breastplate riding on a chariot. Akhenaton writing a decree on papyrus. He was floating above an obelisk with a golden pyramidal top etched with hieroglyphics. Carefully, he ran one of his palms over the markings. A buzzing vibration emanated from the glyph as if it were alive and breathing. He blinked. The spots behind his eyes morphed into wooden masks. Ebony skinned people bowed, genuflecting from waist to ankle. Then came a star brighter than the night sky. An unseen force pushed him forward. He bobbed from side to side like a ball attached to a paddle with a rubber band. Now, he was on the banks of a river. The Niger? No. An Oasis in the middle of the Sahara. Then, he sat astride a camel, its hump, a hairy mess of matted gold. He held his nose shut. Thick jungle. Endless green. Heat. Heavy humidity. He was sweating profusely. A waterfall tumbling into a massive pool. Birds gliding through the bluest sky he'd ever seen. Ocean. Castles of white stone. Spots. First black, then red. Red spots pulsing. *Whoosh!* A vibrating force tugged at his navel. His heartbeat slowed to a crawl. He backstroked though the air though he couldn't swim. Home. His eyes flew open.

"Was it to your liking?" Mama Cool clucked her tongue and smiled.

Elliot bent over to catch his breath. He removed his glasses and took out a kerchief. After wiping his lenses clean, he bit on the arm of the frames and stood silent for a moment, replaying the experience in his head. He'd traveled through time. He didn't believe what had happened, yet it had. He held onto one of the booth's walls to support his weight. "Intense," he said groggily.

"Good."

"Can you teach me how all of this works?" He gathered his wits as the scientist in him returned. Whatever this was, he had to learn. He had to know more. Elliot pointed to the threads of crystallized sugar wrapped around the fork. "What is it?"

"Spells and sweets. Sweets and spells." She narrowed her eyes.

"No. I mean specifics. What is the chemical makeup? It's time travel and sensory overload in a bite!"

"The secret is in the weaving." The old woman placed another candy cloud in a metal bowl.

"Elliot, come on!"

He looked up to see Clair waving in the distance.

"Okay, one second," he called over his shoulder.

He watched as she hurried through a pair of doors. He turned back to Mama Cool. "How long was I gone?"

"Two minutes, give or take." She tugged at her shawl and wrapped it tight around her shoulders before pointing toward the ceiling. Turtles and stingray zipped through a tangle of colorful coral. "The keys are there."

"The water? What's in there?" Elliot stared up at the dome.

"It's a river inside a rainforest. We call it The Grand Menagerie."

"What kind of animals are in there?" Elliot asked, measuring his words.

"What kind of animals would be on display in a magical park?"

"Animals from Africa?" He shrugged. "I don't know."

"Come on, you're smarter than that," Mama Cool said, studying her nails.

"Magical creatures?"

She snapped her fingers. "Ah, I knew you were sharp! The animals are real, but there aren't too many folks who actually believe in them."

"You mean there are sphinxes in there," he stammered.

"Yes, a sphinx guards the entrance." She held her chin in her palm. "And trust me, you wanna be prepared for her. She's quite a character—"

Elliot's heart leapt. "I'm making a formula. Once perfected, it would change the way people think." He looked at the tank. "Is there something in there that can help?"

She looked both ways before speaking though it was clear no one was within earshot. "You will meet a Jengu. Tell her your story."

"Jengu? What's a Jengu?"

She chewed on her lip. "I can't tell you everything. You're a scientist. Research!"

"But, how can it help me?"

The woman put an index finger to her lips. "That is all I can say. Good luck young man."

In an instant, the woman pulled a curtain of red beads closed with a snap. Elliot backed away from the booth and hurried down the corridor, his brain jumbled with thoughts of Jengu and mythological creatures, cotton candy, and magic. He took one last glance at the tank above his head. A creature with glimmering green scales beckoned him with an index finger. He stopped, removed his glasses and wiped them with his kerchief. When he looked up again, it was gone. No matter what, he had to get inside the Grand Menagerie. With a determined sigh, he hurried toward a set of doors in the distance.

EIGHT

GARVEY'S AIRSHIP

"Wow. Never thought I'd see one of these in real life." Omen looked on, mouth agape.

An airship floated in the center of the room. Large enough to seat a small army, it was fashioned after a 17th century pirate ship. Black oars trimmed in gold jutted out of its sides, and its wooden body shone a brilliant green. A massive black balloon speckled with tiny red stars hovered above it. The words: *Dogon, The Black Star Line* had been painted on the balloon's side in golden letters. Thick ropes attached the balloon to the ship and anchored it to the floor.

"I told you this would be anything she wanted it to be. She's a Time Thief." Clair ducked beneath one of the ropes, climbed aboard the ship, and plopped on one of the benches on deck. She glanced at the empty space next to her. "Come on, climb in."

Still skeptical, Omen ran one of his palms along a giant oar. Clair hopped from her seat and walked the ship's perimeter. Every now and then she'd tug on the ropes, knock at one of the structure's benches, or poke at a gear or screw. Finally, she muttered an inaudible chant. After the inspection, she strolled back to her seat. "It's reinforced with spells."

Elliot appeared with his arms folded across his chest. "You sure this thing is safe?" He threw the ship a side-long glance.

Omen poked at one of the ropes. The only modes of transportation he'd experienced in his short life were his uncle's old pick-up and the Model T. Now, he was poised to ride on an airship. If only his pop could see him now. "How do you know?"

"She knows because she's a Taint." Brenda stared at the balloon before taking a seat. Omen followed as Elliot brought up the rear.

"Thieves, Shifters, Artists, and Sages, right?" Elliot chimed in.

"How'd you know?" Brenda cut her eyes in Elliot's direction.

"My best friend has a thing for Taints. He knows all about them." Elliot smirked as he replayed his best friend's shenanigans in his head.

"Well, I still don't know." Brenda looked between Clair and Elliot. "What are they?"

Clair shifted her weight. "In our world, there are four orders of magic folks: Sages, Shifters, Artists, and Thieves. Dr. Djinn is a Thief. I'm a Sage."

"When did you find out?" Omen twirled his thumbs.

Clair paused. "I think I've always known. Sages have vivid memories. We remember things no one else can. Past lives. Events down to the tiniest detail. Birth. Death."

With a snap, a wooden pillar rose from the middle of the ship. Pamphlets jutted from deep grooves on its sides.

"Nice map," Brenda said as her jaw dropped to the floor.

A world atlas covered the ceiling. Tiny lights illuminated what Omen imagined were cities and landmarks.

Elliot craned his neck for a better view. "Do you notice how large Africa is—"

"Yes! The sheer size of Africa has long been understated and she is equally massive in wonder!" A voice boomed from the entranceway.

"I am Baba Ali."

Omen, Brenda, and Elliot stifled their laughter as a round man dressed as a 17th century explorer struggled to adjust his heavy sword and costume. One of the plumes in his bicorn hat had become stuck between two ropes and a golden button from his coat snagged on a column. By the time he'd situated himself, he was out of breath. He smoothed his pants and stood up straight.

"Historian and magic enthusiast. I also enjoy seafood, long walks, and sea foam green." He chuckled at his own joke and ducked beneath the ropes. "I'll be your tour guide."

"Tour guide?" Omen gave the man a quizzical look. "I thought we weren't getting a tour."

Elliot shook his head. "Right. First we're getting a tour, then it's an adventure, now it's a tour again." He threw up his hands.

"Please remember to keep your limbs inside the ship at all times." Baba Ali hurried toward a raised deck at the front of the ship and tugged on the giant ropes, loosening them until they fell to the floor in a heap.

Omen pretended to stretch his long arms until one of them lay draped around Clair's shoulder. She shot him a cold glare.

"Did you ask if you could put your arm around me?"

"I—I'm—" He stammered and laid his hands in his lap.

Her glare softened as she pulled his arm back around her shoulder. "Next time, ask."

Suddenly, the room shook. A fissure formed in the wall ahead of them and a blinding beam of light seeped through. They shielded their eyes as the wall cracked open allowing warm sunlight to bleed through.

Baba Ali climbed a short flight of stairs on the ship and grabbed hold of a golden wheel surrounded by buttons and gears, all of different shapes and sizes. He pressed a button and spun the wheel. All at once, the heavy ropes anchoring the ship to the floor loosened and it lurched forward and into the outside world. Omen took a look over the side of the ship in shock. Though they'd just left a room inside a building rooted to the ground, they were now flying at least fifty feet in the air.

"Up ahead is the Sculpture Garden of Antiquity. It's five square miles of winding paths and documented history."

The ship followed an intricate path above a collection of larger-than-life monuments. Omen swelled with pride as they hovered near Abraham, a Black Seminole leader, depicted with his famous walking stick and head garb. Enormous twenty- and thirty-foot monuments jutted into the sky, each with their own quiet defiance.

"Up ahead is Harriet Tubman." Baba Ali piped up in excitement and gestured toward a giant statue holding a rifle aimed and ready. "And to her left is Denmark Vesey."

Denmark carried a bible under one arm and a rifle under the other. Next to him, Makeda held her hands on her hips, and the Warrior Queen Nzinga sat upon a throne with Portuguese helmets crushed beneath its base.

Brenda and Elliot launched into a contest of identifying the statues before Baba Ali could announce their names. Elliot was a tad bit quicker, which made Brenda visibly annoyed. Menelik II, Toussaint Louverture, Jean-Jacques Dessalines, Nat Turner, Zumbi of Palmares, Captain Cudjoe, Hatshepsut, Dahia al Kahina, Nanny of the Maroons. Expertly manicured bushes of emerald green carved out sharp paths leading to historical facts plastered on pillars. Omen felt a sense of pride bubbling inside him. He'd always been taught to study the Black Seminoles of his father's line and the descendants of enslaved Africans in his mother's lineage. He came from resistance and freedom fighting.

"The Honorable Marcus Mosiah Garvey says the Black skin is not a badge of shame, but rather a glorious symbol of national greatness." Baba Ali opened his arms wide. "This park was built on land that was toiled by our ancestors. Each statue was designed by Archibald John Motley, Jr., a close friend of Dr. Marvellus Djinn."

"My father owns two of his prints. He's a legendary artist," Elliot chimed in.

Baba Ali tipped his hat. "The man has great taste."

Omen looked out at the miles of twists and turns making up the maze. Though stunning from above, he imagined how difficult it would be to complete on foot. "This maze sure looks challenging."

"It is. Luckily there are different levels of difficulty for our guests. Each group will be accompanied by a guide."

Omen, Brenda, and Elliot glanced at each other and smirked.

"Whose idea was it to have an airship in the park?" Brenda grasped the railing as they swerved around the top of a pyramid nestled next to Pharaoh Hatshepsut's chariot.

Baba Ali stroked his chin. "That would be Ms. Bessie Coleman."

Brenda's jaw dropped. "*The* Bessie Coleman?"

Baba Ali smiled. "Yes. She's been on our board of directors for the last year. Dr. Djinn sought her out when we talked about how we'd transport guests throughout the park." He patted the ship's railing fondly. "We call this *The Dogon* because it will also be used for park guests to study the night sky. It will leave each night at dusk."

Omen took note of the copper telescopes lining the deck along with bins filled with compasses and other instruments he didn't recognize. While Baba Ali rambled on about dates, materials, and inspiration, Omen could barely tear his eyes away from Clair. He glanced at the definition of her cheek bones and the smoothness of her dark skin. It was a deep brown with a hint of red, kind of like the rich Florida mud his younger siblings liked to slosh around in after it rained. He glanced at her eye patch and wondered the story it told. Had someone hurt her? When had it happened? Was it an accident at all? Finally, he turned back to Baba Ali. He swallowed a yelp as the ship drifted a bit too close to the massive crown of Mansa Musa, the wealthy king of ancient Mali. Clair squeezed his hand. The entire park, a sprawling one thousand acres, stretched beyond their view. At one end of the park, a glass sphere glowed gold near the sun. On the other, a waterfall spilled over a steep cliff and into the ocean.

Omen used his hand as a visor to shield his eyes. "Wow."

"I never knew there were hills this high along the Virginia coast." Elliot peered over the side of the ship.

Baba Ali chuckled. "There aren't. That's our replica of the Eastern Rift and Mt. Kilimanjaro. If you think this is impressive, you should see what's inside."

As expected, *The Motherland* was full of everything a theme park should have: a Ferris wheel, bumper cars, games, eateries, roller coasters, and other rides that were either safe and predictable or completely terrifying. Regardless of the ride or exhibit, the African motif remained front and center. Red, black, and green flags attached to tall poles rippled in the wind. Baobab trees stabbed the clouds in the sky. Not a single detail had been forgotten. In the shadow of Mt. Kilimanjaro, a vast savannah dotted with wide acacia and short bushes spread for miles. Only the picnic tables and tents signaled this was not the continent itself.

"So, how did this come together?" Omen stared at the churning waterfall.

"Dr. Djinn's story starts in an unlikely place with the most unlikely people," Baba Ali replied in a distant tone. With the push of a button, he put the ship on autopilot. He hopped down from the ship's wheel, leaned over the pillar, and removed a metal case. Inside was a weathered piece of parchment. A glob of red wax with an intricate looking symbol sealed it closed. After removing the seal, he unfurled it carefully. "To understand this park, you must first understand Dr. Marvellus Djinn." He looked at each of them until his eyes settled on Clair. "Sixth generation Sage?"

"As far as I know." She gave him a once over. "Shifter?"

Baba Ali winked. "Third generation." In an instant, he changed his visage to an older woman, bald, with sagging jowls. Next, his skin took on a copper hue and he sprouted jet black hair and striking cheek bones. Omen stared into his father's eyes: two coal black stones. Finally, he morphed into a teenager with wire-rimmed glasses, a girl with an eye patch, and another with giant puffs. When Omen found himself staring at his own image; he recoiled in his seat.

"You're gonna have to give us a warning before you do that." Omen rubbed his eyes as Baba Ali morphed back into himself, or at least what he presented when they'd met.

"I apologize." He bowed his head and presented the parchment to Clair. "You're a Taint. And only a Taint can read this."

Clair took her time unfurling the document. She gazed at the delicate script and held the parchment as if it were a newborn baby. After a deep breath, she began to read.

NINE

40 ACRES AND AN AMUSEMENT PARK

My dearest granddaughter,
For a long, long time, I didn't know what free-
dom was. Not in the sense that we know it today. I was
born a slave. I watched my momma make the beds and
cook the meals in the Big House while I played. Mama
was a quiet soul. She was content with her cooking and
tending to laundry and the house on the outside. But on
the inside, she was a thunderstorm. And once I became
old enough, she'd take me to the edge of the woods
where she'd show me roots, herbs, charms, stars, hexes,
angles of the moon, and different chants to get my way.
She made sure I knew how to protect myself.
It was around that time that one of Massa Arm-
strong's daughters saw fit to teach me to read and write.
Her name was Charity and we was about the same age.
Reading and writing made me stronger than I ever
thought it would. I saw things differently. We did a good
job of keeping my reading and writing a secret for a few
years.

DR. DJINN

The first time we were caught, it was the Mistress. She was upset, but she also loved and cherished her only daughter. She made us both promise we would be more careful because she knew Massa Armstrong wouldn't be so nice if he found out. The lessons kept on for about 5 more years. By now, I didn't really need Charity to teach me anymore. We were about as equal as a slave child and a white child could be in that right. We were learning side by side. Momma had always known. I didn't keep much of anything from her. In fact, I'd sneak books and teach her what I'd learned after I was finished with Charity's studies. Momma loved it. She soaked it all up like a sponge. Soon, she was writing down recipes for tonics and medicines for folks to remember after she died.

One day, Massa caught us reading by the light of a fire in the woods. And when he asked where we'd learned it, neither of us spoke up. The next day, he paraded us in front of the plantation and whipped us side by side. Charity did her best to save us. She screamed and hollered as the blood dripped down our backs in slick currents.

After the whipping, momma became even more defiant. She worked roots on Massa and his family until the rain got stingy and the crops shriveled up and died. Soon, the Mistress fell ill and died of an aggressive form of gout. And on account of our beatings all those years ago, Charity refused to speak to her father ever again. By the time word came that we were all free, Massa was on his death bed and surrounded by irritable slaves, his big ole plantation was in disarray, and he had no family or friends to speak of. He could hardly talk in those final hours of his life. It was like he was passing in and out of a paper-thin veil with every breath. I watched momma feed him hominy. About two weeks after freedom came, she grabbed my hand and gave me a silver skeleton key.

She told me to run downstairs to Massa's study to a cherry wood writing desk in the corner. There, she said I'd find his last will and testament.

The desk was easy enough to find, but the will was not. In his old and ailing age, Massa had become a hoarder. The desk was full of old books with funny markings, coins, enough dollar bills to buy more land, and sale slips for all the slaves he'd ever owned and sold. Underneath it all was a brown leather bible as soft as a baby's bottom and inside that bible, was his will.

I high tailed it up the parlor stairs and handed it to my momma who was sitting by Massa and holding his hand real tight and secure. Next to her was a tea kettle with steam puffing from its lip like cold breath on a winter morning. She held a kerchief over Massa's eye and was talking real low underneath her breath in a hum. I opened the bible and handed her the paper and a quill. He held the quill real shaky in his hands. Then, she chanted a little bit louder and motioned for me to come closer. By the time I reached the edge of the bed, I saw him signing the will. That's when she took the tea from the kettle, poured it in a cup and put it to his lips. She smiled, but with eyes as hard as stones. By the time he saw those eyes, black as pits, it was too late.

And since then, this land is our land. Make this land a refuge for our people. Make sure it is an ode to our accomplishments and beauty. This land can remind us of who we are. I know you will do what's right. I know you will make us proud.

With love,

Lily Armstrong

"So, this land belonged to the people who en-slaved Dr. Djinn's family?" Elliot asked as he leaned forward.

"And thanks to her grandmother, the land now belongs to her."

Omen tore his gaze away from the parchment as the ship moved beneath the shadow of a glass sphere. He looked down.

"And coming up ahead, one of the crowning jewels of *The Motherland*, the Grand Menagerie!"

The Grand Menagerie was a large sphere made entirely of circular panels of glass. Inside, shadows of tall trees crawled up its sides while flashes of lightning illuminated the glass in short bursts. His stomach dropped.

"Is it raining in there?" Elliot asked, tapping his foot nervously.

"Probably. It's a complete replica of a rainforest in every way: dense jungle, swamp, mythological crea-tures…"

"Creatures?" Brenda peered into the sphere.

"Grootslang, Abada, Jengu, —"

"Groot who?" Omen raised an eyebrow.

"Did you say, Jengu?" Elliot craned his neck overboard.

"It's a theme park designed by a Time Thief. What would you expect?" Baba Ali stared at the sphere as if he expected something amazing to reveal itself.

"Wait, is this the same rainforest we saw inside the theater?" Omen rubbed his eyes and squinted through the haze.

Baba Ali grinned. "Why yes, yes, it is!"

"How?" Brenda turned around on the bench and pointed toward the maze behind them. "The theater is back there—"

"My brain hurts thinking about this." Omen shook his head.

Clair sighed. "Anything that can happen, will."

"She's right. Everything you think you know, will be challenged." Baba Ali's eyes shifted. "And the lightning you see isn't from a storm. It's more than likely from the Impundulu. Lightning forms in their droppings."

"Didn't Dr. Djinn mention an Impundulu in the picture show?" Brenda frowned.

Baba Ali skipped across the deck to the ship's wheel. After switching off the autopilot, he maneuvered the ship, so it hovered a few feet from the glass. "Try out the telescopes. They can be used during the day, too."

Omen walked to the edge of the ship and sat on a wooden stool as Brenda and Elliot adjusted their telescopes with ease. He twisted the ocular lens to sharpen its focus. A yellow insect with orange wings zoomed into view before landing on a hanging tree branch. He counted the wings. Two, four, six, eight, ten, twelve...*twenty*. The thing looked like a cross between a dragonfly and a ladybug. He watched as it climbed a twisting lavender vine. Then, it reared back on a pair of spindly legs, took flight, and hovered above a pulsing flower before touching down again. Both its pincers and wings were slick with dew. It turned its oblong body around to face him. Omen's breath caught in his throat as he stared into its eyes. He pushed the telescope away.

Clair leaned over. "You okay?"

Omen shivered. "I'm fine."

"Is that a mermaid? Nah, couldn't be." Brenda twisted the scope's lens.

"If it looks like a mermaid, it probably is." Clair quipped over the top of her telescope.

"What you are seeing is a Jengu." Baba Ali held up an index finger.

Brenda and Omen exchanged puzzled looks.

"West African mermaids. Half fish, half human. Their scales create a magical wax that can be used to seal anything. And their tears and the oils from their hair heal disease." Baba Ali gazed at the sun fondly. "I fell in love with a Jengu once." His full lips stretched into a wide smile. "Sure, those fins are beautiful to look at, but they get in the way of a whole lot to be honest." He cleared his throat and snapped back to attention.

"Look at this, now!" Elliot shouted over the chatter. He took a step back as the others crowded around his stool.

Brenda tip-toed toward the telescope and peered inside. Her breath hitched in her throat as she covered her mouth with her hand. After gazing into the scope, Clair motioned for Omen to come closer. He did so reluctantly. What he saw made his stomach drop. Lumbering into view was a monstrous beast. Its head was covered in wrinkly gray skin dusted with a silvery shimmer. Precious jewels floated in the creases. Ruby, diamond, emerald, sapphire. The thing would have been regal had it not been so startlingly grotesque. Ringlets of jade twisted round and round its ivory tusks like jeweled adornments. And then there was its torso, part elephant, part snake. Its tail was the width of a large tree trunk. Omen fiddled with the lens and gulped as it reared back its massive head. The floppy ears folded over themselves with each movement. When it let out a massive roar, the scholars scrambled from their stools.

TEN

A LABYRINTH OF DOORS

Baba Ali twirled his fingers, waddled across the deck, and grabbed hold of the wheel. "We'd best be getting on now."

Brenda held onto her seat as the ship edged backward before turning away from the sphere.

After a few moments of uncomfortable silence, she spoke up. "So, what's the purpose of having a thing like that in a park?"

"Everything has its place," Baba Ali said. "The Grootslang is a terrifying creature, but it is necessary." He kept his eyes trained on the approaching waterfall and spun the wheel, causing the ship to and dip east. A mist crawled aboard as they moved closer to the falls. He pushed another button and with a grinding hum, glass panels extended from the sides of the boat, enveloping them in a sealed carriage. Tiny droplets gradually became a thunderous stream sliding down the panel sides.

Brenda gazed into the falling water. The scene reminded her of a story her Uncle Rufus read to her when she was younger. The story was about the patience of nature and every season having its time. Whenever she'd done something to disappoint her aunt and uncle, they would respond with a parable. Sometimes, she and Uncle Rufus would sneak down to the basement after Aunt Squeak was asleep and pine over his old books. The large basement in Philly had a library that took up three of the four long row house walls. She snapped out of her reverie when she spotted a rainbow reaching its long arms from the top of the cliff to a billowing cloud of mist below.

"Take a look at this." Elliot walked toward the opposite deck. As they cruised beside a cliff of alternating jagged rocks and prickly bushes, a glittering wall appeared. He snatched his glasses off and cleaned them quickly with a cloth. "What are those?"

Brenda leaned forward until the tip of her nose touched the glass. "What? Where?"

Elliot pointed to a ledge above her sightline.

"Souls." Baba Ali flicked a switch and the ship slowed to a halt. Elliot and the others leaned in for a better view.

"Souls? What do you mean souls?" Brenda wrinkled her nose.

Upon closer inspection, a portion of the hill had been cut away to reveal an innumerable number of Jars perched on countless shelves. The Jars swallowed the sun's rays and, in turn, reflected kaleidoscopic light. Brenda cocked her head to the side and thought back to the ingenuity competition in Charleston. These were exactly like the Jar she'd used to demonstrate the uses of her Fire Needle. The mere thought of how close she'd gotten to a soul detached from its body made her cringe.

Baba Ali shrugged. "Everything has a place. And if its place is here, trust it's for a reason."

Brenda struggled to tear her gaze away from the discovery. "Ok, but what is this exactly? It's gotta have a name."

Baba Ali glanced at the Jars. "This is the Shelf of the Damned."

"The Damned?" Omen shoved his hands in his pockets.

Clair whistled. "I've heard about these."

Baba Ali glanced at his dangling pocket watch. "Time, time, time . . ." he yammered. "I gotta get better at this keeping time thing," he let out a nervous chuckle. "Guess that's why I'm a Shifter and not a Thief. Anyway, Professor Blue will tell you more."

The airship glided through another cluster of cascading falls and rainbows. Brenda watched as the golden sunlight played a game of hide and seek with prisms of color.

"I don't think I've ever seen anything so beautiful," Clair murmured.

Omen turned to look at her. "Really? I have."

She blushed as he tightened his grip around her shoulders. Brenda smiled as she watched Omen and Clair lean into one another as they sped toward a dark cave. Once they pulled inside, the glass panels retracted with an echoing thud.

"It was a pleasure and an honor being your tour guide. I trust your stay here at The Motherland will be inspirational." Baba Ali stepped away from the ship's wheel.

"What's next?" Elliot asked with a raised eyebrow.

"The day is only beginning," Baba Ali replied as he exited the ship and onto a gravelly landing. "What's next, is teamwork."

They followed his lead into the dimly lit cave. As Brenda surveyed her new surroundings, she noticed the glimmer of crystals lodged inside the rocks. The roar of churning water beyond the airship echoed around them.

Brenda watched as Elliot ran his fingers over the walls. Clair looked on, suspicious.

She hurried to Elliot's side as Omen climbed off the ship. "Wait, don't touch any—"

"Good luck." Baba Ali bowed low as his bulky cutlass scraped the floor. With a pop, he disappeared.

Brenda looked around in shock. Everything was gone, the falls, the cave, the airship. Everything.

"What the—" Brenda shrieked.

"Hush!" Clair held up her hand.

They were in the middle of a room filled with doors: square, circular, rectangular, triangular, octagonal, and diamond shaped. Each door had been marked with golden symbols.

Clair ran her palm across one of the symbols. Each time she made contact, it shifted, inverting itself backward, upside down, and inside out, changing from gold to silver and back. A rustling sound accompanied each shift. "Shift sorcery."

Brenda turned to face her. "Hope that means you know how to get us out of here."

Clair shook her head. "No. It's Shift Sorcery. Remember, there are four orders: Artists, Thieves, Sages, and Shifters. I'm a Sage. I know a little something about each order, but not enough to get us out of here."

Brenda sucked her teeth. "Well, one thing I'm great at is puzzles. Let's put our heads together and see how we can get outta here."

"Is there anything you know about Shift Sorcery that could help us? Anything we should keep in mind?" Elliot inspected a bright green door in the shape of a pentagon nearest him.

"Well, at the root of all Shift Sorcery is...a shift. Sounds elementary, I know, but be prepared. This'll all change soon. At least that's what my gut is telling me."

"Shift? You mean the way Baba Ali shifted back on the ship?" Omen asked as he examined another door in the shape of a triangle.

Clair shook her head. "Yup. We need to find the trigger."

"Trigger?" Elliot turned to Clair.

"A password." She mopped her forehead with a kerchief. "It'll trigger the doors to shift. That'll lead to a way out."

"How in the world are we supposed to know what the password is?" Omen groaned.

"If we solved the clue at the theater, we can solve this one," Brenda said as she cracked her knuckles behind her back.

Clair turned in a circle. "Shift Sorcery. What would a Shifter use to trigger a door? Could be a word or a sound or a spell—"

"Or it could be an invisible clue," Brenda cut in. She scanned the door facing her. Her heartbeat quickened. She hadn't had this kind of rush since she was back in Philly unlocking clues to Benjamin Banneker's inventions with Uncle Rufus. A sly smile spread across her face. "I think I may have something that'll help." She pulled her briefcase over her shoulder and set it down.

"Do Ain't inventions work in the Taint world?" Omen asked as he peered over Brenda's shoulder.

"Good question," Elliot said as he bit the arm of his glasses. "Guess we're about to find out."

Brenda pressed a silver button on the briefcase's side, causing it to double in size. Elliot's eyes grew wide as the case morphed into a four-foot pyramid of drawers, pockets, snaps, clasps, zippers, and moving gears. After its transformation, the case hummed like a well-oiled machine. Quickly, she lifted the clasp on a long, rectangular drawer. Lying on a velvet cushion was a pair of goggles with tinted lavender lenses. She lifted the goggles from the cushion and tapped a button on the frame. With a soft whoosh, a dozen lenses of various sizes appeared. With another tap, the lenses retracted. She pulled the goggles over her head and walked toward one of the doors.

"Are those—" Clair covered her mouth with surprise.

Brenda beamed. "Yup. I made a few enhancements, but these are the glasses you saw in the vision."

Elliot and Omen exchanged confused looks. "What vision?" Omen frowned.

"Oh yeah, we forgot to tell you—" Brenda waved her hand.

"We met before," Clair cut in.

All eyes followed Brenda as she moved through the room. Every now and again, she'd push a button and the lenses would twist, spin, or retract in circles before rearranging their order. Elliot attached himself to her side, his eyes glued to her every move.

"Gimme some space," she spat, glaring at Elliot.

"Sorry," he mumbled and backed away with his hands up.

After a few minutes, she pulled the goggles from over her eyes. "The symbols are riddles."

"All of them?" Omen asked as he looked at the doors on the ceiling.

"All of them."

"Okay." Omen stretched his hands above his head. "Where do we start?"

Clair stroked her chin. "At the top." She pointed at a door directly above them.

"How do we get to it? I'm over 6 feet and can't reach." Omen stood on his tiptoes.

"I have a feeling we won't have to worry about that." Brenda pulled the goggles back over her eyes. Again, she pressed a button. A green lens repositioned itself in front of one of her eyes. "What falls and does not make noise?"

Elliot knit his brows together in thought. Omen scratched his temple.

"Night?" Clair answered with a snap of her fingers.

CRACK! The ceiling door swung open on its hinge and a staircase materialized before them like a shimmering mirage.

Brenda and Clair exchanged a wink while Omen circled the staircase. Elliot pulled on the railing to measure its sturdiness.

"I didn't think it would be that easy." Elliot folded his arms across his chest.

"Neither did I," Omen said as he applied his weight to the bottom stair.

One by one, they climbed. Brenda hit a switch on the side of her briefcase and it shrunk back to its original size. She slung the case over her shoulder and followed. Once at the top of the stairs, she surveyed the room. Her shoulders slumped. Once again, they were inside a doomed room filled with doors. It was as if they'd never left.

ELEVEN

TAINT HISTORY: 101

Elliot threw his head back and groaned. "I knew it."

"Shift Sorcery begins at the end," Clair whispered.

Brenda turned to face her. "What?"

Clair bit her lip. "It's an old story, not sure it'll help us but—"

Elliot rubbed his temples in frustration. "Talk it out Clair. Outside of those goggles," he pointed at Brenda, "we don't exactly have a bunch of leads."

The others nodded in agreement.

Clair sat cross-legged in the middle of the floor. After a deep exhale, she spoke. "Taints were almost always free. They started their own towns and businesses." She smoothed her skirt. "But of all the Taints, Shifters have always struggled, even in our world."

Elliot and Omen stopped their pacing to listen. Brenda took a seat next to her.

"Shifters live mostly underground. Always have. The poor, the homeless—" Clair rubbed her temples.

"Most of 'em are Shifters. If you saw them twenty years ago, they were in Freak Shows or circus acts. I don't really know how it all started. The story changes depending on who you talk to, but one day a Shifter and a Thief got into it pretty bad. Back then, Shifters would steal people's faces and even their lives. Some still do."

"So, what's the difference between a Shifter and a Time Thief?" Omen folded his arms across his chest. "Sounds like they both steal."

"True, but it's different," she said slowly. "Time Thieves have strict laws. They only steal what's owed to them. They take things: resources, knowledge, power. They're cast out if they break the laws. The Shifters were stealing faces whenever they wanted."

"I'd steal too if I was poor and homeless," Brenda muttered under her breath.

"And if I'm really honest, folks didn't like Shifters because," she counted on her fingers, "they weren't proper enough, they weren't classy enough and they made too much trouble."

"Sounds like my Aunt Squeak." Brenda shook her head.

"Hush! Let her finish," Elliot hissed.

Brenda rolled her eyes and turned her attention back to Clair.

"Well, before we knew it, a civil war broke out. The Thieves and Artists joined forces against the Shifters."

Omen folded his arms across his chest. "Two against one? That ain't no fair fight."

Clair added a dark chuckle. "Shifters outnumber all other Taints two to one. Trust me, it was fair alright. Things got really bad when Artists started denying Shifters their Marks. Lots of folks died."

"Marks?" Brenda leaned forward on her elbows.

Clair turned so that the base of her neck was visible beneath her hair.

Omen squinted at the three green bars tattooed below her hairline. "All Taints have them?"

Clair let her braids fall back over her shoulders. "Yes, Taints without Marks are outcasts. That's why it led to war when the Artists stopped Marking the Shifters. Artists are the only Order capable of Marking us all. The decision was major."

"Are all the Marks different?" Brenda piped up.

"Yup. Sages are Marked by the three stripes." She gestured to the Mark at the top of her spine. "Time Thieves have infinity symbols wrapped around their wrists. The Artist Mark is an octagon on the palm of the hand. And Shifters have a diamond on their lower back."

"My brother and my best friend told me that a few weeks ago. Now, what were you saying about the war?" Elliot knelt down so he was at eye level with Clair.

"Oh yeah . . . sorry I got sidetracked." She shifted her weight and the ruffles from her skirt cascaded down her shapely legs. "Sages stayed neutral as always. We don't have a choice. It's a part of our laws to be intermediaries. We don't fight unless our lives are in danger."

"Why couldn't the Sages conjure a spell to stop the war?" Elliot shrugged.

Clair took a deep breath. "Doesn't work that way. We have free will like everyone else and there isn't a spell for everything. Some things are out of our control."

"Control . . . like control your impulse to ask questions and let her finish," Brenda snapped.

Elliot glared in her direction but said nothing.

"The Shifters gained some ground when Dana Spade, one of their generals, captured a Thief city in South Carolina in 1890. Dana and her resistance movement held the city for over a year and won. It wasn't until then that Shifters were recognized as full members of Taint society."

"Hold on, capturing cities, generals, movements?" Elliot shook his head in disbelief. "All this was happening under the government's nose?"

"Yes and no." She tilted her head to one side. "This was right after Reconstruction, so the government made it look like Colored folks were out of control. The Taint Wars were also used to justify the Klan."

"But, how did—" Elliot began.

"Hush!" Brenda cut her eyes in Elliot's direction. "Let her finish."

Elliot frowned, but fell silent.

"On June 16, 1890, discrimination against Shifters was declared illegal and their lives were finally made legitimate. Shifters consider themselves reborn on that day. It's a day of celebration for all Taints, but especially for them. It's the day they were recognized as human. We need to find the symbol that begins at the end. That's the riddle we need to solve."

"So, there's bigots in the Taint world too, huh?" Elliot shook his head. "Disappointing."

"We're not above mistakes or bad decisions. And I wish I could say the war stopped the resentment, but I can't. There are still Thieves and Artists who think they're better than Shifters. It's tough."

"I have a question." Omen stuffed his hands in his pockets. "Taints were free right?"

"Yeah, unless they were Shifters," Clair said as she studied the doors. "Time Thieves, Sages, and Artists were almost never slaves."

Omen's thick eyebrows knitted together. "The letter you read on the airship said Dr. Djinn's grandmother was a slave, yet the rumors we've all heard and the picture show says she's a Time Thief. Does that sound right to y'all?"

"Sounds suspicious." Brenda stopped to think before she rose from her seat on the floor. She pushed another button on her goggles.

"Definitely sounds fishy." Elliot stood and shifted his weight from one foot to the other.

Clair shrugged. "It was rare for Artists, Thieves, and Sages to be slaves, but maybe she comes from one of those families."

"Could you use Sage magic to find out?" Omen asked.

"Can we get outta here first?" Brenda shot Omen a look. "One puzzle at a time."

Omen ran his fingers through his hair. "Ok. You're right."

"Do Shifters use their own number or alphabet system?" Brenda called over her shoulder. By now, she was moving from door to door, inspecting each symbol.

Clair stopped to think. "Yes. They have their own language, too. It's a mixture of different magical languages."

"Like the Gullah language or Patois in Jamaica?" Elliot asked.

"Yeah, that's a good comparison."

Brenda put her hands on her hips. "Would you recognize it if you saw it? Could you read it?"

"Yup. I don't have access to the source of their magic, but I speak the language." A small smile spread across her lips. "My last boyfriend was a Shifter. I speak it pretty well."

Omen shifted his weight uncomfortably.

"Well then, you take the lead." Brenda pulled the goggles off and handed them to Clair.

After fiddling with the lenses and finding the right focus, Clair studied the doors. The others watched as she stomped her foot with either disappointment or glee. After a few minutes of silence, she returned to the group.

"Each symbol has a number. I say we try the year of Shifter inclusion, 1890. That would be four different doors, four clues."

Brenda threw her hands up. "Sounds great. Where's door number one?"

Clair pointed to a green door and waved a palm over the symbol. It shifted before their eyes in an intricate dance of glitter and gold before dissolving into a puddle of smaller symbols. Quickly, the symbols rearranged themselves and formed the number one.

Clair tapped the goggles and two additional lenses sprouted from its sides. "My dwelling has neither windows nor doors. What am I?"

The scholars mulled over the riddle for a moment or two. Finally, Elliot spoke up. "An egg. It's an egg."

The others smiled as the door creaked open. Brenda rushed to her briefcase. With a push of a button, it shrunk down to size. She secured it to her middle and darted inside. Omen followed with Clair and Elliot bringing up the rear. The door closed behind them with a snap.

Clair peered through the eerie mist. Giant trees towered above them. Tall, thick trunks spiraled high into a darkened sky. A swollen river rushed a few feet beyond the door and a flash of lightning lit up the dome.

"Must be one hundred percent humidity in here." Elliot tugged at his collar.

"There's more doors." Omen thrust an index finger at a row of doors a few feet away. Not unlike the doors they'd already inspected, these also had shifting, golden symbols. The only difference was there were fewer doors and they were covered with twisting vines.

Quickly they hurried along the riverbank. The sounds of rushing water and screeching birds echoed around them. They huddled close to the wall. Clair pushed a button on her goggles. With a click, a bright green lens repositioned itself in front of the others.

"We're looking for the number eight!" Brenda yelled.

Lightning lit up the dome. They linked arms to form a semicircle around Clair as she inspected each door.

Again, Clair ran her palm across a red door in the shape of an oval. The symbols shifted in a golden dance before forming the number eight. Thunder shook the room.

Elliot leaned into the circle. "I have a feeling we're inside that sphere."

Omen turned to meet his eyes. "The Grand Menagerie?"

Elliot pointed upward.

Another flash of lightning revealed the curved outline. "I think you're right." Omen reached under his shirt and rubbed the alligator tooth dangling from a chain around his neck.

"I am neither outside nor inside, but I'm in every house!" Clair shouted over the raging river.

Lightning flashed. Elliot squinted through his glasses. "What's that in the water?"

Feet from where they stood, a wave zipped through the river. Then came a tail: long, lizard-like, and enormous. A head with a diamond in its center attached to a thick body moved into view. From what Brenda could gather, the thing was a dragon covered in mirrored scales reflecting everything around them. She covered her eyes as a flash of lightning refracted from the creature's skin into a blinding, brilliant light. It extended its long neck, threw its head back, and roared. They covered their ears. Out of the corner of her eye, she spotted something heading toward them from above. "Duck!"

A bird the size of an adult human swooped close to where they stood. Its feathers crackled with electricity from talon to beak.

"Neither outside nor inside, but in every house! Think!" Clair repeated.

The ground shook as the bird landed on a tree limb above the dragon's head. Brenda kept one eye on the bird perched in the tree and the other on the mirror-scaled dragon as it lumbered toward them. Roughly the size and girth of an elephant, the dragon slithered through the water like a snake as the bird's wings and talons sizzled and popped white-hot electricity from up high.

"Doors! A door!" Elliot yelled.

The door flew open, nearly knocking them all to the ground. The bird and dragon took notice and gave chase. One by one the scholars barreled inside. Omen kicked it closed with less than a second to spare as the winged creature snapped at his foot, electric sparks shooting from its beak.

"Oh God! What kind of place is this?" Elliot held on to his side and sucked in short breaths.

"I don't know, but I was almost eaten by a giant electric bird." Omen laid flat on his back, his forearm still covering his eyes.

Brenda and Clair lay entangled in a corner. "The minute I see Dr. Djinn, we're gonna have a talk about these creatures," Brenda said through pants as she sat upright.

"All magic ain't good magic." She dusted off her skirt and stood. Another dome shaped room full of doors. This time, most of the space was white. The room appeared to go on forever. Clair spun around as the others gathered themselves. Her line of vision homed in on a sloping wall covered in a kaleidoscopic pattern. A steady hum filled the room.

"Are we near the cave?" Elliot covered his ears.

"I think so." Omen pointed toward rays of iridescent light skirting the wall in the distance. "Looks like we're on the other side of—" he squinted as if trying to remember. "What did Baba Ali call it?"

"The Shelf of the Damned," Clair spoke up. "Whatever you do, stay far away. That's not the kind of magic any of us can handle, not even me." She pivoted back to the doors. They looked like distorted rectangles with golden hooks. She took a step closer, located the number nine and began reading. "Who has a house too small for guests?"

Brenda yanked on one of the hooks. A low rumble echoed throughout the room. They froze. Clair bent her knees to steady herself. Her eyes flew around the room. "Grab one of these hooks," she shouted. No sooner had she spoken did the room begin to turn, slowly at first, then picking up speed. Brenda held on tight as they were whipped around like ragdolls.

Clair swallowed a scream as her insides pulled against gravity. The humming soon became a sawing blare. "Who has a house too small for guests? Think!"

"A turtle!" Omen blurted out. And as suddenly as it started, the room came to a screeching halt. They landed on the floor in a disheveled heap. Glasses askew, Elliot vomited on the ground beside him. Brenda did the same.

"I don't know if I can survive this place," Omen croaked and doubled over.

Clair limped around in a dizzying circle before falling to her knees. Instead of creaking open, the door quivered like an oasis in the middle of unfathomable heat and dissolved.

Omen rushed to Clair's side. Brenda wrinkled her nose at the sight of vomit near Elliot's shoe, but extended her hand anyway. He hoisted himself up from the floor and looked away in embarrassment. Omen poked his head through the door and took a peek before signaling them to follow. One by one, they ducked under the threshold and into a dark room illuminated by pinpricks of light. Brenda put her hand on one of the walls. It was soft to the touch, like a down pillow covered in velvet. Directly across from them was another door outlined by soft white light.

"At least there's only one door." Brenda smirked.

"Thank God," Clair huffed. "This should be the last one."

"Right. I'm waiting on the trick. You know she's got something up her sleeve," Elliot replied as he took a few cautious steps forward.

On cue, a buzzing sound echoed through the room. The scholars froze. After the sound stopped, Brenda turned around in a circle. "Hey Clair, you think you can get to that door quickly and read the next clue?"

"Let's get outta here." She pulled the goggles over her eyes and rushed toward the door.

Elliot shook his head. "I don't like this." He glanced at the ceiling stained with brilliant stars. "I think the room is getting smaller."

Omen raised his hands above his head. His fingertips grazed the ceiling. "Talk to us Clair. We're about to be squished."

Clair ran a palm across the symbols. For the last time, the golden dust settled into the number zero. "What is it that cannot be counted?"

The room compressed around them like a shrinking closet. They crept next to Clair as she shouted the clue out loud again. "What is it that cannot be counted?" Her heart slammed against her chest. "Stars. Stars cannot be counted. Stars!"

The last door dissolved before them like a shimmering mirage and the room expanded as if it were made of rubber. Clair and the others looked around suspiciously before standing up straight. In front of them, a shadow of a man appeared. An ornate monocle of golden gears and lenses covered one of his eyes. He held up a cane with a silver topper in the likeness of a sphinx.

"Everyting criss?"[3]

---

[3] In Jamaican Patois, this question is asked to check on a person to see how they are doing.

TWELVE

THE SECOND LIBRARY OF TIMBUKTU

"So, you're saying it's too dangerous?" Professor Blue walked briskly down yet another dark hallway. Everyone except Omen struggled to keep pace with his long strides. "Dr. Djinn was convinced the labyrinth would be a perfect attraction." He shook his head. "Are you sure?"

"Yes. Quite," Elliot quipped as he smoothed his slacks. He glanced at the tiny vomit stain on the bottom of one of his cuffs and grit his teeth. The seething embarrassment rising in his chest threatened to materialize into a coughing fit. He did his best to beat the emotions back.

"Diamond and Shock don't normally behave that way. I'll have to speak with Dr. Djinn about their diets. Can't have our guests scared to death." Blue turned to meet their eyes. "What were your thoughts about the airship?"

"Gorgeous. And breakfast was great." Brenda offered.

The Professor raised an eyebrow. "But . . .?"

"You have a Grootslang on the premises and an Impundulu and a dragon that almost ate us alive. We could have died!" Clair blurted out in a huff.

The Professor stopped in his tracks, causing the scholars to nearly topple over like a row of dominoes. "Sadly, I voiced those same concerns to Dr. Djinn before your visit." He fiddled with the monocle over his eye. "Well, we can't get rid of Jade. The Grootslang will be one of the park's biggest draws." He picked up his pace as they entered a long, never-ending corridor. "And Diamond will be confined to a secure area. She's a Ninki Nanka. They're found in The Gambia." He popped his collar. "Located her myself. In fact, I've uncovered all of our creatures here in the park. It's a hobby I've taken up. Whenever I go out ghoul gathering, I try and find a little something to take home, a souvenir of sorts."

"Sounds like a dangerous hobby," Brenda muttered.

"But Shock is another matter entirely. I'll see that he's returned to South Africa where he belongs. Lightning Birds are unpredictable." The Professor drummed his fingertips on an exquisite railing attached to the corridor wall. "It was worth a try."

Elliot raised an index finger in the air. "Two questions. What's ghoul gathering? And where is Dr. Djinn? I thought we'd see her by now."

"Ah, the ancient art of ghoul gathering." He swung his cane beneath his arm and formed a tent with his fingers. "It's the removal of a soul from a cadaver."

"Great. More souls," Brenda grumbled.

"And Dr. Djinn?" Elliot held the Professor's gaze. "Where is she?"

"She's away—urgent business. She'll make her grand entrance. I guarantee you that." He cleared his throat. "It's settled then. The Impundulu will be transported back to South Africa. Its place is in the wild. Thank you for your feedback. After all, that's what you're here for."

No one replied. Professor Blue waved a hand. "Quick, quick. So much to see."

For the next five minutes or so, they walked through regal hallways decorated with potted plants and antique pictures. It looked like one of the Smithsonian's museums back in DC. Everything around them was rare and expensive. Much of the excursion was completed in silence except for their footfalls on carpet, concrete, and marble. Finally, they came to a halt in front of a door in the shape of a triangle. A heavy, silver knocker in the shape of a lion materialized before them. The Professor muttered something Elliot didn't understand and the knocker shifted into a sphinx identical to the one perched on top of his cane. The door swung open on its hinge.

They ducked inside a dark room illuminated by constellations. Directly ahead, another door frame bled white light around its edges.

"We just left this room." Brenda slapped her forehead with her palm.

Professor Blue rubbed his palms together. "Are you sure?"

Brenda shifted her briefcase to the opposite shoulder. "Yup."

The stars and constellations flickered as the room went black. Professor Blue clapped his hands together and light flooded the space. Elliot blinked in surprise. His heart nearly leapt out of his chest.

Shelves upon shelves of books spiraled high into a dome of concentric circles. There were so many floors, Elliot couldn't begin to count them all. Jade bannisters trimmed in gold flanked the stairs. Maps, chalkboards, paintings, and shadowboxes filled with rare objects covered the walls. He marveled at all of it, from the wide, majestic windows bathing them in natural light to the freshly polished cherry wood floors gleaming beneath his feet.

"I could stay here forever." Brenda's eyes darted around the room. "I could live here."

"Same." Elliot grinned. "I've never seen so many books in one place in my life, ever."

The Professor waved them ahead. "Sections are marked by the signs at the top of each staircase. Twenty-six floors. One floor for each letter of the alphabet. The elevator's in the corner." He turned to Elliot. "If my memory serves me correctly, you're a chemistry whiz. There's a chemistry collection up on floor three."

Elliot could hardly contain himself. He whisked down the main hall toward the staircase and took the stairs two at a time. When he arrived on the third floor, the first book to catch his eye had a spine of glass. *Chemical Magic: A History of Science and Sorcery.* A pair of plastic gloves covered in green feathers were attached to the book's front cover.

Sharp! Wear these while reading.

Elliot removed the book from its shelf, sat it carefully on a nearby table, and pulled on the odd-looking gloves. After reading the introduction, an animated story of the periodic table of elements began. The pages, each a smooth sheet of glass, clanked softly as he turned.

"Fascinating."

He jumped.

Brenda held her hands up. "Sorry. Didn't realize your nerves were so bad," she called over his shoulder, peering at the book. She chuckled and waved a hand. "It's ok. Books do that to me, too. My uncle owned an antique shop with a library in the basement back in Philly. It was my favorite place."

Elliot stuck his head back in the book, careful to disguise his stare. This was probably the nicest thing the girl had said to him since they'd arrived.

He watched as she pulled a new pair of goggles over her eyes and flicked a switch. An orange lens popped out in front of the others with a subtle click. Clearly, the girl was some kind of genius—and pretty in a way he hadn't considered. But he didn't like her. She was haughty, arrogant, and always armed with a slick comeback. She reminded him of someone. He removed his glasses, bit the arm, and rifled through the cast of characters he knew back home. *Art!* That was it! Brenda was the female version of his brother. He balled up his fists and shook his head. But she was also undeniably brilliant. The feelings were difficult to sort out.

"What kinds of settings do you have on those?" He pointed to her goggles.

She stood on her tiptoes, ran a palm over a row of thick purple volumes, and muttered to herself.

"What kinds of—"

"I heard you," she shot over her shoulder before adjusting another lens on the goggles.

Elliot sunk deeper in the ruby red cushions of his chair and turned his attention back to the book.

With a grunt, she pulled a volume from the shelf and placed it on his table. "They're not as advanced as the ones I gave to Clair, but they're close. Hers have twenty-four customizable lenses. These only have twelve." She pulled the goggles over her head and tossed them in his lap.

After fumbling the catch, he pushed the glass tome aside to take a closer look.

"Makes math and science equations easier to solve. I mostly use them to cut the time it takes to build an invention. They can also translate dozens of different languages. Very efficient." She pulled up a chair.

Elliot turned the goggles over in his hands. Multiple lenses extended from each end. Cogs snapped and spun, forcing the front lens to retract and the one behind it to move in its place.

"Impressive."

Brenda shrugged. "I was excited about the tour, but it's the scholarship that means the most to me. It's what my Uncle Rufus would have wanted."

"Yeah. The scholarship is all that matters to me too and now here we are." He looked up, their eyes locking. "Running from magical creatures, interpreting symbols, escaping shrinking rooms . . ."

Brenda's lips upturned into a smile. "I didn't expect that either."

"I heard you made a siphoning invention for your competition. Mind telling me about it?"

"Who told you that?"

Elliot folded his arms over his chest. "I asked around."

Brenda smirked and turned a page. "Yeah, it siphons, but it also acts as a container that holds harmful substances. Wait, I can show you better than I can tell you." She retrieved the invention from her briefcase and turned to Elliot. "Watch and learn." After a quick demonstration, she laid the fire needle on its velvet cushion and pushed the drawer closed.

"Benjamin Banneker is your great great great uncle?" He pushed his glasses up the bridge of his nose.

"Yup."

"What's that like? He's one of the greatest Colored men to ever live. He's an inspiration."

Brenda bit her lip. "Of course, the whole family is proud."

Elliot turned his attention to a book lying next to her briefcase. "Mind if I look at that?"

"Sure."

Elliot inspected the script on its spine. "I saw this in the bookstore outside the theater. *Fangs, Feathers, and Folklore: Africa's Amazing Beasts,*" he read.

When she turned the page, a miniature dragon leapt in the air and thrashed its long, mirrored tail back and forth. The pages shook. After roaming around in circles for a few seconds, the dragon settled down, looked up, and snarled in their direction. Brenda pulled the goggles over her eyes.

The Ninki Nanka

The Ninki Nanka, or West African Dragon, is native to The Gambia River. Often described as dragon-like with reflective scales covering its massive body, the Ninki Nanka can grow to nearly thirty feet long. West African Dragons are extremely dangerous, often attacking unsuspecting prey from underwater at night.

Elliot shifted in his chair. "So that's the thing that almost bit us in two, huh?"

"Yup. I won't ever forget it as long as I live." She peered at the miniature dragon and shivered.

"Wait a second. Are these in alphabetical order?" Elliot flipped through a few of the pages.

"Looks like it."

He pointed to the guidewords in the upper right-hand corner. "Turn to the Js."

She did as he asked. A mermaid with thick silver braids and dark skin climbed from the margins. Elliot hunched down low in his seat so he was eye level with the animated figure. Graciously, it took a seat on the edge of the book and dangled its silver fin over the edge.

The Jengu

Found in Cameroon, West Africa, the Jengu are characterized by their dark skin, gap-toothed smiles, wooly hair, and profound beauty. The Jengu are kind and empathetic creatures who often act as intermediaries between the human and spirit world. Known as natural healers, these creatures possess sacred oils and cures for illness and disease in their hair and scales. The Jengu accept offerings of fruit and beautiful objects in exchange for their protection.

They watched as the Jengu climbed from the edge of the book and dove into an adjacent page as if it were a body of water. Then, it melted back into its picture resting on a rock.

Elliot pointed at the creature. "I need some of those oils and I think your siphoning invention can help," he stammered, barely able to contain his excitement.

Brenda put a hand on her hip. "Say what?"

"I saw one. Right after we left the courtyard. We saw them from the airship," he sputtered. "Remember the telescopes?"

"Okay, but why do you need the Jengu?"

"Look, I have this—" he paused to lower his voice, "I have this tonic I'm working on. It's what got me here. I think it can change the world."

Brenda lowered her goggles, so they swung around her neck. Elliot babbled on for several minutes, discussing The Black Gaze and how he'd been forced to enter it into the competition after his brother's antics.

She whistled. "Your brother, interesting cat, huh? Why do you think he would do something like that?"

"What do you mean? Art never has a reason to do what he does. It's how he is." Elliot shifted in his chair.

"There's always a reason. Might have to do some digging to find it, but it's there."

"You don't understand." He studied his shoes.

"Maybe not. Or maybe I struck a nerve. But that's for you to figure out. My Aunt Squeak always says, hit dogs holler." She went back to searching the shelves while Elliot stewed in his seat.

The truth was, he and Art hadn't always been rivals. There was a time when he wanted to be like his older brother. And then, last summer happened. Elliot closed his eyes. Everyone grieves differently and their uncle's death tore the family apart. Some blamed his father for leaving that night. And a part of Elliot believed he blamed himself as well. The accusations led to infighting and everyone found themselves taking sides. Art hadn't really spoken to their father since it all happened. He'd become mean and distant. No one could get through to him, and Uncle Baron, the only person who could, was no longer alive.

Elliot looked up. "You remind me of my brother."

"Oh yeah."

"Your Uncle Rufus passed away, right?"

Brenda cut her eyes in his direction. "Yes."

"How did you handle it?"

"I—I don't want to talk about that right now."

"I understand." He caught a glimpse of something shiny in the window and froze. "Are those policemen?"

She turned to look through the window. Sure enough, two policemen, one short and stout, the other lean and lanky, were making their way through the bushes. The large one lumbered along, his many stomachs a hindrance as he ducked beneath the low boughs of a tree.

He frowned. "Those officers look like—"

"The policemen from the picture show!" she shrieked.

He looked at the exit sign. "Wanna check it out?"

THIRTEEN

BOYS IN BLUE

Brenda and Elliot crept through the bushes, careful to keep their distance behind the trespassers.

"Think this is about Dr. Djinn's land?" Elliot whispered.

Brenda dropped to her knees and crawled near a row of hibiscus flowers. "What else could it be?"

"They're headed toward the sculpture garden."

Side by side, they snuck over footpaths and through flowerbeds. Finally, they arrived at a massive tree. Brenda stopped in her tracks.

The Baobab. The pictures hadn't done it any justice. Uncle Rufus had mentioned it was the most wondrous of all trees. She'd seen it in pictures, but never like this. It didn't disappoint. Surrounded by a copper fence, it was clear Dr. Djinn had spared no detail. Tiny carvings decorated the trunk.

"Psst, let's go!" Elliot waved her to where he squatted behind a bench near a hedge.

"Over here," said a voice.

Brenda scurried toward the bench.

"Come on! There's no one around. Get a few pictures and let's get out of here! Then, we'll plan from there," a different voice replied.

Brenda hurried behind the thick hedge of cherry laurel. Bending low so as to not be seen, she met Elliot's wide, serious eyes. She pointed to the other side of the trunk. Heart racing and surrounded by waxy leaves, they peeked through the open spaces in the bushes.

"I'm telling you, this here land belongs to the Jefferson brothers by right," the heavy policeman responded. "All we gotta do is prove it. Gotta be something here to do that."

Brenda turned to Elliot. "You said it," she whispered.

"I don't know about this, Sheriff," his companion mumbled in a shaky voice. "Seems we're trespassing without a warrant and that ain't good."

"Trespassing? Whoever heard of anything stopping a sheriff from trespassing on a Colored's so-called land?" The sheriff thrust a fat finger at the shiny badge pinned to his chest. "We're the law."

"Yeah, but . . ."

Sheriff Dodge walked toward the Baobab tree and hiked his pants up from beneath his bulging stomachs. "Well, I'll be damned. What in tarnation is this?" He reached up and removed his hat to reveal a splotchy patch of pink surrounded by twigs of straw blonde hair. "This is 'bout the biggest tree I ever did see in my life." He turned back to his partner. "You reckon you ever seen such a thing?"

The other officer stopped. His eyes followed the massive trunk up into the air. He whistled. "Can't say that I have, Sheriff Dodge. Can't say that I have."

Dodge removed a kerchief from his shirt pocket and mopped his forehead. "Where d'ya think it's from? I sure ain't seen nothing like this in South Carolina."

"Don't know." The smaller officer stepped inside the open gate and edged closer. "Look, there's pictures and words." He held up one of his hands and guided a palm over the markings as if he were reading braille. "Whoa, it's—beautiful." He continued to walk the wide circumference of the tree, leading with his hands.

"Don't matter none, Officer Goode." The sheriff flailed his fleshy arms in all directions. "All of this is gonna be a pile of rubble before long." He hiked his pants up, took a step inside the copper gate, and spat. "I reckon we're done here for now, but I got news for Dr. Djinn. Won't be no grand opening if I got anything to say 'bout it."

FOURTEEN

THE ANCIENT BOOK OF EPOCHS, ERAS, AND EONS

Omen stood near the jade banister on the landing of the library's fifth floor. He looked up, mouth agape. A golden letter E had been engraved on the circular ceiling. "You wanna look around up here?"

"No. There's a book I need to find down here," Clair shouted as she poked her head around one of the marble pillars.

"Okay," he called back. "Anything you want me to grab while I'm up here?"

"Yeah, *The Ancient Book of Epochs, Eras, and Eons,* if you can find it. That's the book of the Time Thieves. We're gonna need them both."

"Gotcha."

The books were of all kinds, shapes, and sizes. Some were round with feathered pages. Others were blocks of stone or as thin as paper mâché. There were books in English, French, Hausa, Igbo, Patois, Swahili, Aramaic and magical languages she'd seen, but couldn't understand. Some of them were written in a delicate script, others with a clumsy hand or neatly typed. Most contained spells and sorcery far beyond her knowledge. Clair had taken a more practical approach to touring the library: twenty minutes per floor. This way she could pace herself and avoid becoming overwhelmed by the world class collection. Judging from what she'd seen so far, the library had a right to be named after the structure in ancient Timbuktu. She thumbed through a book with a spine of cracked, brown leather. The majority of the volumes in their midst had either been stolen from centuries ago or from the far future and technically hadn't been written yet. Now, she was nearly two hours into her own self-guided tour. To her delight, Omen had been her shadow the entire time.

"See, I'm good for something." He flashed a dazzling smile and pointed to *The Ancient Book of Epochs, Eras, and Eons* on a nearby table.

"Thanks," she said. "Now, can you grab that one over there?"

"This one?" He stretched one of his long arms in the direction of a shelf filled with books that buzzed as if they'd been plugged into electrical sockets. He stood on his tiptoes to reach it. The book was easily the width of three large books bound into one. He dragged it from its place on the shelf with both hands and held it high above his head before bringing it down to his chest.

"Here, I got it." She held out her arms.

His biceps bulged as he demonstrated a few curls. "This thing is at least a hundred pounds. Let's find a table," he grunted.

"We can find a table later. Hand it over." She motioned toward the book. When he again refused, she visualized the book in her head, just as large, but easier to lift and carry.

Instantly, it sagged in his arms, as light as a feather. "Lemme guess, Sage magic?"

"We're not as cool as the Time Thieves, but we hold our own." She winked. *Art's Great Equation.* The book was a think of legend. There weren't many books in the Taint world that were more important and the Artists have always been the most mysterious order of them all. A dozen and a half more floors and she'd have the opportunity to examine the sacred book of her own order, *The Book of the Blind Limbs.* But for now, the Artists.

Omen took a seat near the edge of the table as Clair went to work. First, she took the logical route and tugged at its front cover. Nothing. Then came the muttering and inaudible chants. Still, the book did not respond.

"Okay, here goes nothing." She took a deep breath, blew a stray hair out of her face, and pulled the goggles over her eyes. "Let's see your secrets," she whispered. Just as she'd done while in the labyrinth of doors, she combined Brenda's invention with her own sage spells. Twenty minutes later, she still hadn't cracked the Artwork, the sorcery of the Artists. It sat on the table, as blue and stubborn as it had when Omen pulled it from its shelf.

"Why don't you take a break?" Omen suggested as he twirled his chain between his fingers.

"Maybe, I should." She sighed. "I'm not used to this."

"Used to what? A challenge?" He formed a steeple with his fingers.

"Yeah and no. That was a challenge back there with all of those doors, we could have died," she shook her head. "But I'm talking about magic right now. Sage spells shoot from the hip. Artwork is different. I feel like I've been tryin' to learn a whole new language in twenty minutes."

"Give it a minute, rest your brain or whatever you need to rest to do magic." He smiled and fiddled with his chain.

"Why are you always rubbing that? What is it?"

"Legacy."

There was that smirk again. Half mystery, half unapologetic ambition. She'd never let on how much she enjoyed his brand of charm, but she was certainly a fan. "Oh yeah?"

"I come from Strongmen. Some of the strongest in the South. My grandfather wrestled a gator and won." He held the chain up high. The chunks of turquoise off-setting the tooth gleamed against the sunlight. "This tooth came from that gator. Been passed down from my granddad to my pops to me. I earned it when I won Dr. Djinn's strength competition in Florida a few weeks back."

"That's impressive." Clair leaned in to look at the chain up close. She appreciated a hint of arrogance. It was what had initially attracted her to Lonnie. But Omen's arrogance was different. It came from another place. Where Lonnie was all hot air and sorcery, Omen was grit, like he knew the importance of hard work, but still had more to prove. And that's what kept him humble. It also didn't hurt that he was easy on the eyes with his high cheekbones and skin like a copper sun.

"Thanks."

"What will you study at Hampton?"

Omen twirled the tooth between his thumb and index fingers. "Blacksmithing or agriculture. Haven't decided yet. Gonna run it past my pops before I make the final decision. You?"

"Business. Been selling things for years."

"So, what's the story behind that? How'd it happen?" He focused on the black patch covering her eye.

She motioned for him to come closer. "A curse from my father."

He reached for her hand. "I'm sorry."

"The old folks say the curse can jump to young men with ill intentions." Her voice crumbled into whoops of laughter.

His eyebrows knit together in confusion. "What do you—"

She slapped her knee before lifting the patch over her eye. "Relax. It's a trick. It's all a part of the show!"

"What do you mean?"

"Look, I'm a Sage, but I'm also a businesswoman. And this patch," she said as she flipped the patch up to show a perfectly symmetrical and healthy, brown eye, "is good for business. I'm a seventeen-year-old orphan who sells tonics in Charleston. I gotta make ends meet."

Omen sat back in his chair, listening.

"This patch is part of my legend. It's my legacy." She gestured toward his chain. "Folks been comin' from all over to see 'bout the half-blind colored girl who can read bones in bowls and bring good fortune to folks who been down on their luck." She shrugged. "And it works."

Omen wagged his finger in her direction. "Smart, beautiful, and funny." They locked eyes as he moved closer, their lips centimeters away.

Clair's stomach did a backflip. Quickly, she turned back to the book. "Remember when I said Time Thieves need Era Ports?"

"Yeah," he said, collecting himself.

"I think there's one either here at the park or close by. I'm sure it's hidden though." She chewed on her bottom lip. "That's where this comes in."

"So, this book will tell us if there's an Era Port here?" Omen peered at its binding. It looked like a fish's scales, rough and worn from age.

"That's my theory."

"You said you were a little familiar with the Shifters. What about the Artists?"

Clair shook her head. "They're secretive. The smallest order of all Taints. I've never actually met one in my life."

"Feel like trying again?"

"Might as well."

For what seemed like an eternity, they huddled in silence. Clair fixated on the embossed lettering, visualizing open pages in her mind. Finally, the title flickered, then glowed.

"You got it!"

The book vibrated then burst open as if it were alive. Clair emerged from her trance and stared at an open map covered in zigzags and dots.

"What's this?"

She drummed her fingers on the tabletop. "It's a map of all the interdimensional doors in the world. My theory was right."

The sound of footsteps echoed through the room. Clair and Omen looked up as Elliot and Brenda skidded to a stop, out of breath. Omen and Clair exchanged a look.

"Where were you two?" Clair asked.

Elliot closed his eyes, hands on his knees. "Cops," he managed between pants.

Brenda nodded vigorously. "From the picture show," she cut in.

Omen steered Elliot and Brenda toward two chairs. "Say what now?"

Brenda sucked in air. "We saw two cops wandering around in the sculpture garden." She pointed to a window. "Turns out it was the cops we saw in the theater."

Elliot caught his breath. "They're trying to take Dr. Djinn's land. They're trying to sabotage the park before it opens," he sputtered. "It was just like the picture show."

"Was anyone around?" Clair leaned on the edge of a table.

"No. We followed them for a little while, but there was no one around." Brenda added. "No one but us."

"This ain't a coincidence," Clair added.

"How do we help?" Omen looked between Brenda and Elliot with serious eyes.

"Redneck cops are always poking at Colored folks." Clair sucked her teeth. "Gotta make sure we stay in our place."

"If only you or Elliot could whip up a cure for rednecks," Omen muttered.

"What's that?" Brenda wandered over to the map. "Coordinates?"

"Yep, coordinates from *Art's Great Equation*."

Brenda flung open her briefcase and grabbed her goggles. She pointed at one of the lights. Clair followed her fingertip. "This is where we're standing right now."

"Would you be able to pinpoint exactly where that dot is in the park?" Clair chewed on her bottom lip.

"More or less. I'd need a map of the park to figure out our exact whereabouts."

Clair clapped her hands together and pointed at the wall directly behind them. "How about that one?"

Brenda spun around. "Any closer and it would have bitten me." She strode toward the wall and pointed at a spot smack dab in the middle of a mountain. The words *Mt. Kilimanjaro Roller Coaster* were etched between two peaks. "There."

Clair stroked her chin. "Makes sense."

Omen and Elliot looked at each other, then at Clair. "What makes sense?" Omen asked.

"If there's no Artist to create a door, you need a Bump. I'm guessing Dr. Djinn doesn't have any Artists here, so she had the park built over a Bump. It's a natural doorway inside the Time Continuum." Clair paced in a small circle. "That's where the Era Port is—beyond the Bump." She smiled again. "And the coaster is how you get there."

"So, we'd get to the Era Port by riding the coaster? Seems easy enough." Elliot bit the arm of his glasses.

"Can't be that simple." Brenda squinted at the map. "The park is for both Taints and Aints. I can't imagine Dr. Djinn would want Aints discovering an Era Port."

Clair studied the map closely. "Time Thieves have Sirius Marks that give them access to time travel. Everyone else would need an Era Dial."

"What are they?" Omen leaned against a wall.

"The dials are made of Grootstones and leather. Without an Era Dial, it would be a regular roller coaster ride." She traced a finger on the map between the two mountain peaks. "The Era Port wouldn't appear."

"But if you had an Era Dial, that would mean—" Omen began slowly.

"Access to the Era Port beyond the bump and boom! Time Travel," Clair interrupted. "But I need more information. I'm not a Time Thief." She rushed back to the table and rifled through the pages of another book.

"What's the name of that book?" Elliot pointed.

"It's the most important collection among the Sacred Order of Time Thieves. It's the *Book of Eras, Epochs, and Eons.*" She turned to the table of contents.

Brenda leaned over one of the book's thin pages. "Try page 1,015." She pointed to a subtitle. *Interdimensional Doors, Portals, and Dials.*

Clair rifled through the pages and read. "It is the duty of the Time Thief to enact vengeance, retribution, and justice," she read in a hushed voice. "Go, take what is owed to us, whether it is in the ancient past, present, or far future. Whether it is money, resources, or ideas previously stolen by imperialists, colonizers, masters, overseers, kings, or queens."

"Vengeance? Retribution? For what?" Omen looked on in confusion.

"For what we've lost. For what's been taken from us," Brenda answered darkly.

Elliot leaned forward in his chair. "What hasn't been taken from us?"

"Not much." Clair pushed a braid away from her eye.

Vengeance." He removed his glasses again. "We all deserve it." Elliot spoke in a soft, serious tone. "I know my family deserves it."

"Mine too," Clair whispered.

Elliot leaned forward and cleared his throat. "Last summer, I went to South Carolina to study plants with my pop, uncle, and brother." His voice dropped. "My Uncle Baron had recently come back home from the war and he took a liking to photography. Pops thought it would be good for him to take the trip with us and practice. Pop was studying Gelsemium sempervirens."

"That's yellow jessamine," Clair cut in.

Elliot continued. "After we got to the low country, we set out early looking at plants, flowers, and trees. The smell of the swamp is something I'll never forget." He looked up at the others. "Smells like fresh air and sunlight." He laced his fingers behind his head. "We came up on an embankment covered with yellow jessamine. You shoulda seen it. A riverbank covered in sheets of gold. Of course, Pop wanted to take some samples of the petals and the root. It's poisonous, so it had to be handled carefully. Then, Uncle Baron wanted to take pictures."

Clair sat and crossed her legs, her face settling into a soft smile.

"Foamflowers, Fire Pinks, Passionflowers, Coral Honeysuckles—" His eyes glazed over as the tears threatened to fall and he wiped them with the back of his sleeve. "So, Uncle Baron set up the brand-new camera he bought and he went crazy taking all kinds of pictures. He really wanted pictures of the Lyreleaf Sage before sunset. He swore he could win a photography prize."

Clair covered her eyes, sensing what was to come. These kinds of stories rarely ended well for Colored folks. Happiness was something they were always chasing, regardless of where they were from.

Elliot took a deep breath. "By the time we got back to DC, we were told that Colored folks needed to lay low. A White Woman had accused two Colored men of trying to take her umbrella and harassing her. This riled up the White army and navy vets in the city and they had been attacking Colored folks randomly for more than 24 hours. They were shooting from terror cars, dragging us off the street, and beating us in mobs."

Brenda's shoulders slumped. "Uncle Rufus was up all-night last summer reading those headlines. I remember."

"We tried our best to get Uncle Baron to leave his place and come with us, but he said he was an Army man with a rifle and could hold his own. He wanted to help protect his neighbors. So, we dropped him off. The minute we got back to our house; my brother, my pop, and I were on patrol around the clock with our pistols making sure we protected our house. I don't remember ever being so scared in my life. The gunshots and shouts and the blood bath outside the window. That Sunday, we got the news that Uncle Baron had been shot from one of those terror cars. He was dead before they could get him to one of the Colored hospitals."

The joy had been squeezed from the room. Everyone hung their heads.

"Pop developed those pictures. Had them blown up. Now, they're on the walls of the house. Funny how a man can serve in a war thousands of miles away, win that war, come home, and be murdered like a dog in the street by the people he enlisted to protect," Elliot said, his eyes shining with tears.

Brenda looked up. It all made sense. She dabbed at her eyes as Clair stared at the floor. Omen fixated his gaze on a tree swaying in the window. "The Black Gaze. The Era Port. Vengeance," she said in a hush. "A redneck cure. That's it. That's how we can help."

Clair and Omen exchanged confused looks. "What's the Black Gaze?" Omen asked.

"It's a tonic that I developed. I think it can cure racism. It needs one final ingredient," Elliot added.

Brenda rushed toward the open book and cleared her throat before reading. "It is the duty of the Time Thief to right wrongs, one visit at a time. Each Thief is Marked as either a Ghoul Gatherer or Soul Keeper. The Sirius Mark, an infinity symbol found on the wrist, communicates this marriage between time and space."

Elliot's eyes narrowed. "The Shelf of the Damned."

Clair stroked her chin, deep in thought. "Time travel is propelled by the substance inside the Soul Jar stored on the Shelf of the Damned. The souls are from people who led wicked lives on earth: Slavers, murderers, colonizers. The souls are the fuel."

"Like gas in a car," Elliot murmured. He rubbed his hands together.

"Professor Blue— I demonstrated my siphoning invention on one of his Soul Jars!" Brenda gasped.

"The picture show," Omen cut in. "They were wrestling with one of those things. They trapped it in a Jar."

"Travel through time and space requires a propellant. A damned soul has the energy make-up to propel the traveler forward and through." Clair slapped herself on the forehead. "That's why they have a Grootslang here at the park!" She turned to the others. "The Grootslang guards Grootstones, the stones we need to make an Era Dial."

Elliot's eyes widened. "So that would mean--"

"We'd have to make one from scratch which would require that we enter the Grand Menagerie and get some of those stones," Clair interrupted.

"And have a talk with a Jengu about the Black Gaze," Elliot cut in. "If I can be sure my formula works, we can use time travel to stop the sheriff."

She reached for her eyepatch. "I think I need both eyes open for the rest of this adventure."

"But—" Elliot took a look at Clair's eye without the patch for the first time and sighed.

"Don't feel bad," Omen said as he thumped him on the back. "I just found out thirty minutes ago."

Brenda pointed at the table of contents. After scanning the page quickly, she thrust an index finger at a subtitle. *The Era Dial: A Guide for Construction.* She turned to the appropriate page and nudged Clair. "Think you can handle it?"

Clair winked. "As sure as I am Colored and Southern."

FIFTEEN

DINNER PLANS

"So, what's the plan?" Omen asked after scarfing down a slice of cake.

Brenda sipped water from a glass. "I say we leave early in the morning."

"The earlier, the better," Omen said between bites. "What time are you thinking? Four? Five?"

"Midnight," she said and helped herself to a tart.

"But, it's seven o'clock right now," Elliot pointed to his watch. The others stopped mid-chew.

"I know, but hear me out. We need to do this under the cover of darkness. Less interruptions. It's the safest way."

Clair buttered a slice of bread and exhaled. "She's right."

Brenda rubbed her hands together and grinned, her eyes wild as a mad scientist. "Take a look at this." She pulled a page from her briefcase and spread it on the table in front of them.

"How'd you—" Elliot began.

"I call this a put back." She held up a metal tool and smiled. It looked like a cross between a butter knife and a scalpel except the handle was comprised of buttons and gears similar to those on her goggles. "This lets me remove and put back a page from a book effortlessly."

Elliot swiped the instrument and examined it up close. "Solid."

Brenda winked and began reading from the orphaned page.

The Grootslang
Found in the limestone caves of the Richtersveld in South Africa, the Grootslang, or great snake, is said to have the tail of a snake and the head and torso of an elephant. It lures its enemies and the unsuspecting alike into its cave and devours them. Deep in the abyss, the Grootslang sits upon a giant hoard of precious metals and stones. The creature is as old as the world itself. Because of this, the precious stones from its hoard (Grootstones), contain bits and pieces of time. Naturally, Grootstones are the prime materials used to create Era Dials, used by Time Thieves. The only way to escape the clutches of a Grootslang without injury is to barter with precious metals or jewels.

As with the other pages, an animated elephant with a snake's tail lumbered across the page before burying itself in a pile of jewels.

"Like Clair said earlier, we'll need Era Dials if we plan on traveling through time. Era Dials need Grootstones." She surveyed each of their faces. "And who's strong enough to face a monster, grab some stones, and return in one piece?"

Omen felt three pairs of eyes boring into him.

"You're our strongman." Clair rubbed him between the shoulder blades. "There isn't anyone else with your skillset."

Omen turned to Elliot who held up his hands.

"Don't look at me, I'm a scientist," he said before polishing off a glass of juice.

Omen rolled his eyes, defeated. "Fine. Tell me what I need to do."

Brenda scanned the next page. "Says here it's all in the body language. Careful movements. Always slow and steady. And as frightening as it sounds, keep eye contact. That will gain the creature's respect."

Omen reached for his chain. "If my grandfather can wrestle a gator, I can handle a Grootslang." He took a deep breath.

Brenda pulled out a miniature version of the map they'd seen on the wall in the library.

"How'd you—" Elliot pointed at the map.

Brenda held up a palm. "We start at this little supply house and grab some protective gear. Then, we head to the Grand Menagerie." She pointed to a sphere. "There's a sphinx at the entrance, so make sure you put your thinking caps on."

"Mama Cool said—" Elliot interrupted.

"Hush!" Brenda placed a finger over her lips. "I ain't never in my life met a scientist who doesn't listen as much as you!"

Elliot shot Brenda an irritated look.

"If we can't answer the riddles, we run," she continued. "The sphinx can only fly a short distance. I'll lead the way. Then, we speak to the Jengu about Elliot's formula and hopefully bottle up some tears. Finally,

Omen enters the cave and grabs the stones. Once we leave the Grand Menagerie, we head up the hill." She traced a winding path with her fingertip. "We'll take the elevator up through the Haunted Obelisk."

Clair licked her lips. "Yup. The map says there's a lab at the top. I can make the Era Dials there and Elliot can add the tears to his formula."

"Then, we board the Kilimanjaro Coaster through the Bump and we're at the Era Port." Brenda grinned, pleased with herself.

"Are we going forward or back in time?" Elliot cut in.

Clair leaned back in her chair. "I say we go back to earlier today. That way, Elliot or Brenda can slip the formula to the sheriff."

"We'll get in, get out, and be back in time to start the next part of the agenda at 9 am." Brenda clasped her hands together.

"Anything else we need to keep in mind?" Elliot said as he smoothed his mustache.

"Beat walkers," Clair said as she piled her silverware on her plate. "Security guards in the Era Port. Might be a nuisance. Make sure you keep your Era Dials visible and don't take anything." She glared at Brenda. "Stolen goods will set them off."

Brenda held up her hands. "Okay, okay, I hear you!"

"Anything else?" Omen ran his fingers through his hair.

"Yes, keep track of the trains. There are two kinds." Clair counted on her fingers. "Next and Then. Next trains take us to the future. Then trains take us to the past."

"Simple, right?" Brenda asked, beaming.

"Oh yeah, sounds easy," Elliot rolled his eyes.

"Good. Get some sleep." Brenda grabbed her tool and the page, shoved them both in her briefcase, and closed it with a snap.

SIXTEEN

THE STORY OF FAT FRIDAY

"You like him, don't you?" Brenda pulled back the covers on her bed and sat down.

"Who?" Clair raised an eyebrow.

"Really?" She fiddled with another one of her contraptions, pressing buttons and twisting gears. "I think you know who I'm talking about."

Clair sighed. "That ain't even the reason we're here."

"So what? That never stopped anyone from falling in love before," Brenda said with a sly smile.

"Whoa, who said anything about falling in love?" Clair shot back.

"Think about it. It would be a great love story." She hopped from the bed and sat cross-legged on the floor.

"He's nice, but I'm just getting out of something . . ."

Brenda looked at Clair, eyebrows raised. "Do tell."

Her eyes shifted. "Oh . . . yeah, well he was my boyfriend for over a year."

"What was his name?"

"Lonnie," Clair stared at the ceiling. "And he's probably the most interesting boy I've ever met."

"Interesting like how?"

Clair shrugged. "We kind of clicked."

Brenda's mouth stretched into a smile. "He was cute, wasn't he?"

Clair smiled. "Of course, he was, especially his real face."

"What do you mean, his *real* face?"

"Lonnie's a Shifter. He played with different faces and builds and looks. But I liked the regular ole Lonnie. Didn't have a bunch of muscles. Wasn't the finest thing this side of the Mississippi, but he was perfect for me." She stroked her chin. "Don't think I ever told him that."

"Why was he perfect for you?"

"We ran a business together and he taught me the ropes. It worked out, for a while."

"What kind of things did you sell?" Brenda looked up from a pile of cogs and screws.

"Mostly spirits. Lonnie had all the connections. People respected him." Clair rolled over and fluffed her pillow. "He'd find out when a shipment was coming in. We'd go down to the docks at night, pick it up, then we'd sell it."

"Sounds like my kind of guy," Brenda grinned.

"One night about a year ago, Lonnie had a contract to buy bourbon from a White man named Fat Friday. Funny thing was, Friday hated Colored folks. I told Lonnie it was too risky, but he insisted we do it...and a little extra."

Brenda froze. "What was the little extra?"

"Lonnie called it a two for one." Clair winked. "Fat Friday was the king of the Charleston underground. If you wanted to bootleg, you had to go through him. Everybody who was anybody knew it." She cleared her throat. "We got Lonnie's big brother Rich in on the plan. The cut was too big to turn down. Five hundred dollars split three ways."

Brenda's jaw dropped. "Five hundred—was Rich a Shifter too?"

"Yup. And he was also our driver. I was the lookout and Lonnie made the deal. Lonnie took on the face of a White man to get in with Friday's gang down on the docks and things went smooth, at first."

"What happened?" Brenda uncrossed her legs.

"It was a perfect spring night: Cool air—not too hot, not too cold—a breeze off the ocean, and an orange new moon. Me, Rich, and Lonnie went over the plan at least twenty times. So, Rich drove down to the docks and let Lonnie out while we stayed a ways up the road with our headlights off. I couldn't see much from where we were parked, but I watched Lonnie slip inside one of those old buildings near the pier. Next thing I knew, he was high tailing it outta there."

Brenda held a hand over her mouth. "So, what happened next?"

"Turns out Fat Friday had a Shifter in his gang that Lonnie didn't know about, and Shifters can easily sniff each other out. It's like they have a scent or something. So, Lonnie ran out of that building with a knapsack full of bourbon toward the car. By then, Rich was revving the engine. Then, we saw the other Shifter running after him calling him all kinds of low-down darkies and such. So, I hopped in the back seat and threw open the other door so Lonnie could jump inside."

Brenda shrieked. "Oh my God, did y'all make it?"

Clair shook her head. "We did, and we still managed to make a decent amount of cash off those bottles. If it wasn't for Lonnie, I wouldn't have gotten my tent."

"What about the two for one?" Brenda egged her on.

Clair smirked. "Though me and Rich tried to convince him not to, Lonnie went back. This time, he took the face of the Shifter that chased him. Turns out the guy was only a mono-morph and Lonnie's a polymorph."

Brenda frowned. "What's that?"

"Monomorphs can only shift once every twenty-four hours. They're kinda like one-trick ponies. But polymorphs can shift into anything at any time. They're rare . . . and dangerous."

"Wow." Brenda leaned forward. "What happened next?"

"He set their hide-out on fire." Clair stifled a chuckle. "Lit up the place. Nobody died, but let's just say Fat Friday's still trying to recover his losses. And of course, he blamed the Shifter in his gang."

"Whoa. That's something else."

"It was crazy is what it was." Clair's jaw turned hard as if she'd been shaken awake from a dream.

Brenda shrugged. "Who am I to judge? I tried to steal from you."

Clair snorted. "Glad you're not judging, but that ain't the same."

"Why not?

"This ain't really about stealing." Clair sucked her teeth. "I, for one, don't give a damn about stealing from a redneck who sees our kind as less than something on the bottom of his shoe."

"Then, what's it about?" Brenda countered.

"Let's see." Clair paused to think. "Even though it's sad and all that your uncle died, you still have an aunt who loves and cares for you. You do what you do because you like acting out. I did what I did because I gotta survive."

Brenda swallowed hard. "Survival? How?"

"Been on my own since I was twelve. My parents died so my Big Ma took care of me. I came home one day, and she was dead. That was five years ago." Clair shrugged. "Like I said before. It's not the same." She pulled the covers up to her chin. "Anyway, seems you and Elliot have a lot in common. He's a chemist. You're an inventor. And y'all both got that briefcase thing going on."

Brenda swallowed a smirk. "I guess. What do you think we'll see tomorrow at the Era Port?"

Clair propped herself up on her elbows. "Too much."

"What do you mean by that?"

"The future and the past ain't to be toyed with."

"So, why go?"

"Because we can change the world." Clair adjusted her pillows. "Because we can."

Brenda leaned back on her elbows. "Because we can. I like that."

Clair rolled over on her stomach. "We all do things we shouldn't. Sometimes, we do them because we can. Let's hope this'll all be worth it."

"Think we'll see Dr. Djinn tomorrow?"

Clair shrugged. "Don't know. Something tells me this is all a set-up. It's like we're inside a maze and she'll show up as the prize at the end.

"Right. I expected to see more of her, ya know? Wanted to pick her brain." Brenda swallowed a smile. "Tomorrow, we travel through time."

"Yeah . . ." Clair said in a faraway voice.

"Can't wait!" Brenda stood, turned off the lights and clambered underneath the covers. In one hand, she held an additional page from *The Book of Epochs, Eras, and Eons*. In the other, she held an instrument that looked like a flashlight.

SEVENTEEN

INSOMNIA

Clair sat up at the sound of the *tap, tap, tapping* on the bedroom door. Careful not to wake Brenda, she pulled back the covers and tiptoed across the floor. When she pushed the door ajar, she saw a tall, muscular frame bathed in moonlight. *Omen.* He stood there with his arms folded.

"Feel like talking?" he asked in a gruff voice. "Can't sleep."

After rubbing the sleep from her eyes, she grabbed a shawl and followed him out into the black of night. The full moon was now a circle of white light puncturing the velvet sky. She watched as the fireflies darted between the trees, pulled the shawl tight around her shoulders, and took a seat in a rocking chair on the cabin's porch.

"How you feeling?"

Omen rubbed his hands together. "Ok, I guess."

"Just ok?"

"Nah. Not really."

She turned to him. "I believe in you."

"Up until a few minutes ago, I believed in me too." He rocked back on his heels. "Do you think we should do this?"

"I don't know. I was the one who mentioned the Era Port. No one would have known what it was if it wasn't for me."

"Yeah, you mentioned it, but *should* we do it? What are the consequences?" He twirled his chain around his finger.

"Dabbling in time is always a gamble. Usually the price is losing time." She leaned forward in the rocking chair.

Omen frowned. "Losing time...like actual time?"

"If we get caught, yes."

He raised an eyebrow. "So, I guess that means we've gotta be careful."

"I guess we should think about the possibility of losing those scholarships."

"Right. The park is great and everything, but school is the real prize." He held his head in his hands.

"Do you think Elliot will be able to handle it?"

"I think so." He leaned against the banister to support his weight. "He shot a rifle from a rooftop last summer. He may not have known it when he won, but vengeance is why he's here."

"Yeah. True." She concentrated on a firefly and its zigzagging path of light. "You scared?"

"There's a saying in my family. Strength is the—"

She wagged an index finger in the air, cutting him off. "That ain't what I asked. I asked if you were scared."

He took a seat on a stair. "I don't know."

"What do you mean you don't know? Either you're scared or you're not."

"All my life, I've been training. It's what the Crows do. We wrestle and lift dumbbells and compete. It's how we make our living. We're Strongmen. Have been for almost a century." He pulled at his chain.

"Is that the source of your strength?"

He made a face. "This?" he asked pointing to the tooth.

"Yeah. Is that where you get your strength?"

"No...I mean yeah, but—"

"But what?" She clutched the chair and rocked forward.

"I mean, it's a symbol."

"So, if it was taken from you, you'd be ok?" she prodded. "If tomorrow you couldn't find it, you'd still be brave enough to go on, right?"

"If someone took your patch, could you go on?" he shot back.

She sat up straight. "That's different."

"You're damn right it's different. That patch ain't connected to legacy or bravery or family." He folded his arms across his chest. "It's just business."

"Well, I—"

"Strength is my family's business. It's who we are. It ain't a costume."

She pulled her shawl tight around her shoulders. "I'm scared."

"You'd be a fool not to be. This ain't no average enemy. This ain't somebody I can size up and prepare for. This here is some kind of magic I ain't never known." He laced his fingers above his head. They sat there for a moment, engulfed in a cocoon of silence and the songs of insects.

"Good to know neither one of us are fools," Clair said in a shaky voice.

Omen inhaled. "Yeah, good to know."

"I never took you for no fool. Not when I laid eyes on you."

"That's right," he smirked. "You got that gift. I keep forgetting you can read me and what not."

"More like feel you," she corrected. "I'm a tele-kinetic. I can move things. And to do that, I gotta feel them first."

"So, what do you feel about all of this?" He gestured in the direction of the towering obelisk lit up like a lighthouse and the shadow of The Grand Menagerie looming in the distance.

She shrugged. "I didn't feel any of this. Didn't feel any of it coming." She looked away. "And that's what makes it scary."

"You didn't feel nothin'?"

"Nope. I got the letter like you and everyone else. I knew there would be some surprises, but this?" She spread her arms wide. "Had no idea we'd be solving a mystery we ain't even sure of."

He cracked his knuckles. "Right. And the fact that Elliot and Brenda saw the same cops from the picture show snooping around the park—I think this is what she wanted. Is that impossible?"

"Everything is possible." She turned to look him in the eye. "But I do feel you're gonna beat that thing in there."

"What else do you feel?" He reached for her hand and kissed it.

He was even more beautiful framed by the moonlight. "I feel like you're trying to tell me something."

He placed a palm on her cheek. "I think I'm trying to show you something instead." The last thing she felt was his breath on her neck and a kiss that felt like a dream.

*

"Is this how you spend your nights? Researching under the stars? Reading while everyone else sleeps?"

Brenda flinched as a voice interrupted her late-night book binge. Elliot stood in the doorway of the front steps, flashlight in hand.

"Pretty much," she said and continued to read.

"What's your favorite book?"

"Can't choose," Brenda sighed. "That's like asking me if I have a favorite eye or a favorite tooth."

"True. Mine is *The Odyssey* by Homer."

"*The Odyssey*? I expected you to say some science book." She looked up.

"Nope. *The Odyssey* is about adventure and loyalty and choices. I like that. Today, I was Odysseus. Running from creatures, solving riddles, making choices—"

"Today was an adventure," Brenda chuckled.

"Mind if I soak up some of that knowledge you've been packing in that brain of yours?" He gestured toward her briefcase.

"If you wanna see what's inside, say so." She closed the book and opened the briefcase, spreading its contents across the porch's wooden slats.

Elliot dropped to his knees. "What's the story behind this thing?"

"A gift when I turned twelve."

He ran an index finger over the leather. With a click, a drawer opened to reveal a contraption that looked like a small, hand-held mirror. He pushed a button and a hidden compartment opened to reveal an expensive-looking ink pen studded with rubies, onyx, and emeralds. He lifted it from its cushion. "You got this briefcase from Benjamin Banneker?"

"I don't know anymore." She looked up at the moon. For the first time in her life, things were starting to add up. All the pieces of the puzzle were shifting into place. She wished Uncle Rufus was here.

"But you said—"

"I know what I said. I just think this may have been my Uncle Rufus's doing all along. Kind of like how adults convince kids to believe in Santa Claus." She shrugged.

He turned to the mirror and lifted it gently from its velvet cushion. "What's this?"

"What's it look like?"

"I know what it looks like but knowing you the way I think I do; it's got to be more than a mirror. Right?"

She extended an open palm and he handed it over. The mirror was silver with cogs and buttons on its handle. With a click, the glass slid open to reveal a hidden compartment behind it. "Nothing special. Extra storage."

"What about this?" He held the pen up to the moonlight.

A smile crept across her face. "A pen."

He cocked his head to the side. "Really? Looks like it's worth a fortune."

"Probably is, but it's not practical. Uncle Rufus believed it was an heirloom."

"Why do you say it isn't practical?"

"It doesn't write. No ink and no way to add any. Part of the mystery, I guess. That one came to me already assembled. It was the only invention I didn't have to build. Still not sure what it does. It's beautiful though."

"You scared?" He paused. "About tomorrow I mean."

"Not really. I think the only thing that really scares me is getting caught."

"Right."

"You?" She pulled her knees to her chin.

"Kind of. I mean, I'm not a Taint, but I do know there's consequences when you break a law. And time traveling has to have laws, ya know?"

"Of course."

"You're brilliant." He scooted closer.

"That's saying something from the boy who invented a cure for bigots."

"Not yet. Won't work unless we meet up with a Jengu."

"Besides cures for racism, what else have you made? Anything practical?"

He pulled his shoulders back. "A cure for bigotry isn't practical? I didn't know that." His laugh dissolved into a serious smirk. "Science is magic, too."

"I guess so, but what kinds of simple things do you make?"

He shot her a side-eye. "Simple? Like you invent simple things!"

"Okay, okay. You're right," she laughed.

"I make oils for hair and skin. It's made with lavender and coconut oil. My pop taught me how to use plants and flowers for everyday use. And my mom's a teacher so lots of learning and experimenting goes on in our household."

"Get out! Do you have any with you?"

"Sure do. Got a bottle back in the room."

"Good. Keep it with you."

"Do I need to make sure I smell good for the Jengu or something?"

"You never know. Might come in handy. Science is magic, too."

EIGHTEEN

THE GRAND MENAGERIE

Omen and the others crept around the perimeter of the sculpture garden after rising at midnight. The park was much different on foot. He had to remind himself that they'd toured the park the day before by airship, a means of transportation much faster than two legs. Though the sun had yet to pull itself up over the shoulders of the world, the heat hadn't gotten the memo. Even in the early morning hours, sweat trickled across his brow. Luckily, he'd packed a cold, wet rag from the cabin for relief. He reached for it and dabbed at his temples before ducking beneath a group of trees next to the bumper cars.

Brenda stopped and pulled out the map. "We're here." She circled the area outside the theater and courtyard with her fingertip. "The Grand Menagerie is ahead. But we need to stop here before we go in." She pointed at a squat building off to the sphere's side.

Together, they ducked around a carousel with "horses" that looked like lizards and through an outdoor plaza of games and tents. Finally, they stood beneath the shadow of the Grand Menagerie and in front of a building the size of a small shack. Brenda retrieved a gadget from her briefcase, which was now the size of a wallet, and picked the lock on the door.

Inside, the room looked like a smaller version of the lecture hall they visited at Hampton Institute. Omen turned around in a circle. A chalkboard covered in a pearl-like substance stretched across one of the walls. He pulled on his chin hairs as the shiny particles shifted to reveal another map.

Clair stood next to him. "It's the inside of The Grand Menagerie."

Sure enough, he recognized the great swamp semi-surrounded by doors on one side and the churning river dividing the globe in two unequal parts.

Brenda pointed to a square on the map. "This is the South entranceway. We enter here. Remember, there will be a Sphinx." She looked at the group. "We'll probably need to solve at least three riddles. We can do it. If not, run." She tapped the map again. "The South entrance is also where they keep a Mokele-Mbembe. I researched him last night. He's enormous, but completely harmless." She scanned their uneasy faces. "I need you to trust me." She pointed at a waterfall upstream of the river. "This is where the Jengu gather." She looked at Elliot who pulled Brenda's Fire Needle from his shirt pocket.

"We can stop there before moving toward the Grootslang's cave." She turned to Omen. "It sleeps 10 hours each day. It's midnight. You'll have about ninety minutes to retrieve the stones from her hoard." She tossed Omen a silver net. "That's to keep the stones safe once they're collected. The stones and metals absorb the Grootslang's body heat, which can reach up to two hundred and twelve degrees. Collect as many stones as you can, at least thirty. Emerald, onyx, ruby, diamond, and platinum ore are best. No matter how small, don't pass up the platinum."

"Since when did you become an expert on all of this?" Omen raised an eyebrow.

"Couldn't sleep." Brenda shrugged. "How good is your strength and balance?"

"Well, I train all year, but what does that have to do with gathering stones?"

"There's a Wonder Hole. You'll have to lower yourself inside. It's the only way in." She avoided his eyes.

"Lower myself?"

"And take this just in case," she said and tossed him an expensive looking pen bejeweled with rubies, emeralds, and onyx.

"In case of what?" Omen turned the pen over in his hands.

"For bartering. If it wakes, you can trade the pen for your life."

"Great," he grumbled.

Brenda pointed to a table of tools and equipment. Out of the corner of his eye, he watched as Clair pulled on a pair of studded rubber gloves that looked like torture instruments. Brenda leaned over his shoulder, examining the display. "None of this equipment was available yesterday."

He shook his head in agreement. "Sure wasn't." Omen surveyed the tools in front of him: a flashlight with a copper handle, a pair of goggles with kaleidoscopic lenses, a clear raincoat, large ear muffs made of lavender and orange feathers, a thin, black rope, and a pair of those hideous gloves. He placed the necessary items into a plain knapsack and tossed it over his shoulder.

* * *

They crept toward a sign hanging beneath a glass archway. *The Grand Menagerie.*

"Keep your eyes peeled and voices low. You'll need your goggles." Brenda crouched down to the ground and motioned over her shoulder.

They tiptoed along until the oily blackness gave way to a golden haze. Omen steadied himself through the marsh. A loud buzz took him by surprise. With a wild swing, he swatted at an insect the size of his palm. The bug zigzagged away in a noisy panic. Tangles of low brush and branches descended into grassy nooks and spinning whirlpools. Nests of orange feathers peeked from the arms of giant trees. Golden placards with the names of animals, plants, and insects thrust from the sodden ground.

Omen froze as a massive gray tail slithered between two nearby trees. He held his breath as it slipped noisily over the moss and through a knot of bushes before moving out of sight.

"That's the Mokele-Mbembe," Brenda whispered. "The name literally means, "one who stops the flow of rivers." She crouched near a plant with wide, prickly leaves.

Not far ahead, he saw the river. There, the animal revealed its massive body, first the head, then the neck, torso, and so on. Its neck must have been at least fifteen feet long. Omen watched, slack jawed as it stood up on front legs as big around as tractor trailers. After an ear-splitting screech, it munched on the leaves from a tall tree and returned to the river with a resounding splash. Finally, it released a furious snort, shooting water high in the air from a blowhole on the top of its head.

"I could have sworn dinosaurs were extinct," Elliot whispered.

"There she is," Brenda hissed. "Let's go. Follow my lead."

A few feet from where they knelt, a creature with the head of a woman and the body of an adult lion lounged on a pedestal. Feathered wings stretched from its shoulders and lay idle at its sides. It smoothed its mane with its paw. Sensing the group as they approached, the Sphinx rose on all fours.

"Welcome to the Grand Menagerie."

The voice that exited the creature's mouth could only be described as rushing water, wide and deep like a void with no bottom. Immediately, Clair and Brenda avoided its purple-gray eyes and knelt on the mossy ground with Elliot and Omen following suit.

"Oh, mighty Sphinx, Queen of riddles, secrets, and lore," Brenda said after a deep breath. "We humbly ask for entrance."

It responded with a vicious growl. "Look at me," it commanded, "all of you!"

Omen sucked in air before he lifted his eyes to meet the creature's gaze. His shoulders slumped in surprise. The sphinx had a face like his mother, with skin the color of bronze, thick features, and eyes as wise as a legend. But still, there was a wildness present that Omen had never witnessed. A part of him wondered if his grandfather had these thoughts while wrestling that gator. There were differences in the two scenarios though. His granddaddy's gator couldn't speak.

"You may pass if you answer these riddles correctly."

His heart slammed against his chest as the creature chewed absently on a blade of grass.

"I am always spinning, but I have no clothes," the sphinx boomed. "What am I?"

Omen frowned. "A spider."

Clair squeezed his hand.

The Sphinx sat back on its hind legs. "Good, another," it said while pacing back and forth. "I have a friend who teaches me things but does not speak. Who is my friend?"

The sounds of the forest intensified. Omen gulped as the seconds ticked by. The river rushed in the distance. A large bird flapped its wings from its perch high above in a tree. An insect buzzed near his ear. He swatted a palm in its direction. Seconds later, he exchanged nervous looks with Elliot, Brenda, and Clair. The Sphinx glowered at each of them, one by one. Omen looked away.

"Well, it seems I cannot grant you passage. What a shame—"

"Run!" Brenda hissed and dashed around the pedestal. Omen scrambled to his feet and followed close behind Elliot and Clair into a knot of trees leaving the stunned Sphinx behind, fangs bared in an angry snarl.

NINETEEN

SWALLOWING MONSTERS AND MERMAIDS

Elliot sucked in air as he darted between tree trunks. In the distance, he could hear the low growl of the sphinx as it gave chase. His heart slammed against his ribcage as they zigzagged through the muddy terrain. He peeked over his shoulder to be sure Clair and Omen were keeping up. Thankfully, they were all on a tear driven by fear and pure adrenaline. His instincts told him to look down. Luckily, he sidestepped a tangle of tree branches, poking from the ground. The Grand Menagerie was a swamp with unsteady footing. He had a feeling being in the field with his dad would come in handy someday. Spiraling roots and marsh disguised as piles of unsuspecting leaves were among his father's specialties. As he veered around a bush with waxy leaves as sharp as knives, the rushing river made an appearance on his right. He stole a glance at Brenda up ahead and hoped she knew where she was going.

"The raft!" she panted.

Sure enough, a round river raft attached to a wooden dock by a thick, heavy rope moved into view. Brenda hopped aboard followed by Clair and Elliot. Omen leaped over a thicket of pink cacti before diving inside.

Together, Omen and Elliot hoisted the rope inside the raft. Out of the corner of his eye, a golden paw swiped at him from above. Omen tumbled backward, rope in hand. Elliot looked up into a pair of piercing lavender eyes and a terrifying snarl. As the sphinx bared its fangs, the current caught hold of the raft, whisking them off into the swirling, white capped river. Elliot slammed into one of the empty bucket seats. Quickly, he clambered to his feet, kicked the rope aside, and grabbed hold of a leather belt dangling from the seat. The raft dipped over a mini-cliff and into a stretch of vast, churning water. Meanwhile, the sphinx hovered over the dock in the distance, its wings spread wide like a prehistoric butterfly. Elliot exhaled in relief as the creature pulled its wings back to its sides, touched down, and stalked back in the direction it had come.

They held on for dear life as they spun like a top. Omen was the first to secure himself in his seat by tying two of the water-logged belts across his lap. He assisted Clair while Elliot fumbled with Brenda's straps as she clung to her briefcase.

Elliot squeezed his eyes shut as the raft dipped between a clump of rocks and plants. All the while, the river grew wider. Soon, the banks dwarfed in the distance. The roar of foaming rapids, fierce and unyielding, rushed on all sides. By now, at least a half mile of water stood between them and the riverbank. To one side, he spotted a waterfall spilling over a sizeable cliff, on the other he spied a cave, illuminated by soft amber light. It was a toss-up as to where they'd end up.

"Oh my God!" Brenda screeched.

The raft spun counterclockwise as two heads attached to elongated necks rose from the foaming water on opposite sides. Elliot swallowed a scream as the creatures lumbered dangerously close in their quest to reach a tree rooted near the riverbank. Its bright yellow leaves splayed over the river like fistfuls of umbrellas cradling ruby red fruit. The Mokele-Mbembe took turns munching on the leaves. Finally, as if bidding them goodbye, one of the beasts shot a geyser through its blowhole, engulfing them in a heavy mist. Elliot struggled to see through the droplets fogging his lenses as the raft bounced off one of the creature's massive torso of wrinkly gray skin.

Forward momentum pushed them further downstream. Elliot clenched his fists around the seat as they spun in dizzying circles. Then, after what seemed like an eternity of thrashing back and forth, the river grew calm.

"Never have I ever been this close to death on consecutive days," Elliot said, glasses askew.

"Me neither." Omen grimaced while rolling his chain between his thumb and forefinger.

"This wasn't a smart plan." Elliot shook his head.

"So yesterday, it was brilliant, and today it's dumb?" Brenda said, clutching her briefcase to her chest like a last meal.

"We almost died," Elliot spat through clenched teeth. "And for the record, I said you were brilliant, *you*, not the plan."

"So, what do you suggest, Wise Guy? Should we paddle between those monsters, sneak around the sphinx, and back to our cabins like nothing happened?" Brenda shot back.

Elliot avoided her eyes.

"Exactly," she scoffed. "We get those tears and stones. We get to the Era Port. We make the leap and we change the world. What do we have to lose?"

"A lot." Clair cleared her throat and glanced at Omen. "We have a lot to lose. A whole lot more than you and Elliot."

"Why would you say—" Brenda began.

"We're different," Clair cut in. "If we're caught, what happens?"

Brenda shifted uncomfortably in her seat. "I don't, I mean—" she stammered.

Clair held up a hand. "If y'all are caught, you go back to making inventions and formulas in Philly and D.C. If we're caught, we go back to strugglin' in the south." She shook her head. "So, quit it with this back and forth and think about how we can survive."

Brenda and Elliot exchanged resigned looks as they floated along in silence. Soon, the river narrowed again, now no more than twenty feet across. Elliot craned his neck. They were headed toward the cave. His gaze swung to the riverbank. A placard surrounded by powder blue leaves sprouting from the wet sand caught his eye.

Chipfalamfula: The River Shutter (Mozambique)

"Chipfalamfula," Clair said. "The River Shutter."

"What's a River Shutter?" Omen asked.

Brenda rubbed her eyes. "Sounds familiar. I think I read about it, but I'm not sure."

The inside of the cave was a newfound wonder. Signs indicating rare and mythical plant life poked from the shore. Elliot struggled to read them all. Instead of rock as he'd expected, the walls were covered in a thin tissue paper infused with meandering lines like veins poking under skin. Wild plants and giant, prehistoric trees gave way to smaller flowers and short blades of emerald grass. Sterling silver bushes and stunted trees covered in Venus Flytraps opened and closed. He thought of his Uncle Baron, his camera, and all the pictures he'd never get to take.

"What's that?" Omen pointed over Elliot's shoulder.

Elliot squinted at the shore. A dozen tiny creatures smaller than the palm of his hand trotted alongside the raft. Some rode on the backs of lizards, others kept pace on tiny legs. All were armed with spears and shields made of fish bones and bark. They huddled around the bottom of a stake attached to another placard stuck in the sand.

Abatwa: The Tiniest of All Fairies (South Africa)

"Glad I'm human. Those things look fierce." Elliot shook his head.

Omen let out a deep sigh. "Gotta give it to Dr. Djinn, this is one helluva park."

They drifted deeper inside the cave. Instead of hitting a wall, the raft turned, drifting closer to the opposite bank and back in the direction they'd come.

"Are those hills?" Brenda said as she squinted through the orange glow. "Couldn't be."

"A cage in a cave?" Clair thrust a finger in the air.

Up ahead, a glass box dangled from an invisible hook. A snake with iridescent scales slithered inside. Elliot looked on, slack jawed. The thing had to be as thick around as both of his thighs.

Aido Hwedo: The Rainbow Serpent (Benin)

Sensing their presence, it undulated like a ribbon on the end of a dancer's wand. Before long, it extended its tongue like a strip of silver lightning. Then, it disappeared, leaving behind a shimmering rainbow in its wake.

"Wow, I never thought I'd see our source," Clair said in a low voice.

Omen turned to Clair. "What do you mean?"

"Each order is associated with a creature," she said, shifting in her seat. "The old folks say Sage wisdom comes from the great rainbow serpent." She covered her mouth with her hand. "I can't believe I'm seeing one in the flesh."

"Look!" Brenda pointed at a hill of smooth, gray stones stacked high. Gold droppings dotted the rocks like splotches of regal paint.

"What's that smell?" Elliot sniffed the air as they approached a thicket of nests stuffed between the stones. Some were filled with smoldering golden powder and molten feathers of reddish gold. "Myrrh and frankincense? In a cave?"

Omen thrust his finger toward another sign.

Bennu: The Phoenix (Kemit)

On cue, a majestic bird let out a piercing screech before touching down on a stone. A flock of red gold birds gathered a few feet from where they drifted. Suddenly, an unseen force sucked them backward. Elliot's heartbeat stalled. Seconds stretched like a rubber band and the raft sprung from the cave in a wet, revolving heap.

Elliot swallowed bile as they catapulted forward into calmer waters.

"Now, I remember," Brenda said through heavy breaths. "Chipfalamfula is a swallowing monster. Completely harmless, but it has a world in its belly."

"Thank goodness it wasn't hungry." Clair ran a hand through her soaked braids.

Elliot peeked over the seats. Sure enough, the "cave" was the mouth of a giant fish. Two eyes covered in a grayish film sat above its mouth while its fins splashed in the river. With another guttural belch, its mouth opened and closed. Elliot held his breath, fearful of where the frothy current might take them. To his surprise, they bypassed the Mokele-Mbembe, who were again wading on the far side of the river and headed toward tall cliffs with nooks of crystal pools. Omen looked at the dome above. Rays of moonlight poured through the glass in prisms.

Another dock loomed ahead. "I think this is our stop." Elliot reached for the rope and flung it toward the dock. The toss landed perfectly.

"Nice toss." Brenda rolled her eyes. "Glad you're good for something."

He shook his head and extended a hand to help Omen, Clair, and finally, Brenda, from the raft. With a sigh of relief, he flopped to the ground. In thirty minutes, they'd been chased by a Sphinx, sprayed by two dinosaurs, and toured the inside of a swallowing monster. They deserved a breather. Omen took a seat next to Elliot and removed his shoes.

Brenda made a face and held her arms out from her sides. "Soaked."

"Better soaked than eaten," Elliot shot from over his shoulder. He watched as Clair muttered under her breath.

Omen patted his trousers and shirt with his palms. *Dry.* His soggy shoes were clean and good as new. He looked around at the others as they realized the wonder of Clair's magic. Though they'd been tossed and turned to an inch of their lives, no one would have ever known it.

"Thanks!" He gave her the thumbs up sign.

Brenda secured her briefcase over her shoulder and looked at the flashing gadget attached to her wrist. "Jengu then the Grootslang. Let's hurry."

Here, the river trickled into dozens of tiny streams. They hurried past shallow pools with tourmaline stones and spider webs woven between bushes drenched in dew. A bridge with a glass bottom stretched over one of the streams. Elliot looked down in time to see a school of red fish. In a flash, the school swam out of sight and beyond the sphere's curved edge in the distance. Once they crossed the bridge, the terrain changed to red clay dirt, then to shimmering white sand. Smooth, black boulders poked from the ground as they trekked up a steady incline.

The north side of the menagerie wasn't consumed by tall trees and endless green. The thick humidity had disappeared. Here, the air was light and crisp. Tall cliffs of black boulders huddled before them. Elliot glanced from the sand to a cave above a brisk waterfall. They'd climbed at least thirty feet. His gaze drifted back to the waterfall. Wide lavender fins poked out of the frothy cascades. A creature with dark skin, brown eyes, and kinky silver hair climbed onto a rock. Her fin shimmered as rays of moonlight knifed between the trees.

"Psst! Do you see that?" He thrust his finger in the direction of the fins.

Brenda pulled her goggles over her eyes. The lenses clicked into place. "Fascinating." She bent down for a better view.

Several Jengu congregated below the bridge. Elliot steadied himself as he climbed down a steep, sandy embankment. They looked more intimidating up close than from afar. Some had thick copper braids, others kinky silver clouds that surrounded their heads like halos. A Jengu with ebony skin and silver braids folded her arms across her chest.

"State your purpose," she hissed.

Elliot took a step backward in surprise. According to what they'd read, the Jengu were benevolent creatures. He hadn't expected any pushback.

"I—I need your help," he stammered.

The creature studied her nails. "Would you consider this a personal matter?" The other creatures gathered around, listening intently to the conversation.

Elliot stood tall. "Well, I'd say yes because—"

"We're not interested unless your request involves the good of all," she snapped. "We have no time for selfish requests."

"This isn't selfish. It's probably the most unselfish request you'll ever hear." The words tumbled from his lips before he could sort them out. "Please, hear me out."

Her face softened. "Fine." She held out a palm. "Your offering?"

"I don't think, I—" Elliot fumbled with the button on his shirt pocket as Brenda made her way down the embankment, half skidding, half falling to his side.

"We have an offering." Brenda extended her arm. In her hand, she held the mirror from her briefcase.

The Jengu leader studied it before passing it on to the others who'd gathered around.

Elliot reached for a small bottle in his pocket. "And these—oils made from coconut and lavender."

After rolling the bottle around in her hand, she opened it and took a whiff. Her eyes fluttered. "Thank you. These offerings please us. I'm listening. *We're* listening."

After a deep breath, Elliot launched into the grisly tale of his trip to South Carolina and the riots that took the life of his uncle in Washington, DC. He watched them carefully as he spoke. They floated, some bowing their heads, others recoiling and grabbing hold of one another in reaction to the horrible details. By the time he'd completed the tale, their faces were slick with tears. The leader rose from the stream, settled on a rock, and reached for Elliot's hand.

"We need your help." Elliot's voice cracked. "Your tears…heal."

The Jengu watched as Brenda retrieved her fire needle from the briefcase. She removed the plastic container inside and collected a vial of tears.

"I hope our tears can heal these wounds," the Jengu said, wiping her eyes. "Promise you'll let us know the outcome?"

"I promise." He tucked the samples inside his shirt pocket.

TWENTY

BARTERING WITH A GROOTSLANG

They followed a rocky path to Jade's lair. Steel plaques with facts about the beast guided their way. The sphere was closer now and the full moon cast a brilliant light over their shadows.

"Ready?" Brenda turned to Omen with expectant eyes.

Armed with a rope and harness, he stepped forward. A final plaque protruded from the ground outside of the cave.

Grootslang are among the most dangerous creatures in the park. Please speak softly and do not place your hands, arms, or legs over the rail for your safety.

"Great," he muttered to himself.

"Gather as many stones as you can," Brenda called over his shoulder.

Clair patted him on the arm. "You can do this. I believe in you." She winked. "You ain't no fool."

Brenda approached with an outstretched hand. She handed him a pair of goggles. "Take these. Trust me."

"Thanks," he said before turning toward the cave.

Once inside, he pulled the goggles over his eyes. With the push of a button, a pair of orange lenses appeared. Immediately, the cave's outer rim came alive with foreign markings invisible to the naked eye. Excited, he pressed another button.

Almost Doesn't Fill a Bowl-Zulu Proverb

With a click, a new pair of lenses jutted from the frame, replacing the old. This time, a dark purple tint washed out amber light. He took another careful step. The cave reminded him of a volcano with a steep summit, open crater, and a cone leading to a deep, dark core. He looked up. To his surprise, a large oval covered with a sheet of glass had been cut in the top of the cave. This explained their ability to see the beast from the airship the day before. All but a sliver of moonlight had been swallowed up by the clouds.

Cautiously, he made his way around a circular walkway. A thick, steel railing attached to sturdy poles secured him from the dangerous drop down. Every few feet, polished black telescopes attached to the railing poked into the abyss. He removed the goggles and peeked through one of the scopes. Flashes of metal and gems gleamed in the darkness and a wrinkled, gray trunk rested atop mounds of jewels. A soft growl enveloped the cave as the beast snored below.

Strength is the family business. He knelt down, rummaged through his bag, and pulled on a pair of fur-lined gloves. In one corner of the cave, a sturdy hook poked from the rock wall. *Locate the hook and attach the rope.* He rolled the rope between his palms. It was rubber to the touch but had the strength of a hippo's jaws when taut. *Next, knot the rope around the hook and connect to the utility belt. Finally, lower yourself into the abyss, collect the gems, pull yourself up, and out.*

Omen secured the rope to the hook and rifled through the goggle's lenses until he found a pair that fit him best. "Here goes nothing." He tugged at the rope, tapped the alligator tooth one more time for luck, and swung his hulking frame over the railing.

The creature's snores grew louder as he dropped, inch by inch over the gleaming hoard. *A little bit lower.* The toes of his shoes grazed the top of the mound. Beneath him, the gray trunk and a pair of tusks poked from under the stones. A monstrous snake-like tail coiled around the side of the cave. By the time he felt secure enough to walk, pure adrenaline kicked in. Quick and in a hurry, he snatched as many stones as he could. Small, large, smooth, and jagged; he grasped emeralds, rubies, diamonds, and hunks of platinum ore by the fistfuls and stuffed them in the net. *More than enough.* He tossed it over his shoulder, tugged on the rope, and grunted as he pulled himself up. The lantern attached to the wall rattled and flickered. A shadow appeared in front of him and the sound that followed turned his blood cold.

The cavern shook as he let go of the rope, landing in a heap. He struggled to get his bearings. *Kneel. Offer. Back Away.* He managed a few steps on the unsteady surface and knelt on one knee, head bowed. Before he could react, the Grootslang hoisted itself up from its resting place atop the massive mound. A shower of jewels rained down on his head and shoulders. First, he saw the long, ivory tusks studded with topaz and ringlets of jade bracelets. Then came the enormous gray foot. The creature growled. Still, Omen held his ground as the sound of its tail slithered over the stones. Still kneeling, he gazed into the thing's beady eyes. The monster moved slowly, extending its heavy trunk until it coiled around his shoulders and waist as he trembled. Its skin was like sheets of seething hot leather left out in the summer sun. His body rose from the hill of jewels as the creature lifted him from his feet. He held his breath as the monster opened its mouth. A stench like sewage and rotted meat flooded his nostrils. Tears welled in his eyes as he gagged. Never had he experienced such unspeakable terror. Somehow, he summoned calm even in the clutches of a thing that would gladly make him a meal. The beast roared again and set its sights on the silver chain dangling from his neck. *Strength is the family business. Strength is the family business.* His heart stalled. *No. Not this.* The beast growled again. A cascade of white-hot jewels fell over his back and shoulders.

"Put me down," he croaked. "Put me down and you can have it."

Slowly, the monster released its grip as if it understood. Visibly shaking, Omen removed the chain and thrust it forward in his open palm. The creature trained its beady little eyes on Omen and inched closer. He resisted the urge to vomit as its fetid breath fogged up his goggles. Then, it snatched the chain with its trunk and retreated. Omen backed away, chest heaving. Covered in sweat, he kept his eyes trained on the monster as it stared back at him, daring him to make a sudden move. With trembling hands, he hoisted his body out of the hole, unhooked the rope, and bolted from the cave. A stabbing sensation ricocheted through his thigh. Brenda's pen poked from his pocket. He bit his lip, retrieved the pen, and tore down the hill.

TWENTY-ONE

THE HAUNTED OBELISK

Brenda sprang into action the moment Omen sprinted from the cave. Together, the scholars side-stepped mud puddles and ducked beneath wide fronds until the dense foliage thinned. A dirt path that veered dangerously close to a waterfall moved into view. Her heart skipped a beat. This wasn't on the map. Yet, they couldn't leave the same way they'd come, not with an angry Sphinx guarding the entrance.

"Wait, let's regroup," she panted. "I wanna take a look at the map—"

A sudden sensation of falling, then sliding overtook her senses. The trees blurred and the cliff dwarfed in the distance. Her shoulders slammed into the sides of a tube winding below the rushing waterfall, through the river, and now, underground. In a flash, she slid between gleaming fins and beside the belly of a partially submerged beast. It took everything in her to swallow her screams and hope for a soft landing. Her stomach dropped somewhere near her knees and the world lit up in silver sparks. Pillars of light twisted around the tube as she careened feet first into oblivion.

Plop! She lay near Omen's knapsack on an oversized cushion in a cavernous void. Elliot and Clair zipped through the tunnel and landed beside her. Thin pillars of light poked from the cavern's ceiling alongside jagged stalactites. The slide had taken them through the boughs of the Grand Menagerie to the underbelly of the entire park. A wide cavern spread before them for as far as the eye could see.

"That would have been fun if I was prepared for it," Elliot said as he struggled to sit upright.

Clair hugged herself tight. "Where are we?"

"Underground," Elliot said while wiping his glasses clean on his sleeve. "In a giant cave."

Brenda pulled the briefcase from around her shoulders, opened a drawer, and pulled out the map. "I didn't think this place was on here." She shined a tiny flashlight over the paper.

"Like the Era Port," Elliot chimed in.

"Something tells me we can take that to the other side of the park." She pointed from a faint line on the map to a row of mine carts waiting on a wooden track. The track wound from the landing deep into the illuminated darkness.

"Doesn't look like we have much of a choice." Elliot's eyes slid from the mine carts to the plastic tube and shrugged. "I was never good at climbing up the slides on the playground."

"What are those lights?" Brenda took a step toward the railing.

"Roots," Clair whispered.

"What do you mean, roots?" Brenda squinted at one of the spiraling lights before pulling her goggles over her eyes.

"It's the root of the spell. The park was designed by an Artist, *an Architect*, to be exact." Clair looked on in awe.

"I thought there were only four orders." Elliot held up a hand and counted on his fingers. "Time Thieves, Shifters, Sages, and Artists."

"There are two kinds of Artists: Writers and Architects." She moved closer to the railings to examine one of the root spells. "Writers draw Marks or write spells and Architects build magical structures like doors, bridges, and buildings. The roots anchor the magic to the world, like a tree to the soil below." Clair waved a hand. "Come on, let's go."

Brenda peered at the pillars of light and climbed into one of the carts with the others. The makeshift coaster maintained a moderate speed as they meandered around jagged rocks and iridescent light. Up close, she spotted letters, numbers, and symbols spiraling in a chaotic rhythm inside the pillars. Every now and then, they'd collide into tiny silver stars only to begin the dance again. After about twenty minutes, they cruised to a stop at the foot of a massive baobab tree climbing skyward from inside the cavern. The glow of the full moon illuminated the branches up high and a moving walkway encircled its trunk, leading back to the surface.

"Looks like we're here," Brenda said as she stepped on another landing.

Exquisite symbols were carved in the walkway's railings. She grazed the metalwork with her palm and a bird with its head turned backward caught her eye.

"Sankofa," Clair murmured. "Go back and fetch it. Always remember the past, where you've come from. It'll help guide you in where you need to go."

One by one, they boarded the moving walkway. Brenda frowned at the heavy nooses hanging from the branches. Two stone walls flanked the tree like an open book. Each wall listed names, too many to count, too many to read. She leaned over the railing to read a plaque nailed to the tree.

"The Honorable Marcus Garvey says, 'A people without the knowledge of their past history, origin, and culture is like a tree without roots.' This tree is in remembrance of our ancestors," she read. "These are our strange fruit. All the men and women and children who've been taken from us by lynch mobs. May they receive the justice they deserve." Tiny sparks appeared over an empty space on one of the walls. In seconds, another name appeared.

Clair pushed a braid behind her ear. "Everything here will show you who we were, who we are, and who we will be. This tree's been covered with Sage spells. *It feels*. It's adding names in real time."

Brenda thought of how Uncle Rufus and even Aunt Squeak would have reacted to the tree. She pictured her uncle combing through a newspaper as he sat in his favorite armchair, his glasses slipping to the tip of his nose. She had no doubt he'd be in awe of this strange and incredible magic just as he was the mysterious birthday gifts and the briefcase that, in many ways, had become a secret weapon since she'd arrived. She clutched it tight. Finally, they reached the surface.

"Does it feel like we're this high up?" Elliot nudged her in the shoulder.

She took a few steps and peered over the edge of the walkway. The tree had been a distraction. A dizzying drop of a few hundred feet stared at her from below.

"Not at all," she said and sucked in the night air.

"This magic stuff is something else." Elliot shivered and shook his head.

A rocky path stretched ahead once they reached the surface. The moon hung high in the sky and a glass needle rose high above their heads like a weapon threatening the midnight sky.

"The Haunted Obelisk," Omen read aloud a cursive script scrawled above the entrance.

"There are two kinds of Time Thieves," Clair began. "Keepers and Gatherers. Ghoul Gatherers collect the souls trapped in limbo. Then, the Keepers store them in Jars on the Shelf of the Damned until they're used for fuel."

Elliot examined the base of the obelisk to its tip, a pyramid shimmering red, black, and green. "How much you wanna bet some of those souls were let loose inside?"

"Wouldn't shock me. Any park that's home to a Grootslang and a Sphinx wouldn't see nothing wrong with a few haints floating around to scare the hell outta folks." Clair took a deep breath. "Remember, the damned can't hurt the living." She waved them inside. "Keep that in mind and you'll be ok."

Brenda removed the goggles from her eyes and filed inside. The heavy glass door shut behind them with an echoing thud.

Inside, the obelisk felt like a museum, stiff and expansive. A long, red carpet spread to the opposite wall. Marble statues loomed above like wardens keeping watch over prisoners on either side. She felt claustrophobic. Thankfully, the glass panes allowed for plenty of light from the stars and moon outside. A glass elevator awaited them. She glanced at Omen. His once confident and steady posture now looked slumped and unsure. As he walked, she caught a glimpse of his neckline. The chain was no longer there. Her heart dropped. The expression he wore was something between sadness and loss. She connected the dots: the mad dash from the cave, the silence inside the carts. She couldn't help but feel responsible. This had all been her idea, her plan.

"Well, let us pray." Clair took a deep breath and stepped inside the elevator.

Brenda followed. Her gaze stuck to a panel of buttons. Some blinked, vibrated, and buzzed. Others looked like they'd been filled with liquid mercury, blocks of ice, or colorful coral from the depths of the sea.

"The elevator's been covered in protective spells. Hang on tight," Clair said and grabbed hold of a bronze railing. She reached around Elliot and pushed one of the buttons.

Brenda gripped the bar in the nick of time. The elevator rose with lightning speed. Before she knew what hit her, they came to a sudden halt. She looked around at the terrified faces as they hovered like an open umbrella caught in a storm. Anxious, she searched for Elliot's eyes. Before she could find them, a disfigured hand crawled across one of the glass walls. Humans half dissolved with limp limbs scratched at the elevator as it drifted along. Her breath hitched inside her throat as a ghoulish figure stared through black sockets, daring her to look before darting in a different direction.

"They're in different stages of decay." Clair placed a palm on the glass. "My guess is they've been captured from different centuries. Some were murderers during the Crusades of Europe. Others took part in the Middle Passage. Others were conquistadors and colonizers."

"How can you tell?" Elliot asked in a hush. He held his breath as the shadows covered the elevator in clumps, like blood clotting a wound.

"Sages know souls. We can feel them." She pointed toward a deformed figure climbing on the ceiling. "He was one of the men who fought Queen Nanny of the maroons. He was found recently. Feels fresh." She turned to another wall where a woman reduced to a head and torso crawled along the glass. "This one was a slaver during the Indian Ocean Slave Trade."

Brenda took a step back. "The Indian Ocean Slave Trade? Never heard of it."

Clair stared into the abyss. "Many haven't. But between 1500 and 1900, the Arabs enslaved East Africans. Shipped them from along the Indian Ocean's coast to North Africa and other parts of the world. These are slavers from Algeria and Libya in 1520." She chuckled darkly and pointed at a few souls whipping around the cube in a feeding frenzy. The grotesque bodies slammed into the glass, only to slide off and dissolve into smoke before reforming again. "Not all of them are from the past. Some are from now and others, the distant future." She closed her eyes and placed an ear to the glass. "Some organized lynch mobs. Some took part in the assassinations of our leaders," her voice cracked. "Of course, they never stood trial. But here—this is where they receive justice. They exist in a limbo of sickness and disease. We are the flesh they'll never feast upon. They live half-lives forever."

Brenda watched the spirits hover in sluggish agony. She could feel the bile coat the back of her throat as one of the ghouls struggled to force its heart inside a rotten chest cavity. The dead muscle hardened first into a tangled fist of dried veins and then crumbled to a pile of ash. The act was a broken record skipping a sick song of repetitive gore. "It's like they're our exhibits." She chewed on her lip. "Our revenge."

Clair shoved an index finger in the direction of a soul that looked more like a man than the others. "Sometimes the souls are collected days after death and burial. This one's been cursed by an echo cast. Echo casts continue on until infinity."

Brenda and Elliot huddled together and watched as a baby with pasty flesh crawled forward, matured from infant to toddler to man, then pulled at its throat until strips of smoke melted inside the darkness like flakes of ember only to begin the cycle again.

"Sweet justice," Elliot muttered under his breath.

Brenda laid a hand on his shoulder as he stood there, still as a stone, eyes trained on the specter in front of them. "Justice," she whispered.

For what felt like a long time, they looked on as death crawled around them. Every now and then a moan would reverberate through the space causing a feeding frenzy as the dead feasted on one another. Then came the silence, like a long and drawn-out death she hoped to never know.

TWENTY-TWO
ERA DIALS

Instead of looking into the eyes of the undead, Clair willed herself to concentrate on warm memories. Thoughts of Big Mama and the good times came flying back—the laughter, the church songs, the food. She breathed in deep, hoping the nostalgia would lift the heavy cloak of death shrouding them on all sides.

"We're almost at the top." Elliot pointed toward the elevator's ceiling.

The figures shrank beneath them and the darkness opened to a night sky peppered with stars. In the distance, the moonlight bathed the Grand Menagerie in a fuzzy white glow.

Clair watched as the elevator slid to a stop. A steel track protruded from the obelisk's pyramidal top, dipped out of sight, looped over the churning river below, and disappeared inside the mouth of a cave. Then, the waterfall slid into view. From this angle, the Soul Shelf glimmered like a gift. They were hundreds of feet above solid ground and with nothing below except a host of damned souls floating in oblivion, fear made her shiver again.

"That might've been the scariest stuff I've ever seen in my life," she muttered.

Omen gave her a sidelong glance. "Be thankful you didn't have to barter with a Grootslang."

There was a coolness in his reply. It felt foreign. He'd been warm since their meeting. What would cause such a shift? And then it hit her, she turned and searched for the tooth dangling from the silver chain. *Nothing.* Its absence was a blow. That wasn't just a chain; it was legacy, a piece of him.

"Omen, I—"

"I knew the risks," he said, waving her off.

"I know that chain meant a lot to your family and to you," she pressed.

"Ain't no use crying over spilled milk," he said, avoiding her eyes.

"I'm sorry," she whispered. The apology felt empty as it left her lips, but there was nothing else she could say to comfort him. No other words mattered. She felt tongue tied as he stalked to the elevator's other side.

The doors opened to reveal a dimly lit room. Numbers and equations glowed on the walls. Beakers filled with colorful liquid boiled, smoked, and whistled in concert over ice blue flames. Steel instruments hummed and whizzed. Numerous Soul Jars zipped along a conveyor belt wrapped around the room's perimeter like an eerie assembly line.

"This is where the souls are synthesized to fuel time travel." Clair walked toward the belt and bent low to inspect one of the Jars.

Meanwhile, Elliot reached in his pocket and held the vial of Jengu tears up to a ray of moonlight knifing through a window. Sparks fizzed and popped on the lip of a beaker as he combined his tonic with the final ingredient, secured it with a cork, and stuffed it inside his satchel. On the other side of the room, Omen opened his knapsack and spread the stones on an empty table carved with ridges and symbols.

"This is the timetable." Clair ran an open palm over the polished wood. "It's where all time-related instruments are assembled. "Back watches, Minute rings, Era Dials—"

"Second Swatches," Brenda cut in.

"How'd you know that?" Clair whirled around to face her.

Brenda shrugged. "Couldn't sleep, so I studied."

"Sapphires, platinum, rubies, diamonds." Clair's eyes sparkled as she counted the gems.

Brenda glanced at the timetable. "Did he get enough?"

"More than enough!"

"How many do we need to make an Era Dial?" Elliot spoke up.

"Three per dial." She pointed to a glass bowl filled with strips of leather. "Once I attach the stones to the leather with a spell, we're all set."

"So that's it?" Brenda crossed her arms over her chest.

Clair rolled an emerald between her thumb and forefinger. "The stones have magical properties. And once the spells and stones collide—" She opened her palms wide, signaling an explosion. "Color holds energy and frequency. Match red leather with ruby. Blue with sapphire. You get the picture."

Brenda took a look at her red leather strip and scanned the table for rubies. Once the Dials had been loosely assembled, Clair snapped her fingers. The stones hovered above their strips, then turned end over end before touching back down. Threads of delicate light covered the stones and leather like an ethereal web. Then came a rumbling that left the Dials engulfed in smoke.

"Now we go to the Era Port?" Brenda asked, breaking the silence.

"Not quite." Clair bit her lip. "Gotta survive the bump first."

TWENTY-THREE

BUMPS AND SCREAMS

Elliot scanned the room before raising a hand in the air. "What's a bump again?"

"Yeah, what is it?" Omen's shoulders slumped. "I can't keep up with all of this."

"It's an invisible interdimensional portal. Think of it as an underground tunnel. It's the gate that leads to an Era Port." Clair grabbed her dial. "Go on, put them on."

Elliot rubbed his thumb over the stone in his Era Dial. It was cool to the touch. "How far is it?"

Clair pointed to a wide vestibule on the opposite side of the room. "Everything's convenient. The lab connects to the bump and the bump to the Era Port."

Blinking red lights on the floor guided their steps to a hollowed-out wall where a red roller coaster car awaited on a shiny track. Bulky apparatuses wrapped in black leather had been attached to each of the seats.

"Are these to keep us in place?" Elliot tugged on the bars.

"Looks like it," Omen chimed in. "Does this thing go upside-down?"

"Upside-down, under a waterfall, and there are three drops of more than fifty feet," Brenda interjected.

Elliot shook his head. "But that kind of technology hasn't—"

"—been invented yet?" Clair cut in. "They're Time Thieves," she said and climbed inside. "They take what's owed to them: resources, technology, or ideas."

"She stole this." Brenda waved a hand in the direction of a blueprint and newspaper clipping framed in a shadowbox above the coaster.

Faint mathematical equations had been written under each loop. Elliot stood on his tiptoes to count the loops and dips in the sketch.

"Looks like she found it in New Jersey. Twenty-first century." Brenda pointed at a caption. "There's a theme park there called Six Flags Great Adventure. The coaster has a ninety degree climb and fall. It's over four hundred feet tall. The largest in the world at the time."

Elliot stared at the blueprint. He had a healthy appreciation for science; he was a chemist, but this— what he was staring at now, was unreal. He sighed.

"Try to relax." Brenda lowered herself in a seat and secured her seatbelt. "It's not an exact replica. It's a source of inspiration. Pull the harness down over your head until it clicks."

Elliot shoved his tortoiseshell frames inside his shirt pocket and squinted at the blurred world around him. With a deep breath, and against his better judgement, he climbed inside the coaster and lowered the harness until it fit snugly over his shoulders. Omen and Clair did the same. Immediately, the coaster rushed forward with a violent jolt. He closed his eyes so tight he could see stars behind his lids. *Our father who art in heaven, hallowed be the name.*

Before he could finish his prayer, they'd burst into the darkness. The sticky summer air smacked him hard as the coaster *click, click, clicked* to a crawl before reaching the top of a monstrous climb.

Elliot clenched his jaws tight as the coaster sped toward the river below. His stomach settled somewhere near the base of his spine. They continued at a staggering speed, this time in a loop, once, twice, three times, before charging toward the river. He gulped and opened his eyes. Between the dizzying loops and raging rapids, he was sure this would be his last day on earth. He dug the pads of his fingers into the leather harness and held on for dear life as they soared along. A spray of cool water splashed his arms and a scream lodged in his throat like a glob of phlegm. He peered over the side as the coaster climbed again, this time in a swirling spiral that left him punch-drunk.

"Almost there! Hold on!" Clair yelled over the noise.

The coaster slowed to a crawl and *click, click, clicked* again before entering the mouth of a cave.

"Jesus!" Brenda screeched.

Elliot bit his lower lip as they slipped inside the inky darkness. Invisible daggers stabbed at his ear drums and his breath was snatched from his lungs. Now, they floated along in a cocoon of lavender light. Dizzy and disoriented, he breathed in deep. The *click click click* became a low drone and the coaster glided to a stop. He fumbled with his glasses and blinked for the first time in more than a minute. There was no way they were still in Hampton, Virginia. In fact, there was no way they were in 1920 at all.

PART THREE: FORWARD,
THEN BACK AGAIN

TWENTY-FOUR

THE ERA PORT

After a long exhale, Brenda lifted her harness and peered over the side of the car. Nothing looked familiar. The coaster sat up high on a platform while people, shops, and a set of odd-looking trains darted in and out of tunnels below. Everything bustled, spiraled, and climbed, from bannisters, staircases, and escalators to the symbols plastering the walls.

"Umm." Elliot cleared his throat and pointed to her hand gripping his thigh.

"Sorry." Brenda climbed from the coaster and extended her hand to help him out of the car.

"Look!" Clair pointed at the ceiling. High above their heads, a rotating boulder hung on a thin, silver strand. "It's the Clock of Thieves." Instead of numbers, glyphs and symbols covered its surface. "The symbols are seconds, days, months, centuries, and even millennia."

Brenda squinted at the stones gleaming on the clock's surface. "Are those—"

"Grootstones," Omen said darkly. "Here, take this. Didn't get a chance to use it." He opened his palm to reveal the jeweled pen Brenda had given him before they ventured inside the Grand Menagerie.

Without a word, she offered him a solemn look and zipped it inside a compartment in her briefcase. Her attention swung back to the boulder. "So, this is an Era Port, huh?"

"Yep! Always wanted to see one. Didn't think I would." Clair turned to Elliot. "Meet you down at the trains in thirty minutes?" She wordlessly motioned toward Omen, who'd wandered off with his back to the group.

"You got it." Elliot gave the thumbs up sign before rushing to Omen's side.

"Come on, let's go. We don't have a lot of time." She took Brenda by the hand and headed toward a flight of stairs.

The Era Port was ten times larger than Brenda imagined. It was both a train station and a marketplace. Women sold fresh fruit and vegetables from wooden carts. A street magician levitated a deck of playing cards in front of a group of wide-eyed children. A storefront overflowed with odd-looking newspapers and blinking screens. Stands sold soft pretzels, popcorn, and drinks.

"Come on," Clair shouted over her shoulder.

Brenda hurried to keep pace through the thick crowd. *Used Era Dials (Only a Nickel and Up). Timeless Hats and Head Gear. The Shoes Make the Man.* The Era Port reminded her of Cabbage Row all over again, but with more mystique.

Finally, Clair skidded to a halt. *The Journeyman Times.* A neon sign blinked above the store's entrance. "Let's check this place out."

Inside, customers picked through merchandise and waited in a line to purchase items. A single clerk smiled behind a counter. Brenda turned in a circle. She'd never seen so many newspapers and magazines in one place at one time. They were everywhere. On racks. In bins. On shelves. In stacks. Flashing by-lines floated across screens on small, handheld machines.

"It's past, present, and future news!" Clair shrieked. "We can peek into what's going to happen in ten or twenty years and even a century from now."

"But—"

Clair held up an index finger. "Remember—"

"Right. They're Time Thieves. Gotta remember that." Brenda rolled her eyes.

Clair turned one of the handheld machines over in her palm. "It's called a tablet. The letters, numbers, and pictures are created with signals sent through invisible waves. It's digital." She ran her finger over the screen. It shifted gently with each touch. "This is how we'll get our information next century."

"All of it?" Brenda raised an eyebrow. "Doesn't sound reliable."

Clair wrinkled her nose. "I hope not all of it. I still like the feel of a good newspaper. But judging from what I see, a whole lot of it will be digital." She gazed at the shelves and bins around the room filled with older newspapers.

Brenda skimmed a headline on the screen. *Divided U.S. Gives Obama More Time. November 7, 2012.* "Wait! Go back."

Clair stopped and tapped the screen. She put a hand over her mouth.

"Barack Obama?" Brenda frowned at the picture of a man with slightly graying hair. He was youngish and distinguished looking. But that wasn't what stood out to her the most.

"He's Colored!" the girls whispered in unison.

Brenda scanned the article's opening paragraph. Barack Obama had won his second term as president of the United States and, according to the story, he was popular among the people.

"Wow, a Colored president. I never would have thought." Clair covered her mouth in shock.

Brenda lifted the tablet from Clair's trembling hands and continued to read. "Yeah, well the headline still says the country is divided. That's a clue it still ain't all rainbows and blue skies in 2012." She returned the device to her outstretched hand. "Do you think Omen's okay?"

Clair took a deep breath. "No. I think he will be, but he isn't right now."

"Yeah, I don't wanna know what went on in that cave."

"Had to have been serious. His life was threatened. It's the only way he would've given up that chain." Clair bit her lip. "Didn't you give him something to barter with?"

"I did. Not sure why he didn't use it."

"Take a look at this. *Baltimore Trial Leaves Unanswered Question: What Happened to Freddie Gray? The New York Times. December 14, 2015.* I think you're right. Not a lot changes." Clair scrolled to the next article.

"2015. Ninety-five years in the future and still." Brenda shook her head. "I want to check out those newspapers over there."

Clair nodded; face buried in the screen. "Ok. I'll be right here."

Brenda let out a deep sigh and walked toward one of the walls. It didn't surprise her that time would prove to be stubborn, yet still she'd felt a jolt of disappointment. Ninety-five years was a long time to see such little progress. And a Negro president didn't seem to mean much at all. She wandered down another aisle of tablets. The glow of the screens pulled her into a trace. So much information at your fingertips. So much power. She bit her bottom lip. *Maybe.* Her eyes darted around the store. Everyone, including Clair and the clerk, were occupied. *Why not? No one would miss it.* Quickly, she pulled her briefcase, now the size of a wallet, from her pocket and pushed a button. It expanded in her arms. In a blink, she swiped one of the tablets from its display and shifted the briefcase so it covered her middle. With the press of another button, one of the compartments opened with a subtle click. She slipped the tablet inside before making her way toward a rack outside the entrance. The headline on the front of a newspaper caught her eye. She reached for it on a rotating rack. *Nine Killed in Shooting at Black Church in Charleston, SC. The New York Times. June 17, 2015.*

"Clair, you've got to see—"

"Minutes, seconds, hours for sale. Days, weeks, years if you dare…"

A voice floated above the din.

"Minutes, seconds, hours for sale. Days, weeks, years if you dare…"

Curiosity piqued, she replaced the paper on the rack and followed the voice until she came to a booth. The woman inside had a bald head and a smile she'd never, ever forget.

TWENTY-FIVE

MAMA JUJU'S READING RACKET

The woman's heavily bangled arms rested on a ledge. She had dark eyes surrounded by faint halos of blue. Wrinkled copper skin hung from her jowls as her lips upturned into a smile.

"Welcome to Mama Juju's Reading Racket. How about an hour of time for you?"

Brenda frowned. "An hour?"

The woman leaned forward. "Or a day or a minute or a second I reckon."

Her Aunt Squeak had a saying when too much was going on. She called it "busy." Mama Juju's booth was busier than anything she'd ever seen. Mirrors dangled and danced. Herbs and mangled roots tied together with string hung on the walls. A bunch of bracelets drooped from a hook. Rings with glowing stones and symbols poked from a velvet case. She sniffed the air: frankincense, sage, peppermint oil. The scent reminded her of Squeak's herbal closet back home in Philly and Clair's tent in Charleston.

"How do I win an hour?" Brenda's gaze shifted from the herbs to Mama Juju.

The old woman pointed to a deck of circular cards. "We play a game." Her crooked smile faded. "I read you with cards. I ask a question. If true, you give me time. If untrue, I give you time."

"Time?"

"If I win, you lose minutes, hours, days, months, years from your life. You win, you take the same from me. It is an exchange and time is the reward."

Aunt Squeak's stories of boo daddies, witch doctors, and haints flooded her thoughts. Yet somehow, she wasn't afraid. Something in her gut told her she could gamble and win. "Can we start with seconds?"

Mama Juju smiled through a set of perfect teeth-stained purple on account of her lipstick. She pointed at the four-card spread. "Choose one."

Brenda tapped one of the cards. A soothing vibration reverberated from her fingertip to her toes. She snatched her hand back in surprise.

The woman grinned before flipping it over. A symbol as blue and clear as the ocean shimmered on the face of the card. "Is your birthday in July?"

Brenda slowly shook her head no.

The old woman grunted. "Fine. Thirty seconds to you."

Brenda rubbed her hands together and chose another card.

The woman bit her lip. "Wager?"

She thought for a moment. Though she hadn't come across any of this in her readings, something told her what she was doing would probably be frowned upon in the Taint world. *Play it cool, but not too cool.* "Two minutes." She pointed at a second card painted green. It reverberated a steady pulse, like a heartbeat. Like life itself.

Mama Juju gnashed her teeth together and flipped it over. "Does your aunt have a belief in sorcery and hoodoo?"

"Yes."

Mama Juju clapped her wrinkled hands together, her bangled wrists clattering like miniature cymbals. "Two cards left. Higher wager?"

Brenda rubbed her chin. "How high?"

"An hour? If you dare?"

Her body tensed. *The woman had been wrong before. Perhaps she could win?* Something inside her told her to finish. It would mean something in the end. "An hour." She tapped another card, scarlet red, screaming and sharp to the touch. She recoiled as if she'd been pricked by a razor blade and glanced at her index finger, half-expecting blood.

Mama Juju cleared her throat. "Your uncle died last year. Was he your mentor?"

Brenda stared at her shoes. "Yes," she mumbled.

The woman formed a tent with her fingers. "One day plus all you've lost."

"Fine," Brenda said in defiance. She tapped the last card. This one was white. It left her bone cold and chilled on the inside.

Mama Juju's blue-black eyes darted between Brenda and the card before she finally spoke. "Are you an Artist? Fifth generation?"

Brenda slowly shook her head. "No."

"Are you sure, young lady? The penalty for lying in this instance is severe." Her eyes flashed in anger.

"I'm not lying." Brenda took a step backward.

"Alright. One day plus all you've lost." She turned toward the items in her booth. "Minute rings or Second Swatches?"

It didn't take long to think it over. She needed something small. Something that wouldn't take up too much space. Something she could share. "Both."

Mama Juju pulled out two rings and two bracelets. After cracking her knuckles, she held her palms over the jewelry and murmured under her breath. Brenda watched in silence as the stones pulsed. It was over in less than a minute. If she wasn't mistaken, the woman looked older after she'd cast the spell. There was something about her eyes, the blue crescent moons sparkled a bit brighter and a shadow darkened beneath her lower lids.

She pushed the two rings forward for Brenda to see. "Minute rings. Twelve hours on each," she said as she placed the rings in a small, draw-string bag. "And these are Second Swatches. Thirty-one minutes, fifteen seconds on each." The process reminded her of a teller organizing bills at a bank.

"Thank you." Brenda slid the draw-string bag inside her briefcase.

The woman peered at her over her nose. "You are an Artist, child. I know one when I see one."

"There you are!" Clair grabbed her hand.

"I was—"

"Never mind that now," Clair said as she pulled her through the crowd. "Everyone's been looking for you!"

Brenda struggled to keep up with Clair's long strides as she headed toward a packed escalator. As they descended, she squinted at the glowing tracks below. While the steel tracks she'd seen at home ran horizontally or vertically, the tracks in the Era Port looped in circles, funnels, and curlicues. A long, silver train pulled into the station.

"It looks like something from the future."

"It *is* from the future. It's next century technology," Clair replied.

Now that they'd reached the bottom of the platform, they could fully examine the trains. Wide windows on the sides of each car revealed riders seated and standing. A motherboard of blinking buttons lit up the train's walls. They all stood gawking.

"I've never seen anything like this," Elliot gasped.

"I've never been on a train before." Omen shrugged.

"Everything I thought it'd be." Clair pointed. "Look at the tracks. They're bits of time layered with incantations."

Brenda squinted at the neon maze tacked to the ground below the platform. Warning signs had been posted along the multicolored tracks. Her line of vision followed the length of the corridor to their exits labeled: *Now, Next,* and *Then.*

"Any destination can be sorted into these three categories. And inside those tunnels," Clair continued, "—are doors. Each door can take you anywhere at any time; they're interdimensional." She pointed to three turnstiles up ahead, each marked with signs for the appropriate trains: *Now, Next, and Then.*

Omen stroked his chin. "So, I can go back in time, to any place, down to the minute?"

Clair clasped her hands together. "Let's say you wanted to visit 3200 BC Alexandria, Egypt May 2nd, 2:14 pm." She pointed to Omen's Era Dial. "That allows you to take the Then tunnel to the 3200 BC door."

Brenda flexed her wrist, examining her Dial carefully. "Let's take a look at the book." The scholars hurried off to a bench near a corner and huddled in a circle. Brenda opened her briefcase and removed a few pages from a pocket.

"It all starts with the Master Dial." Clair read. "There are 24 Master Dials in the world. Master Dials were created during a ritual by the first Time Thieves thousands of years ago." She pointed to their wrists. "Era Dials aren't from the original Master Dials, but the sorcery in the stones and the incantation makes them decent knock offs."

Elliot pushed his tortoise shell frames up the bridge of his nose. "Who were the first Time Thieves? Where were they from?"

"It says here they were from Mali, West Africa. They're descendants of the Dogon. Their ancestors studied the stars and constellations. They tried to time travel back then and some were successful in bringing back knowledge from the future to use in their present." She scanned another page. "The boulders were first decorated by the best village artisans, then sealed with spells and prayers. Then, twenty-four female Time Thieves were selected from different Dogon families. The gift is passed down from mothers to their daughters and sons. Time Zones were created from the Master Dials and to this day, one descendent from each family keeps the time in each zone."

"Dr. Djinn is the keeper of time for North America's east coast, isn't she?" Brenda folded her arms across her chest.

"All signs point to yes," Clair replied.

"Excuse me, may I have a word."

Brenda turned to meet a pair of unfamiliar eyes. Two men in official looking suits with infinity symbols etched on each shoulder had them pinned in a corner. The words, *Time Police*, had been sewn on their breast pockets in bold, yellow letters. Her heart pounded in her chest. Between the Time Cops stood another man she'd vaguely recognized. It was the cashier from *The Journeyman Times*.

"We have reason to believe you've stolen something from one of our stores. Please empty the contents of your briefcase onto the bench," the officer said.

Brenda locked eyes with Clair, Omen, and Elliot before pushing one of the briefcase drawers closed. She lifted the case from the bench and then, with the press of a button, it shrunk in size. Before the police could recover, she'd turned on her heels and fled toward the turnstiles. Her breath caught in her throat as she pushed through the crowd. Up ahead, a scanner flashed red as eager travelers placed their wrists over a pane of glass and slipped through the turnstile. She looked over her shoulder to find Elliot's wide-eyed stare with Omen and Clair not far behind. By now, another train had arrived, prompting more travelers to gather in knots. Heart slamming against her chest, she lay her wrist over the scanner. A red light zipped over the Era Dial and *badeep!* she hurried through. The wide steel doors slid open on the newly arrived train and they rushed inside, weaving through a throng of passengers to the last car. Brenda snuck a peek through the windows as the doors closed with a snap. They'd escaped. She leaned against the wall, panting.

"This is your *Next Train*. I repeat, this is the *Next Train*. Not the *Now Train* and not the *Then Train*. If you're looking for the *Now Train* or the *Then Train*, please disembark, climb the stairs to your right and follow the signage. Again, this is the *Next Train* serving the next one hundred years with station stops in 1925, 1945, 1965, 1985, 2005, 2015, and finally 2020. Please choose your destination and hold on to a handrail as we will be traveling at high speeds to get you to *the Next* right now," blared a voice over the loudspeaker.

"No, no, no!" Clair screeched. We're supposed to be taking a *Then* Train!" She rushed toward the wall.

Circles of light indicating the names of cities from here to the end of the earth glowed in alphabetical order.

"Maybe we can get off—" Omen began as the train cruised away from the station.

Clair snapped her fingers and pointed at Brenda. "Pick a year, hurry!"

"Umm, 2015," she stammered as the last headline and year she'd read popped in her head.

"Charleston. Charleston, SC." Clair scanned the words on the wall and selected the blinking red button next to Charleston, SC. Instantly, it turned green. "Hold on."

Brenda grabbed a pole and hung on for dear life. But instead of the rush of speed she'd expected, time slowed to a crawl. As the train coasted toward the *Next* corridor, the lights dimmed. A brass grate between the car and the tunnel slowly rose.

"Hold on to your hats ladies and gentlemen."

The lull before the forward motion pulled her into a false sense of security. Then, her heart climbed inside her throat and she gripped the rail with a sweaty palm. In front of her, Clair and Omen flattened themselves against one of the car's oversized windows. Meanwhile, Elliot struggled to maintain his grip on an empty seat.

Time was flying—literally. She braced herself under the force of tremendous speed.

"Charleston, South Carolina. June 17, 2015."

The train slowed to a stop and Brenda tightened her grip. Clair pulled Omen closer. His cheeks were puffed up as if he was suppressing the urge to vomit. Elliot pressed himself against the back of the seat.

"Charleston, South Carolina *Next*. You have arrived in Charleston, South Carolina June 17, 2015 where the time is 9:00 pm. Enjoy your evening and thank you for riding with us. And remember, keep the pace!"

TWENTY-SIX
BIBLE STUDY

"What did you take?" Clair whirled around to face Brenda on a darkened platform.

"I— didn't—" she stammered, backing into a corner.

"Don't lie. Ain't no reason to lie," Omen seethed. "Just tell us what you took."

"Come on, Brenda." Elliot crossed his arms over his chest.

Brenda kicked a stone on the ground, avoiding their stares. "A tablet," she whispered.

"I told you not to take nothing. I told you!" Clair balled her hands into fists and groaned.

"What's a tablet?" Elliot cleaned his glasses with a cloth. "And why would you take it?"

"It's like an electronic machine. You hold it in your hands. It gives you information. We were looking at the news—" Clair spat in frustration. Omen and Elliot looked at each other in confusion.

"Never mind. Doesn't matter." She threw her hands up. "A *Then Train* arrives in twenty minutes. I guess we—" She looked around the empty tunnel, flustered. "We can walk until then. I need to figure out what's next."

"I'm sorry," Brenda said in a small voice.

Omen shook his head and Elliot sneered in disappointment before following Clair's lead. Brenda lagged behind.

Charleston, 2015 didn't look anything like Clair remembered. The city's quaint charm had been replaced with the hustle and bustle of crowds, traffic lights, and sleek-looking vehicles. The only things she found familiar were the buildings shining in their pastel beauty and of course, the heat. There was no escaping that, no matter the year. Less than twenty-four hours earlier they'd agreed traveling to the past would be the best option. That way, they could use Sheriff Dodge as a guinea pig, slip him Elliot's tonic, and hope for the best. Now, here they were, ninety-five years in the future and in a panic.

"Wow. So, this is what 2015 looks like, huh?" Elliot tugged at the hairs on his chin.

"Wait!" Clair opened her arms wide, impeding their progress. "This is 2015. We're 95 years in the future."

"Um, we've discussed this—" Elliot cut in, impatient.

She rolled her eyes. "Look at us! She pointed at her clothes before gesturing at Omen and Brenda. "We don't exactly fit in!"

Elliot took a look at his clothing. "Guess you're right."

"Let me work a Sage spell so we don't look so suspicious." She stole a glance at a group of teens out for a stroll and closed her eyes, visualizing more era-appropriate clothing for them all. In an instant, Brenda was wearing a knee-length skirt and graphic tee, Elliot and Omen were dressed in khaki shorts and she had on a yellow sundress that flattered her curves. She let out an uneasy breath and surveyed the group. "Better. Let's go."

Everything felt…faster. Cars zoomed down the road. People hurried from here to there. The pounding bass of music blasting from passing car speakers penetrated the humid air like a knife through a stick of butter. Brenda stood slack jawed while Omen strolled toward an expensive looking parked car. The candy apple red vehicle shimmered under the streetlights. Clair stood back to look at the car's hood. The letters BMW were wrapped around a black and white checkered symbol. She whistled to herself.

"Now what?" Omen turned after examining the hubcaps and wheels. "It's a little after 9 pm."

Clair exhaled. "Church."

"Church?" Elliot adjusted his satchel on his shoulder.

Clair shook her head. Something told her visiting her family's church was the right thing to do. If nothing else, she wanted to look at the pew her grandmother used to sit in every Sunday before she passed away. She could see the woman rocking with her eyes closed as she sang a hymn with the rest of the congregation. "Yup. It's the only thing that'll calm me down." She cut her eyes at Brenda. "Follow me."

Charleston nightlife was alive and buzzing even on a weekday. Car horns blared and loud music drifted from open windows as traffic sped by. Still seeing red, she could barely keep her focus as she led the small group down the block. Stately residences were framed by palm trees. Store fronts with wide windows showcased everything from clothing and shoes to seafood restaurants. She breathed in deep. What she wouldn't give for some of Big Mama's seafood stew right now.

"Is that it?" Elliot pointed down the block.

Clair turned away from one of the buildings to
see a familiar structure. Stretched before them was a
gothic church made of white-washed brick. Its steeple
sliced the sky like a dagger in the night.

"Big Ma used to drag me here every Sunday."

"Every Sunday?" Omen asked as he took in the
church's size.

"Yep, Denmark Vesey himself was a founder."

"Wait...*the* Denmark Vesey?" Elliot stopped in
his tracks.

"Yup, *the* Denmark Vesey. You know he was a
Time Thief, right?" Clair headed up the church stairs.

Elliot shook his head. "I didn't."

"Most don't. It was best no one knew. Would've
made him even more of a target." She motioned for them
to follow.

The sanctuary hadn't changed much since she'd
last seen it. Gleaming wooden pews and tall stained-
glass windows made the church feel like a castle. Clair
ran a palm over the soft, red cushions in one of the pews.
Fancy. All was quiet except for the murmuring of a
preacher near the pulpit. She watched as a group of pa-
rishioners shook their heads in unison. She closed her
eyes as the memories flooded back. A rocking chair in
the corner. A heavy pot-bellied stove. The bubbling of a
shrimp boil competing with the summer heat. She
hugged herself tight. Big Mama never missed a Bible
study and the magic never stopped her from believing in
Jesus. In her mind's eye, she pictured her seated in a
pew, pointing to the heavens above. A hand on her
shoulder interrupted her reverie.

"Psst! What's that guy doing?" Omen gestured
toward a center pew.

Clair, Brenda, and Elliot turned in time to see a
youngish, White man dressed in a gray sweatshirt. He

blew a few strands of sandy blonde hair from his eyes and fiddled with something bulky on his lap. The hairs stood up on her arms as she spotted the barrel of a gun sandwiched between his thigh and a hymnal. Then came a ringing in her ears that made her double over in pain. Something was wrong, very, very wrong.

Consecutive pops rang out in eerie succession. Then came the muffled screams and shouts. She bit her lip as a scorching pain shot through her body. Then came two more consecutive pops. Something burned. It was as if she'd been lit on fire. Then came the blood bright red and dripping down her blouse. The sage spells couldn't come fast enough. She murmured a healing chant under her breath as her body fell limp. The room was spinning, fast. Everything left her, the room, the words, and all of her senses.

TWENTY-SEVEN

FUTURE WOUNDS

Omen half ran, half walked back to the station carrying Clair in his arms. By now, the block was crawling with the chaos of a dozen police cars and curious crowds near the church. The entrance to the station was easy to find. Elliot and Brenda hurried alongside Omen as he carried Clair's bleeding body down a narrow stairwell to the next *Then Train*. It arrived just in time. These were the trains he was accustomed to, bulky, old-fashioned, and belching black smoke in the air. Together, they rushed toward a wide seat in the back. Carefully, he lay Clair down on a seat and applied pressure to the gaping wound in her abdomen.

"What just happened?" Omen massaged his temples with his index fingers.

"Gunshots, screams, blood." Elliot bent over, attempting to catch his breath. "He shot those people. He shot them while they prayed."

Omen pushed a strand of hair from Clair's eyes. "I froze. I panicked." He looked down at his palm, now covered in her blood.

Elliot patted him on the back. "It's not your fault."

"I come from strongmen. It's what I am. I'm strong." His lip quivered. "I'm supposed to be able to take that bastard. I'm supposed to dive in front of her." He stroked Clair's hair. "I'm supposed to take that bullet...and I didn't. I didn't do any of it. I didn't protect her. I didn't stop that cracker. I didn't do shit!" He clawed at his neck, naked without the chain. "I lost the tooth. My granddaddy's tooth! I lost it. I'm not strong. I'm nothing. I'm not strong," he croaked.

"Move out of the way," a voice boomed from inside the train.

Omen looked up to see Professor Blue rushing down the aisle accompanied by a boy not much older than him. The stranger immediately fixated on Clair bleeding on the bench. He knelt down, pushing Omen to the side.

"Clair. Can you hear me?" The stranger said in a gruff voice. "Please. Say you can hear me!" His gaze shifted to her wound, now uncovered and pooling with blood. "What happened? What did you do?" He whirled around to face Omen, his face morphing into something large and monstrous. Flames of orange fire formed in the boy's eyes and his frame bulked up to twice its size. Confused, emotionally taxed, and exhausted, Omen balled his hands into fists and prepared for a fight.

The first jab came quickly, but Omen was ready and covered his eyes. After years of training, he'd become adept at predicting the moves of his adversaries, no matter how large. He responded with a swift right hook that connected with the stranger's jaw. Surprised by Omen's strength and skill, the stranger took a step back and squared up. Before Omen could stand and get his footing on the moving train, he landed a punch to his gut. Omen recovered and launched into a flurry of punches to his chest. Then, everything went still. His limbs became too heavy to lift and an unseen force guided the two fighters to seats on opposite sides of the train.

"We don't have time for this!" Professor Blue growled at Omen. "And Lonnie, this isn't why you're here!" The Professor tightened the reins on his spell before releasing them both. Omen rubbed his abdomen, still breathing hard from the rush of adrenaline. Meanwhile, the boy shifted back to his original size.

Omen sputtered. "I—"

Professor Blue held up one of his palms. "Save it." His coal black eyes roved over Clair's bleeding body. Immediately, he grabbed a vial from his coat's inside pocket, uncorked it, and poured a few drops on the injured area. He closed his eyes and muttered an incantation. Omen and the stranger scrambled to Clair's side as the wound appeared to shrink. The stranger laid a palm on her forehead.

"Will she be okay?" Omen said with his head bowed.

"Looks like she's stable," the stranger replied.

"I didn't ask you," Omen seethed.

"That spell was mild compared to what I can do to bind both of you if you can't control yourselves," Professor Blue scowled. He placed a palm over Clair's wound and waved his free hand. A swatch of lattice appeared, thin as a spider's web. "You went to 2015?" he asked before shifting Clair's shirt to one side. Omen watched as he lifted the lattice and applied it to the wound, like a bandage.

Elliot rubbed his temples. "Yes sir."

Professor Blue grunted. "And you saw the church massacre?"

Elliot removed his glasses, fresh tears streaming from his eyes.

"Almost a hundred years in the future and we're still dealing with this," the stranger said and rammed his fist into his open palm.

"This is Lonnie," Professor Blue said stiffly. "He's a friend of Clair's from Charleston. The minute the authorities at the Era Port alerted me of your presence, I traced his whereabouts. The homing spell let me know she'd been shot. I thought it would be best to contact someone who knows her well." His eyes shifted toward Omen. "Lonnie is her next of kin."

Omen's shoulders slumped. The guy knew her. He was her friend. No wonder he was angry. He had every right.

Professor Blue rose from his kneeling position and turned toward the group. "What you did was unauthorized." His voice softened. "What were you thinking?"

"We were thinking we could help." Elliot held his head in his hands.

"Help?" Professor Blue raised an eyebrow. "Help with what?"

"The movie, the policemen, Elliot's cure," Brenda rambled. "It was my fault. I was the one who came up with the plan. There has to be a way to undo this."

"Undo?" the Professor scoffed. "There is no undo."

Omen rubbed the place where his chain should have been. "What?"

"There is no undo and now we've got other things to consider." He glanced at Clair.

"How long do you think that spell will hold?" Lonnie spoke up.

"For as long as we need it. It's sealed with a powerful incantation."

Omen grimaced as Lonnie bent over and kissed Clair on her forehead, now slick with sweat. Avoiding the boy's eyes, he fixated on one of the poles near the front of the train. It was hard to believe that the night before they'd been talking under the moonlight, planning the next day. It was a stupid plan. He rubbed his neck and cursed under his breath. All of this was stupid. None of it should have happened. None of it.

"You must answer for your crimes. You've broken one of our conjuring laws," Professor Blue said in a low whisper.

Elliot slumped in his seat.

"None of you are Time Thieves. It is illegal to travel without the proper permission. But first things first, we tend to Clair."

Omen scooted against the wall of the train, head spinning. Monsters, spells, trips to the far future, this hadn't been what he'd imagined when he'd won the Mighty Biceps Competition weeks ago. And now, Clair was in danger. She'd been shot nearly one hundred years in the future. What were the repercussions if she didn't pull through? He shook the thoughts from his head. He couldn't imagine something like that happening. She would make it. She had to. He willed himself to focus on his surroundings. The *Then Train* couldn't have been more different than the *Next Train* they'd ridden an hour earlier. Instead of the sleek and sterilized look of the future, this train possessed the old-world-style of a nation undergoing expansion. A red velvet carpet stretched down the center aisle, separating polished wooden benches. Each seat had been covered with elegant green pillows with tassels attached to golden poles. They were moving slower as well. He glanced at the armrest and spotted numbers engraved in gold. Elliot leaned over to get a better look. "Another puzzle, huh?"

"Coordinates," the Professor said an cleared his throat. "It's where we plug in our destination. Jamaica is located at latitude 18.109581 and longitude -77.2975082. We're traveling to the 18th century. 1729."

"1729?" Everyone but Lonnie looked at the Professor with questioning eyes. "Why are we going to 1729?"

He leaned forward. "She needs a healer. The gunshot wound is the least of our worries. It's been inflicted in the future, a future where she doesn't exist."

"I don't understand." Omen leaned forward.

Professor Blue grunted. "Our place is always in the present. That's why Time Thieves must be extra careful when Traveling. Injuries jeopardize our descendants. It disrupts the Time Continuum."

Omen chewed on his bottom lip. "So, if she dies—"

"Her descendants are never born," Lonnie cut in.

"Yes. It's a ripple effect." Professor Blue sighed. "But my countrywoman is one of the best. If anyone can help, it's her." He looked at Omen with serious eyes. "Ever heard of Queen Nanny?"

He shifted in his seat. "Yes, sir. Baba Ali mentioned her on our airship tour. She has her own sculpture at the park."

Professor Blue stared out of the train's windows. "Dr. Djinn and I agreed that Queen Nanny's name should ring out far beyond Jamaica."

Omen drummed his fingers on the arm rest. He'd spent his days besting the Armwoods across town. The only history he knew was what had been passed down from his Seminole ancestors. Expecting anything from a seventeen-year-old who'd never even left the state of Florida until a few days ago was a tall order. "What was she queen of?"

Professor Blue used his index finger to flick the numbers up and down until he settled on the correct combination. "I think it's better if you see for yourself."

"She was Queen of the maroons," Brenda replied. "She beat back the British and established a safe haven for slaves in the mountains of Jamaica."

Professor Blue's eyes sparkled as he reached into his pocket and pulled out four pistols. He handed them out. "It's 1729. Many who look like us are still in chains. You may need this if you see something fishy. Know how to use 'em?"

Omen scoffed as he handled the barrel and examined the chamber. Sure enough, he found a slug. "Do gators like swamps?" he said as he placed the heat in the small of his back. "As sure as I love my mama, I know how to handle a pistol."

Lonnie rolled his eyes. "Better question to ask is which kind is my favorite." He rolled the pistol over in his palm, inspecting it like a doctor would a newborn.

They turned to Elliot and Brenda. Elliot grazed the barrel with his thumb. "Sure do. Got firsthand experience."

Brenda took a closer look at the pistol's shiny exterior before tucking it inside her sock.

"Hopefully, we won't have to use them." The Professor shoved his own revolver in a harness.

The train's loudspeaker crackled to life. *1729. We are now arriving at 1729.*

The Professor strode toward the doors, grasping the poles to steady himself on the moving train.

Omen gently lifted Clair's body with Lonnie's assistance. The look of peace and serenity on her face assuaged some of his guilt. He thought back to their talk the night before. If she didn't pull through, he wouldn't be able to forgive himself.

"Last time I took this train, they let me off on the edge of a cliff," Professor Blue smirked as he glanced at his pocket watch.

Omen and the others exchanged worried looks.

"Don't worry, the conductor today is a yardie. I slipped him a little something extra. I think he'll get us closer to the camp than the cliffs. Come." He motioned toward the door as the train slowed to a stop. With a firm pull, he hoisted open the door and hopped from the train. Brenda and Elliot followed, holding their arms out to secure Clair's dangling frame as Omen and Lonnie descended.

Trees dotted the sky for as far as he could see. In the distance, he could hear the calming sound of water crashing against the rocks below. He sniffed the heavy Caribbean air. Something was burning. A fire perhaps? He turned back to the train. *Nothing.* The massive metal dragon belching smoke had been suddenly replaced with a darkening sky as the sun dropped below the hills. Thick shrubs and bushes surrounded them on all sides.

"Where's the—" Omen began.

Professor Blue held a finger to his lips. "All our trains are covered in cloaking spells."

Omen and Lonnie secured Clair between them and took a few steps forward. He flinched at a rustle of leaves. As quick as he was, the maroons were quicker. In seconds, they were surrounded. Omen inhaled, shoulder to shoulder with Brenda and Elliot. At least a dozen pairs of eyes stared at them. Strips of cloth covered their mouths and noses. One of the men stepped forward, yanked away his disguise and chuckled.

"Wah Gwaan! Never can be too careful," the man said in a Caribbean drawl. The two men embraced before the leader of the guerrilla group gestured for his men to lower their weapons. His eyes swung to Clair's limp body in Omen's arms. "Who's this?"

"Our scholars and a friend from 1920 America. One's been injured." The Professor motioned for them to step forward. "Lonnie, Omen, Brenda, Elliot, and the girl who's been shot is named Clair. Two Taints, three

Aints." The Professor looked in the man's direction. "This is Captain Quao, Queen Nanny's brother."

The Captain circled them like a lion would his prey. Omen squared his shoulders and braced himself for a fight. He'd been taught to always be ready. It was the way of the Crows.

Captain Quao chuckled at Omen's response. "Dis one here think he big man, big man!"

Professor Blue put a hand on the Captain's shoulder. "We're here to help them, show them the way, not break them, Quao."

Quao grunted and turned toward the trees. "This way."

They marched about a quarter of a mile from where they'd disembarked from the now vanished, *Then Train*. The company moved in silence and under the cover of dusk and trees covered in flowers and vines. Every now and then, Omen stopped to shift Clair from one of his broad shoulders to the other. As the sky darkened, the Jamaican mountains looked like a tangle of shadows and tall grass.

"You having trouble seeing?" Elliot asked as they crept along.

"Sure am," Omen huffed.

Under the shadow of a hill, the clump of trees thinned to reveal a small village. Shacks with thatched roofs surrounded tents and clusters of rocks. Captain Quao leaned into the Professor's shoulder and spoke. Professor Blue motioned toward Omen and Lonnie. "Come, let's get her inside." He pointed to a dimly lit shack ahead.

Omen and Lonnie followed with Elliot and Brenda trailing close behind. A woman in white rushed toward them.

"Ay! Lay her here," she hissed.

Omen and Lonnie took great care to lie Clair on a cot near a wall.

Professor Blue greeted the woman in white with a deep bow. "She's been hurt."

Nanny looked at him with stern eyes. "Where was she?"

He looked away as if embarrassed. "2015."

Queen Nanny stared at him with pleading eyes. "Two centuries? You want me to heal two centuries?" she replied in the same thick Caribbean accent.

"Please, anything you can do." Omen hadn't planned on saying anything, but his lips were moving anyway.

The old woman shook her head. "I'd need time. A few hours at least."

Omen frowned and looked at the Professor. "What does she mean? Why wouldn't we have time?"

"She needs hours. She needs time. Extra time." He glanced at Omen. "We don't have it to give Nanny. What can you do?"

"Nothing without time, Blue. I'm sorry." She bent over Clair's body and gently peeled back the bandage.

"I have time." Brenda stepped forward with a shaky voice.

Omen and the others turned to face Brenda as she stepped forward from the shadows.

"You don't understand, Brenda. Time is not something you may simply give—" Professor Blue began.

She lay her briefcase on the ground, opened a compartment, and retrieved a velvet pouch. "I won this at the Era Port." Carefully, she opened the pouch and laid out the Minute Rings and Second Swatches on a table.

"What do you mean you won it?" Elliot frowned.

"I gambled with a woman. She had a Reading Racket stand. I won a little over twenty-four hours."

"You met Mama Juju?" Professor Blue folded his arms across his chest.

"Yes, she has a stand in the Era Port."

"You gambled with a Time Thief, and won?" Queen Nanny raised an eyebrow. "And you're not a Taint?"

"Yes, I won," Brenda responded in a tiny voice. "And no ma'am, I'm not a Taint."

Professor Blue and Queen Nanny exchanged a look.

"Mama Juju has long been cast out of the Order," Queen Nanny said with a far-away look in her eyes. "Did she tell you that?"

"No." Brenda shook her head.

The woman pointed to the minute rings. "Give me two hours. I may be able to make a miracle."

TWENTY-EIGHT

THE COUNCIL OF ETERNITY

The night was speckled with stars, each a reminder of how far she was from home. Brenda rested her head in her hands. So much had gone wrong. And most of it, no, *all of it*, was her fault. She'd been the one who'd stolen the map, stayed up and studied spells. She was the one who'd convinced everyone else that time travel was a good idea. She had even gambled her life with a stranger! Yeah, she won, but what if she hadn't? All of this was her doing. *Her mess.* Uncle Rufus had passed on along with her mother and father. She pictured her Aunt Squeak tugging at her hemline or blouse and smoothing a few hairs too stubborn to lie down the way she wanted. The meddling had always annoyed her. But right now, she would give anything to hear her Aunt's counsel. She'd give anything to have Squeak fix her up and make things right. A fine layer of perspiration lined her forehead. Even in the dead of night, the Caribbean heat was stifling. She kept her face buried in her hands. Where were they? What year? In a matter of hours, they'd traveled, what? 300 years? Suddenly, everything was heavy and she couldn't recall ever feeling so help-less, so small, so weak. That's what time does, makes you smaller. It makes you realize what a speck you are in the grand scheme of things.

When she looked up, Captain Quao, Omen, and Professor Blue had emerged from the shack. Wordlessly, they headed back in the direction they'd come. Brenda stood and fell in lock step alongside the men.

"Where are we going?" she asked Elliot in a hush.

He shrugged. "I don't know."

She turned to Omen. "Where's Lonnie?"

"Stayed behind with Clair," he said without meeting her eyes.

They crouched through an open field before making their way toward a thicket of trees. All around them, the night sang an unfamiliar tune. In the distance, she could hear the ocean waves lapping at the shore. Their footfalls became a sort of rhythm in the night, a foreboding pitter patter of their fate. When the image of Clair's bleeding body took up residence in her mind, she swallowed a gulp of humid air and mouthed a prayer. Sure, she'd stolen and lied and manipulated her way out of tight situations, but inadvertently causing a friend's death? For that, she'd never, ever forgive herself.

After a short time, they slowed to a stop and formed a circle in an open space beneath a canopy of trees. Captain Quao stepped forward, cradling a shiny glob of putty in his palm.

Brenda huddled close to Omen and Elliot. "Artists. These are the Taints Clair told us about," she whispered.

Elliot stroked the hairs on his chin. "Right. The interdimensional door designers…"

Brenda watched as Captain Quao transferred the putty from one hand to the other in a smooth, juggling motion. Then, he blew into the substance and rubbed his hands together. Quickly, it crumbled to silver dust and hovered in the air.

"Look, they're numbers," Elliot said, eyeing the scene.

"Letters too," Omen whispered back.

Brenda leaned forward for a better view. Sure enough, the "dust" was actually tiny characters zipping through the darkness. Captain Quao focused on the floating symbols causing them to collide and form threads as thin as hairs. Then, he reached into a pocket in the small of his back and pulled out a black pen covered in golden beads and glittering jewels. One of the jeweled facets caught in the moonlight knifing through the trees. Brenda's breath hitched in her throat.

"That looks like your pen," Elliot said in a hush.

Brenda's eyes remained fastened on Captain Quao as he grasped the threads, weaving braided equations as brilliant as stars. Once the braiding was complete, he situated each thread on an invisible hook to form a doorframe crackling with golden static and fingers of white-hot fire. In one deft motion, he poked a hole in the air with the pen. A stream of golden characters poured through the hole. It was as if someone had turned on a faucet. Quao turned the pen clockwise and pulled. Splinters of white light illuminated the door, cracking open the night like an egg. He turned to the group.

"Taints enter first. As you pass, do not touch the Conjure Pen." He motioned toward the pen which now glowed from its hole inside the door. "The heat can cause third degree burns."

Their company formed a makeshift line with Brenda, Elliot, and Omen bringing up the rear. Brenda stood idle, summoning calm. What she'd experienced would have been a dream come true for Uncle Rufus.

He'd been responsible for fostering her curiosity. All the evenings she'd spent with him pining over books and assembling strange inventions had prepared her for this moment.

"Taints go first." Quao tilted his head in her direction.

Professor Blue turned to the Captain and frowned. "She's not a Taint."

Quao stepped from the front of the line, leaving the doorway pulsing in the nonexistent breeze. He narrowed his eyes. "She's an Artist. She's a descendent of Benjamin Banneker."

The Professor and the others looked on in shock. "Did you know this?"

"I...I didn't," Brenda sputtered. "I mean, I knew about Uncle Benjamin, but I didn't know I was a Taint." She met Elliot's questioning eyes and quickly looked away. Mama Juju's words echoed in her head. *You are an Artist, child. I know one when I see one.*

"Well, you know now," Quao said in a hurry. He took her by the hand and led her to the front of the line. When he yanked open the invisible door, the velvet sky began to crumble into flakes of greenish gray. She felt like she was inside the vestibule of a building being burned to bits. On Quao's command, she hurried through the crackling door. Surrounded by nothingness, she rushed over a bridge made of white noise and static as the others followed behind. Once, she looked over her shoulder to be sure Omen and Elliot were still there. Up ahead, she spotted a speck of green that soon became the solid outline of another rectangular door. It hummed and buzzed like the previous door, only this one shone green instead of gold. Suddenly, she felt queasy. *She was a Taint? Had her uncle known all along? Did Squeak know? Why hadn't anyone told her?* Captain Quao again retrieved the conjure pen from his pocket, poked a hole in the door and pulled it ajar. Brenda took a deep breath, stepped inside, and froze.

"An amphitheater." Elliot took a few steps forward.

Sure enough, circular rows of gray stone separated by strips of grass rose on an incline. The thick, Caribbean air vanished and had been replaced with a welcoming cool breeze. A golden sun glowed above the trees.

Brenda and the others stumbled on a sunken stone stage as dozens of faces looked on. They were surrounded on all sides. Their grim stares all but screamed disappointment. One face, in particular, stood out from the rest. Dr. Djinn, dressed in a white tuxedo, ivory, onyx, ruby cane, and matching top hat stood as Captain Quao, Professor Blue, and the other men in Quao's company found seats among the rest. A snowy white owl was perched on Dr. Djinn's shoulder; its yellow eyes bored into Brenda's face. Elliot and Omen stepped aside so that she stood between them.

"Welcome Brenda Banneker, Elliot Just, and Omen Crow." Dr. Djinn gave each of the scholars a stern look after stating their names. Her words were terse. Though Brenda hadn't seen her in more than a month, it was like she'd never met the woman at all. In Charleston, she'd been serious, inquisitive, and warm. The woman that stood before them now was everything but.

"Please, sit." Dr. Djinn gestured toward three empty stone seats in front of them.

They did as they were told. Brenda noticed immediately that the seat was cold and hard. She shifted, clearly uncomfortable.

"Mr. Crow, Ms. Banneker, Mr. Just, do you know why you're here?" Dr. Djinn leaned on her cane.

They shook their heads no in unison. Brenda glanced at Elliot, sensing his fear. Her stomach sank. A little over a day ago they were on the porch of the park's guest cabin, talking under the stars. He'd even asked if she was afraid. She cringed at her own arrogance.

"Let the hearing begin," she said while addressing the faces in the elevated seats. "The Sacred Order of Time Thieves Council of Eternity does hereby charge Omen Crow, Brenda Banneker, and Elliot Just with an illegal trip ninety-five years in the future resulting in a wounded Taint who is currently receiving medical attention in 1729 Jamaica. All rise, the Honorable Elder Denmark Vesey, presiding."

Dr. Djinn stepped aside as a man rose from a nearby seat. He wore a tan tweed vest and trousers with a red, black, and green bowtie. His footfalls echoed on the stone steps as he made his way to the sunken stage.

Brenda watched he took a seat in a tall chair behind a stone lectern. "Mr. Crow, Mr. Just. Miss Banneker, please tell the members of the Council more about the events leading up to now. Leave nothing out. Your fate will be decided based on the facts you present. Convince us you deserve our mercy."

Omen was the first to speak. He gave a heartfelt speech about the little shack where he was raised in Altamonte Springs, FL, and his grandfather's tooth, given to him by the elders in his family before winning an Odd Scholarship. The Council gasped when he relayed his encounter with the Grootslang. A few tears slipped down his cheeks as he recounted his inability to save Clair from the gunman's bullets. Omen flopped in his seat like a man defeated once he'd finished his testimony.

When Elliot took the stand, the mood lifted a bit. The Councilmen and women chuckled when he spoke of how he outsmarted his older brother in the Boys Chemistry Competition. Unfortunately, the moment turned tearful when Elliot launched into the story of his Uncle's murder and his desire to avenge him with the development of Formula 0619: The Black Gaze. Brenda watched Vesey's eyes as Elliot held up a vial of Jengu tears. Though not wholly convinced it could work, a good number of Council members appeared intrigued, which was all Brenda, Omen, and Elliot could hope for. As Elliot's testimony ended, her mind raced. She needed to wow them, show them the unexpected, make them *feel* something, like Elliot had, but even more. Her life depended on it.

"Miss Banneker, please approach." Vesey turned toward Brenda, his face stoic and unreadable.

Brenda placed a hand on her briefcase and turned toward the council. "May I share evidence?"

A murmur tore through the crowd. Vesey slammed his gavel on the lectern and waved a hand. "Proceed."

Brenda carried the briefcase to a table and began to share how her life as an inventor began in her uncle's basement in Philadelphia. She spoke about the old armoire and the dusty library and the mysterious packages that began arriving a few years prior. Clinging to her every word, she spun the tale of how she'd created the fire needle for the scholarship. The Council appeared impressed with the amount of the sacred text she'd read in a few hours as well as the Era Dials they'd assembled from scratch. From there, she revealed her chance meeting with Mama Juju. A few of the councilmen and women shifted in their chairs at the mention of her name.

"Mama Juju, formerly Elder Adara, is an exile of this Council. We do not mention her name," Vesey interrupted.

Brenda lowered her gaze and continued. After describing the horror of the shooting in detail, she turned to her briefcase. "My evidence is inside."

Elder Vesey clasped his hands together. "Proceed, Miss Banneker."

Like it had numerous times before, the briefcase doubled in size after the push of a button. Brenda bent down to open one of the drawers and retrieved the second swatches and minute rings. Gently, she placed them beside the briefcase. Then, with trembling hands, she pulled out the tablet she'd lifted from *The Journeyman Times* at the Era Port. She held it high above her head for all to see. A few gasps rippled through the amphitheater. Finally, she lowered the device and began scrolling with her thumb. "Things don't get better. Ninety-five years from now, we're still dying." At first her voice was soft and shaky, but with each word, she gained confidence. "'Houston Rally Demanding Justice for Trayvon Martin set for Sunday.' *The Houston Chronicle*, March 24, 2012. 'The Tamir Rice Story: How to Make a Police Shooting Disappear.' *GQ Magazine*, July 14, 2016. 'Minnesota Officer Acquitted in Killing of Philando Castille.' *The New York Times*, June 16, 2017. 'Detroit Settles with Family of Aiyana Stanley-Jones, 7-Year-Old Girl Killed in Police Raid: The girl was shot in the head while she slept on a couch during a 2010 police raid.' *Huffington Post*, April 5, 2019." Finally, she was shouting. "'Sandra Bland's Sister: She died because officer saw her as 'threatening black woman' not human.' *USA Today*, May 15, 2019. 'Puzzling number of men tied to Ferguson Protests Have Died.' *The Star Tribune*, May 21, 2019. 'N.Y. Officer Won't Face Charges After Chokehold Death of Eric Garner.' *LA Times*, July 16, 2019."

When she finished, the silence echoed like a scream. Brenda fought hard against the tears leaking from the corners of her eyes. She hadn't expected the emotion to bubble inside her like a cauldron on a rack above a raging fire. "Nothing changes," she croaked. "Nothing."

The council erupted. Some sobbed while others begged for calm. Elliot leaned over in his seat as Omen held his head in his hands. The bile rose from her throat as she replayed the massacre in her head. The shooter's face, as expressionless as a slab of cold stone. Clair, smiling at the pews in the front of the church, caught in a memory. She and Elliot standing shoulder to shoulder. Vesey struck his gavel against the lectern, yanking her from the memory's clutches.

"Order, order!" he shouted above the commotion.

Brenda stood there, heart slamming against her chest.

"And what would you have us do?" Vesey laced his fingers together.

She raised her hands as if in prayer. "Give us the chance to undo this. Please!" she pleaded. She owed it to Clair. Her bullheadedness, her arrogance, was the reason they were there in the first place. "Please."

Vesey's cold eyes warmed for a second before reverting back to ice. "There is no undo, Miss Banneker. And besides, even if there were—"

"There is a way."

The Councilmen and women turned in their seats in an attempt to locate the lone voice of dissent. Dr. Djinn rose from her seat. "Permission to approach?"

Shock rippled through the amphitheater. All eyes swung in her direction. On cue, the animal let out a rousing *hoot*, before tucking its head under its wing.

Vesey sighed, "I'll allow it."

Dr. Djinn took a breath. "These scholars have managed to do something none of us have even considered. And this young man," she turned to Elliot, "has procured Jengu tears—

healing tears." She paused and paced. "What if we were to open an interdimensional door, allow this young man to complete his formula, and test its effectiveness?"

"Dr. Djinn," Vesey cleared his throat, "this sounds like a complete violation of the Laws of The Sacred Order of Time Thieves. Need I remind you that—"

"The shooter is a descendent of Sheriff Dodge," she cut in. "In 1920, Dodge is Hampton's newest sheriff and he's got a vendetta against me and my park. Leave him in charge, Elder Vesey, and there will be blood, blood we may be able to avoid."

"As Time Thieves, we take what's ours—" Elder Vesey began.

"Ideas, knowledge, *resources*," Dr. Djinn cut in.

"What exactly are you proposing, Marvellus?" he asked, drumming his fingertips on the lectern.

"I'm proposing that we allow Mr. Just to return to 1920 and complete his formula." Dr. Djinn rubbed her hands together. "Before the scholars arrived at my park, Sheriff Dodge visited me with a threat. He vowed to take my land and hand it over to two White men. During this vile exchange, he requested a glass of lemonade. Perhaps that lemonade could be altered with Mr. Just's formula."

Commotion set in. Elder Vesey brought the trial to order.

"There is a saying that bigotry is taught. I tend to believe that family is the first teacher. If Dodge drinks the formula, there's a good change we wipe out a line of oppressors and save a young girl's life as well as nine others." She paced as she spoke. "The plan abides by our laws, wholly and unequivocally."

"Where will they get the time?" Vesey responded coolly. "You don't want them to return to 1920's present day. You're requiring that they return to a few weeks prior. Remember, time must be earned, not given and these three have taken enough. There must be a punishment."

Dr. Djinn turned on one of her heels and lifted the minute rings and second swatches from their velvet cushions. "Let us sort out a punishment that fits their crime at a later date. Miss Banneker has earned time. We may not like the way it was won, but she has earned it."

Vesey shifted in his seat. "And the door?"

"She has my pen," a deep voice boomed through the amphitheater.

Brenda frowned and craned her neck. Her stomach flipped. In the crowd of Elders, a Black man in colonial American dress rose from his seat.

"Permission to approach, Elder Vesey?" the man asked.

Vesey nodded. "Please state your name."

The man approached the sunken stage gracefully and stood next to her. "I am Benjamin Banneker and Brenda is one of my descendants. I willed her my Conjure Pen. It's been in her possession for a few years." He turned to Brenda and offered a reassuring smile.

"Very well, Elder Banneker, but does she know how to use it?" Vesey countered.

"She is an Artist," Banneker replied. "She has the pen. Once given the glue, she can sculpt the door."

Glue? Sculpt? Door? Her nerves unraveled as Elder Banneker moved his fingers along a slender drawer in the briefcase and retrieved the pen.

Sensing her worry, Benjamin Banneker pulled her into a hug. "I'll be sure she succeeds."

Elder Vesey leaned forward in his seat. "What about this formula, Mr. Just presented? Who will see it through?"

"I will, Elder Vesey."

Brenda watched as a heavy-set woman with a gray bun descended the stairs. She'd sworn she'd seen her before but couldn't place her face.

"Mama Cool?" Elliot croaked from his chair.

"Elder Lynk?" Vesey narrowed his eyes. "You'll assist the boy with his formula?"

"I will. I have a feeling we can learn a lot from each other." She smiled in Elliot's direction. "Sugar and spells. Sugar and spells. Sweets and Taints. Taints and sweets."

Elder Vesey gave Mama Cool a confused look and rubbed his palms together. He turned to face Brenda, Elliot, and Omen. "Are you up to this task?"

Brenda exchanged a look, first with Elliot and then, Omen. "Yes, sir," they responded in unison.

"The Council of Eternity hereby rules that Brenda Banneker, Elliot Just, and Omen Crow, otherwise known as Dr. Marvellus Djinn's Odd Scholars shall return at a later date to receive their punishment for their illegal trip ninety-five years in the future. But for now, they are hereby granted permission to return to 1920." He gave them a stern look and rose from his seat. "Best of luck, until we meet again.

TWENTY-NINE

FORMULA 0619: THE BLACK GAZE

After adding several droplets of the Jengu tears to the elixir, Elliot held the vial up to the light. An iridescent explosion erupted inside the glass. The serum took on the appearance of Mother of Pearl. Bits of silver, blue, and pink mingled inside soft green and purple. Elliot could hardly contain his pride. The bottle's contents looked like he'd harnessed a rainbow inside. If only his father and uncle could see him. He beamed with everything he had.

"May I?" Mama Cool asked from inside her booth.

Elliot handed over the vial. This was the final step. Now that the tears had been added, it needed an incantation, some kind of sorcery to "give it a little kick." Mama Cool cracked her knuckles and the concoction boiled as she began an inaudible chant. Seconds later, it bubbled, swirled, and finally turned black as ink with specks of silver.

"But it'll dissolve once it's added to the lemonade, correct?" Elliot chewed on his fingernails. "He won't see the black or silver?

"Odorless and colorless. The only thing he'll taste is citrus, sour, and sugar." Mama Cool grabbed a mason jar filled three quarters of the way with yellow liquid from a shelf. "Pour it in."

Elliot wiped his hands on his pants. The last thing he needed was for it to shatter on the ground on account of his nerves. Brenda and Omen added reassuring looks. He took a deep breath and poured. They watched as it sizzled, fizzed, and popped before settling into a regular old glass of lemonade.

"Here he comes," Elliot whispered as a young boy in overalls made his way to Mama Cool's stand.

He dabbed at his forehead with a kerchief. It had all come down to this, a glass of lemonade. Lemons, sugar, and magic might be all it took to stop death in its tracks. He wished his father and even his brother were here for this experiment. A part of him reveled in the excitement of a possible breakthrough. Yet another part of him wallowed in doubt and what ifs. He was a wreck and he knew the waiting game that followed would be worse.

The young man approached, wiping his sweat-laden neck with a rag, "The new sheriff wants somethin' to quench his thirst. Got any lemonade?"

Mama Cool grinned. "I sure do," she said and handed it over.

Elliot watched the boy disappear over the hill and smiled. Sure enough, science was magic, too.

EPILØGUE

"This is your *Next Train*. I repeat, this is the *Next Train*. Not the *Now Train* and not the *Then Train*. If you're looking for the *Now Train* or the *Then Train*, please disembark, climb the stairs to your right and follow the signage. Again, this is the *Next Train* arriving from the last three hundred years. Please stand back and allow all passengers to exit. Our motto is: we get you to *the Next*, right *Now*."

The station was packed with travelers rushing to their destinations. Omen stepped back to allow a passenger through a narrow aisle. Instinctively, he clawed at his neck. Nothing. He'd done it at least five times per day since the entire ordeal. The tooth and chain were gone, and no amount of magic could bring it back. Still, he gathered himself willing his heart not to jump from his chest as the train approached. And now, he stood beside Elliot, Brenda, Dr. Djinn, and Professor Blue. This would be their moment of truth. The next few minutes would reveal if everything they'd done had all been for naught.

"She'll be here." Elliot thumped him on the shoulder. "I can feel it."

Omen watched as the train pulled into the station. He quickly scanned the giant windows for anything familiar: braids, a long skirt, *anything*. The Travelers disembarked in a blur of colors and faces. He struggled to see. *What if he missed her? What if she didn't remember where to exit? What if she didn't realize where to go?* The countless variables drove him crazy. After the crowd thinned, Dr. Djinn grabbed him by the shoulders and hugged him tight.

"Your guilt is an insatiable beast. Promise me, you will not offer up yourself for its dinner." Dr. Djinn pulled him close.

Before he knew it the tears were falling, one or two at first, and then an onslaught. Brenda and Elliot joined, followed by Professor Blue. Omen had no idea how long they'd been standing there in a long embrace on the *Next* train's platform, waiting for someone who'd never come. And that's when he saw it, a white gown, pooled on the ground near his shoe. When he looked up, he saw the woman from Jamaica, the one who'd been charged with healing Clair. She smiled and wiped away one of his tears. Omen's stomach dropped. Then, the woman stepped aside. And there, standing with the aid of an elaborately carved wooden cane, was Clair. Frozen in place, he stared at her. It was as if he were reliving the moment they'd met a few weeks before. In his mind's eye he saw her climbing from a Model T and extending her hand. She smiled. He closed his eyes tight, half expecting her to be gone when he opened them again. But there she was, hobbled, but alive.

"It's so good to see you again."

Remembering her injury, he stopped himself from hugging her tight, and instead kissed her lightly on the forehead. "Clair—" he croaked.

"I'm right here," she said. "It was tough," she glanced at Queen Nanny who nodded in agreement, "but I'm here."

"What about Lonnie?" Omen sputtered.

"Back in Charleston," Clair replied ,with a small smile. "He's an old friend; that's it."

"To what do we owe the honor of this visit?" Professor Blue beamed at Queen Nanny.

"After listening to this gal talk," Nanny shot Clair a mischievous look, "seems you'll need at a part time healer on staff."

Dr. Djinn, the Professor, and the others chuckled as Elliot guided Queen Nanny toward an empty bench. Omen turned his attention back to Clair.

"I have something for you."

"You're the best gift anyone could—" he began.

"Shh!" She put two fingers to her lips and opened her palm to reveal a silk drawstring bag. She opened it slowly and pulled out a chain. Two chunks of turquoise sandwiched a jagged tooth more than an inch long.

"How?" Omen blinked.

"Sage spells contain telepathy and telekinesis. I conjured this using the stories you told me about your grandfather. It's part will, part memory, but either way, it's very real. Try it on."

Omen did as he was told, sliding the chain over his neck. He rolled the tooth between his thumb and index fingers several times, examining its texture and heft. "I don't know what to say," he stammered. "I don't deserve this." He removed the chain again. "I froze. I could have done so much to help. To stop the bullet…"

"Stop. You did what you could. No one would have known how to react. No one."

Omen pulled her toward him gently and held her as tightly as he could without hurting her. After a few moments, she pulled back and looked up at him.

"What did the Council decide?"

Omen took a deep breath. "We train to become Time Thieves in thirty days."

She frowned. "But I'm a Sage, how can I belong to two orders at once? That's never been done before."

"It's been done, just never documented," Dr. Djinn said with a wink as she strolled toward them. Brenda and Elliot looked up from their conversation with Queen Nanny and followed Dr. Djinn. The four teens watched as Dr. Djinn's features morphed from an attractive thirty something brown skinned woman into a hefty, dark skinned man in a tricorn hat and cutlass dangling dangerously at his side.

"Baba Ali?" Clair narrowed her eyes.

Seconds later, she shifted again, this time into a stout woman with a poof of white hair gathered in a bun on top of her head.

Elliot removed his glasses. "Mama Cool?"

With a wink, she transformed into a woman with copper skin and a bald head as shiny as a freshly polished jewel. Brenda cocked her head to one side. "Mama Juju?"

Finally, as if she were a magician preparing for a grand finale, she shut her eyes and shifted into midnight skin, a muscular build, and a dazzling smile that could light up one's deepest, darkest fears. He rubbed his temples. "Professor Blue?"

The four teens watched intently as the real Professor Blue strode in the group's direction. He stopped once he stood shoulder to shoulder with what looked to be his identical twin. He exchanged a glance with Dr. Djinn as she melted back into her own skin. Professor Blue looked back at her once the shift was complete and winked.

"But I thought," Clair sputtered.

Dr. Djinn put a finger to her lips. "I've been here this entire time. Well, most of the time." She smiled. "I believe in all of you. It's why you were chosen. It's why you won. The Motherland is my way of giving Colored folks an escape. This park is my resistance, one undo at a time."

Omen stared at Dr. Djinn in disbelief. "But Elder Vesey said there was no undo—"

Dr. Djinn turned and flashed a brilliant smile. "Thanks to all of you, that no longer seems to be the case."

APPENDIX

The Four Orders, Their Governing Bodies, and Sacred Texts
Order: **Time Thieves**

- Time Thieves can maneuver through the Time Continuum via interdimensional doors called the Time Stitch to the distant past and far future. However, there are stipulations. Time Thieves may spend no more than 24 hours in travel and the changing of events, past or future, is strictly forbidden. During their jaunts through time, Thieves "acquire" knowledge and resources from the past and future. This practice has allowed them to accumulate great wealth. Time Thieves are often business owners, executives, and politicians. There are two sub-orders of Time Thieves: Keepers and Gatherers.

Sub-Orders: Keepers of the Damned (Keepers), Ghoul Gatherers (Gatherers)

- Keepers of the Damned store the soul jars whose essence propels Time Thieves through the Time Continuum.
- Ghoul Gatherers seek out individuals who lived less than favorable lives (slavers, war mongers, mercenaries, etc.) extract the souls from their cadavers and bring them to Keepers for storing.

Governing Body: The Council of Eternity
- *Duration of Tenure:* Life
- *Election Process:* Determined by Lineage

Mark: An infinity symbol (The Sirius Mark)
Mark Placement: Inside wrist
- Inside right wrist: Keeper of the Damned
- Inside left wrist: Ghoul Gatherer

Conjure Magic: Travelcasting
Sacred Text: The Sacred Book of Epochs, Eras, and Eons
Mythological Creature: The Nommo (The first spirits of the world)
Root Language of Magic: Bambara (Mali)

Order: Artists

- Artists have strong relationships with all Taints but work closest with Time Thieves to maintain the interdimensional doors that ensure time travel runs smoothly. Because their work is always in demand, most Artists live comfortably. The suborders of Artists are Architects and Writers.

Sub-Orders: Writers, Architects
- Writers design and apply the distinguishing Marks worn by Taints. No matter the Order, all Taints will receive their Mark from a Writer. Another sub-set of Writers write the spells used in conjuring.
- Architects design and maintain the interdimensional doors within the Time Continuum.

Governing Body: The Senate of Dogon Descendants
Duration of Tenure: 12 years
Election Process: Elected democratically

Mark: An Octagon (The Art Mark)
Mark Placement: Palm
- Right palm: Writer
- Left palm: Architect

Conjure Magic: Artwork
Sacred Text: Art's Great Equation
Mythological Creature: Jengu/Miengu (West African Mermaid)
Root Language of Magic: Duala (Cameroon)

Order: **Sages**

- Keepers of knowledge and neurological ability, Sages are the wise counselors and philosophers of the magical world. Long ago, when the four orders were created, the Sages were designated the intermediaries of conflict, should it arise. Since then, the Sages have been bound to take positions of neutrality in conflicts among Taints. Sages were responsible for negotiating the Peace Treaty between Thieves and Shifters in the late 19th century.

Sub-Orders: Telepaths, Telekinetics, Omni-Teles
- Telepaths can communicate thoughts without speech using neurological mastery.
- Telekinetics can move objects through space using neurological mastery.
- Omni-Teles are capable of both telepathy and telekinetics.

Governing Body: The Optic Congress
- *Duration of Tenure:* Life
- *Election Process:* Determined by Lineage

Mark: Three Straight Lines, one red, the other black, the last, green (The Three Stripes)

Mark Placement: Shoulder/Neck

- Left Shoulder: Telepath
- Right Shoulder: Telekinetic
- Base of Neck, Above the Spine: Omni-Tele

Conjure Magic: Sage spells

Sacred Text: Book of the Blind Limbs

Mythological Creature: Aido-Hwedo (The Rainbow Snake)

Root Language of Magic: Fon (Benin)

Order: **Shifters**

- Shifters can alter their appearance at any given time and hack into the abilities of Taints in other orders. This "thievery" has caused conflict in the past between Shifters and Taints of other orders. Ultimately, Shifters have experienced a great deal of oppression due to their specific magical abilities. Despite this history, many Shifters have earned success in government, education, and the entertainment industry.

Sub-Orders: Mono-morphs, Polymorphs

- Mono-morphs can shape-shift, but only into one Skin.
- Polymorphs can shape-shift into as many skins as they choose without any stipulations.

Governing Body: House of the Evolving

- *Duration of Tenure:* 2 years
- *Election Process:* Elected by open competition

B. SHARISE MOORE

Mark: A Diamond (The Morph Mark)
Mark Placement: Back
- Lower Back (Right side): Polymorph
- Lower Back (Left side): Monomorph

Conjure Magic: Shift sorcery
Sacred Text: The Heart of the Shift
Mythological Creature: Impundulu (The Lightning Bird)
Root Language of Magic: Zulu (South Africa)
Author's Note:

I became intrigued with magicians and medicine shows after watching Michael Jackson and Paul McCartney's "Say, Say, Say" video as a child in the 1980s. From there, I fell in love with the fantastic worlds of Roald Dahl (Charlie and the Chocolate Factory, James and the Giant Peach, The Witches.) About 5 years ago, I started to research it further and came across a bit of information about Colored Amusement Parks during the Jim Crow Era. During this period, the country was segregated. This was also a time when Black communities thrived. In 1920, an amusement park called Suburban Gardens was built in Washington, DC. The park was designed by H.D. Woodson, a Black architect. To this day, Suburban Gardens remains the only amusement park in the history of Washington, DC. The park had bumper cars, a coaster, a pavilion and sat on seven acres of land. Once I stumbled on this bit of information, I was inspired to create The Motherland.

So much of Black history is buried. This story is my love letter to Black History. Black people have accomplished a great deal, from the great architect, H.D. Woodson to the amazing Garveyite magician, Black Herman (the inspiration for Dr. Marvellus Djinn) to the phenomenal botanist, Beebe Steven Lynk. I hope you enjoyed this story. It was thrilling to write.

~B. Sharise Moore

THANK YOU

To my husband, J. "Owl" Farand, and my son, Peanut: Thank you for your sacrifice. Thank you for understanding my late nights, early mornings, and sometimes mid-afternoons when inspiration hit. You are my magic.

To my mom, Brenda Moore: Thanks to you, books were my first friends. You helped to feed and cultivate my imagination from day one. I love you for believing in me.

To my father, Irving Bolden: Thank you for the stories about my Seminole grandmother and your alligator encounters in Altamonte Springs, FL as a boy in the 1930s. Those stories helped bring Omen to life in a major way. Continue to rest in peace. I love you.

To my Uncle Derrick and Uncle Dwayne: Your support means the world. I love you!

To Cousin Farrah: Thank you for bringing a portion of this book to life! Your conjure pens were absolutely perfect!

To the rest of my family: Thank you for your continued encouragement and support!

To Devan Renea: You were one of the first people to read this short story and encourage me to continue. Thank you for reading those drafts and providing your amazing input! I've always known you'd be a star, but I didn't realize how much you'd end up teaching me. Thank you!

To Cody: Thank you so much for your encouragement and kind words. They have always gone a long way. You are an artist. Keep painting!

To Akande: Thank you for your willingness to read the novel, spread the word, and encourage me in every way you could.

To Gladstone, Dough, and Rahsaan: Thank you for believing in my writing, whether it was poetry or fiction. Thank you for always being in my corner.

To my beta readers Tyhitia Green and Lina Ingram: Your feedback was instrumental in creating a story that worked. I will never forget you taking the time to do this for me!

To Milton Davis: Thank you for taking on this project. I appreciate you.

To my editor, Clint: Thank you for your suggestions and expertise.

To my agent, Laurie McLean: Thank you for seeing something in my writing. Thank you for your kind words of encouragement.

To Marcellus: The moment I saw your art, I knew you'd be perfect to capture this book cover. You've truly outdone yourself. Thank you!

To Sarah: Thank you so much for creating The Motherland map! You climbed inside my mind and placed those visuals on paper. Thank you!

To my former co-workers at DHS, BCPS, and AACPS: Thank you, thank you, thank you! I am so humbled by your support. Thank you for your willingness to not only purchase a copy, but spread the word, too!

To Ann, Marisa, and Tavia at Black Bee Entertainment: Thank you for your unwavering belief in my writing. You came at a time when I desperately need you. I am so grateful you are in my corner.

To my social media friends: I love y'all immensely. Your encouragement over the years has been amazing.

ABOUT THE AUTHOR

B. Sharise Moore is a New Jersey native and graduate of Rutgers University. Moore's poems and short stories have appeared in several anthologies and journals such as Chosen Realities: Summer 2020, These Bewitching Bonds, and Fantasy Magazine.

At present, she is a writer/educator, curriculum designer, the host of Moore Books with B. Sharise on YouTube, and the Poetry Editor for Fiyah Magazine of Black Speculative Fiction. She lives in Baltimore, MD with her husband and precocious young son.

More Young Adult books from MVmedia!
www.mvmediaatl.com

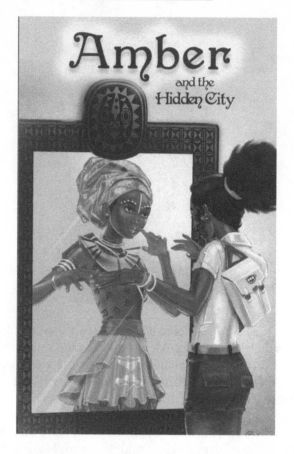

Thirteen-year-old Amber Robinson's life is full of changes. Her parents are sending her to a private school away from her friends, and high school looms before her. But little does she know that her biggest change awaits in a mysterious city hidden from the world for a thousand years. Prepare yourself for an exciting adventure that spans from the Atlanta suburbs to the grasslands of Mali. It's a story of a girl who discovers her hidden abilities and heritage in a way that surprises and entertains.

Clifton Academy is everything Amber thought it would be...
and worse. In addition to trying to fit in at a new school, she
struggles to master her newfound talents. One day she is con-
tacted by Grandma Alake and is told she must once again de-
fend Marai from the sorcerer Bagule and his companion,
Nieleni. The nefarious duo is in search of Sonni Ali's sword, a
talisman so powerful possessing could mean the end of the
ancient and secret city. Can Amber and her friends find the
sword before Bagule and save Marai once more?

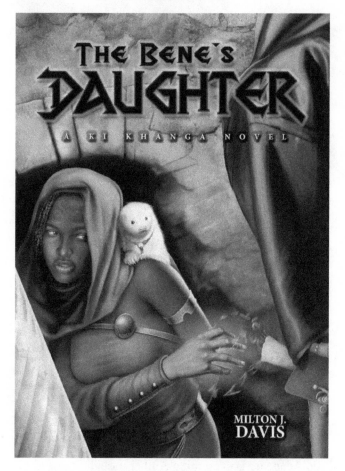

Omolewa lived a peaceful life in the Kiswala city of Nacala with her adopted family, giving little thought of her origins or the family she never knew. But one day a mysterious ship from Zimbabwa arrived in harbor and changed her life forever. Omolewa discovered not only that she was the long-lost daughter of the rulers of Zimbabwa, she also discovered that she possessed powers that could change the fortunes of her family and the destiny of Ki Khanga. The Bene's Daughter is an exciting tale of action, discovery and revelation that will keep you riveted from beginning to end.

CPSIA information can be obtained
at www.ICGtesting.com
Printed in the USA
FSHW010724120521